LOVE TO THE RESCUE

A Dachshund Love Story

Janet Franks Little

ANESSA BOOKS

ISBN:978-1-7322225-1-9

Cover designer: Victoria Landis,
http://www.victorialandis.com/book-cover-design.html

Formatting by Anessa Books, http://anessabooks.com

Published by Anessa Books
Virginia, USA

TABLE OF CONTENTS

OTHER BOOKS BY JANET FRANKS LITTLE

Worth Her Weight
Estate of the Heart
Glass Promises

DEDICATION

This book is dedicated to Maggie May, 9/24/04-12/17/20.

ACKNOWLEDGMENTS

I'd like to thank all the wonderful dachshunds that have lovingly enriched my life starting with Lieben in 1975, followed by Ebbe, Bruno, Mia, Lili, Brewster and, most recently, sweet Maggie.

I'd also like to thank these humans: Patricia Crumpler, Patricia Bellomo, and Elayne Cox of The Mary Jane Critique Group, my friend, fellow writer and fabulous book cover designer, Victoria Landis, and a fellow romance author who did an amazing job formatting and uploading this book, Meredith Bond.

Thanks to author, Roxanne Smolen, who sat with me in a tent at the Coral Springs Festival of the Arts one warm day in March, when the idea for a series of dog lover books came to mind after watching the parade of people and their pets pass by our table of books.

I'd like to impart an important lesson I've learned. When I have a dachshund around, I always have a reason to smile.

Love to the Rescue

CHAPTER 1

"THAT'S NOT FAIR. You let me use balls in the first two wiener races."

The grandfatherly judge, wearing a Delray Beach Dachshund Derby T-shirt, raises his palms. "It was an oversight. But in the final heat, you have to follow the rules."

I brush away a long strand of purple hair that blows across my face. "Was it a sore loser who complained?"

Despite his jolly countenance, firmness tightens the judge's voice. "No, but the man makes a valid point about using a ball."

"But it's not being thrown. I drop it at my feet when Mia gets to the finish line. How is that a violation?"

Behind me, a husky baritone speaks with the mellow richness of my father's finest whiskey. "Because the derby guidelines state no balls."

With an inarticulate noise of annoyance, I whirl around. A tall man with chestnut hair and designer glasses stands with a sheet of paper in one hand. His other hand holds the leash of a red long-haired dachshund with beautiful chocolate-brown markings. My heart flips. At the same time, amusement with the similar colorations of the man and his dog tickles me. "And you are?"

"According to you, some sore loser." He reads aloud from the printed page. "You may not throw balls to encourage your dog to run faster. You cannot use a toy, especially one that makes noise, at the finish line. You may call your dog and use food or dog treats for enticement."

I turn my back on the good-looking complainer and face the judge. "Like I said, I'm not throwing a ball."

The older man grimaces. "He's right. It says only food and treats. The organizers set up the rules. I just follow them. If you've got a problem, take it up with them next year."

"But—"

"My ruling stands. No balls." He lumbers away.

I spin to face my troublemaker. His head is cocked as he studies the Chinese symbols inked on my spine and exposed by the derby T-shirt knotted under my breasts. "What does that say?"

"The ink is Chinese for low back tattoo."

He chuckles with a rumbling growl. "That's rather ironic, isn't it?"

"I thought so, but my mother said it was idiotic." I rock from one foot to the other with a pleading expression. "Listen, about the ball—"

He flashes a smile verging on a smirk. "Sorry you don't like the judge's decision, but rules are rules."

Once again, he appears as uptight as before with jeans sporting knife-sharp creases and a wrinkle-free Ralph Lauren polo shirt. Neat and tidy, even his nails look manicured.

I scowl. "What are you, a lawyer?"

"No. I'm a certified public accountant." Mr. Nitpicker's eyes travel from my purplish black hair to my bare midriff, past the gauzy skirt to my favorite tasseled, white majorette boots. "What do you do?"

"You could say . . . I'm a free spirit."

"Or I could say you're probably unemployed."

Few people understand or accept the normality of my lifestyle. Besides, I need to get back to the issue at hand. "Listen, the final heat will be in about twenty minutes. Let's run it like the quarter and semi-finals. I'll deal with the organizers about the rules next year."

He replies with the speed of a drawn gun. "You bring the racquetball you were using, and I'll make sure your dog is disqualified. No balls. Only food."

I watch the man and his dog walk away then hitch up my skirt. We'll see about using a ball. Racing to where a row of food trucks line the parking lot, behind the third one is a tiny, white-haired woman in a plastic lawn chair under a striped umbrella. A black and tan, long-haired Dachshund perches on her lap. The canine yips and wiggles to be free when I come into view.

The woman hugs the dog to her bony chest. "Hold on, Mia."

With care, she lowers the excited animal to the ground. Mia runs, the leash dragging behind her. I pet my dog's silky head and grab the nylon tether. "Is Rudy inside, Mrs. R?"

The woman nods. "Bang on the door."

The sides of the flaming red food truck proclaim *Great Balls of Fire* in blazing letters with a large decal of Jerry Lee Lewis at the piano. I knock on the rear door. "Rudy, I need your help."

One of the double doors swings open. A small man, with a Fu Manchu mustache and a do-rag over his bald pate, leans out. Emblazoned on his black T-shirt is: *You're Gonna Love My Balls!*

"What's wrong? Is Nonni okay?" He steps down and looks around the corner of the vehicle and his mother waves. "Whaddaya need, Marin?"

"I want you to cook me a plain meatball, no spices or sauces. Make it about the size of Mia's racquetball. And I need it in . . ." I check my Apple watch. "Ten minutes."

"Why?"

"I've been told I can't use a real ball in the final heat, only food."

"You got it!" He hops back inside and pushes past his wife and daughter. "Outta my way. Marin and Mia need my help."

The two women lean backward from the front counter and wave. I waggle my fingers at them.

Rudy's wife, Rita, leaves the cash register and stands at her husband's side. "What can I do?"

He points. "Get me more bread crumbs."

The customer at the open window with money in his raised hand glowers. "What about me? I was next."

Their daughter, Angelina, leans over and snatches the bills. "Hold your horses. This is more important."

Eight minutes later, Rudy hands me a foil-wrapped meatball inside a fluted paper hot dog tray. "I fried it to make sure it's cooked through. But it's not going to taste like a Rosetti *polpette.*"

I squeeze his hand. "Thanks so much. We have to go." My dog and I run to the track.

CHAPTER 2

AN ANNOUNCEMENT BLARES over a loudspeaker. "This is the last call for the final heat. All division finalists are needed at the track."

I shout, "We're here!"

The kneeling handler takes the leash, unclips it from Mia's collar, and hands it to me. He opens the door into the holding box. My thirteen-pound dachshund wiggles from his grasp and runs inside. She quivers like a racehorse anxious for the starting bell.

The track is laid out on a flat meadow-like area of the park. A long panel with portholes covers the fronts of eight boxes for the dogs. Although lane markers are painted on the grass, the racers rarely remain inside the white lines.

I hustle to the opposite end of the track and stand a few feet back from the finish line. When I glance to my left, there stands my nemesis.

He stares at the foil-covered object in my hand. "What's that?"

"My lunch."

"Looks like a ball."

"It's a meatball."

"Riiight," he drawls. "I wasn't kidding. I'll have you disqualified."

I open the foil and hold up the paper tray. "See."

"Looks like meat wrapped around a racquetball." He cranes his neck and scans the area. "Where's the judge?"

I pull apart more of the foil. When the guy looks my way again, I take a bite and chew the dry and tasteless meatball. Rudy is right. It doesn't taste like a Rosetti *polpette*.

When my Doubting Thomas frowns, I lift the food toward him. "Wanna bite? Just to make sure?"

He doesn't answer but turns his attention to where the handler loads the last dog into the gate.

The announcer's voice reverberates over the speaker system. "Okay, folks, we're ready for the final heat. The winner of this race will be crowned this year's Delray Beach Dachshund Derby winner. Ready . . ."

The race volunteers at each end of the front panel grab a lever. I lift the meatball out of the foil.

"Get set."

I place the still too-warm food in my palm. The man next to me bends forward and waves a piece of beef jerky back and forth like a priest swinging a censer of burning incense.

"Go!"

The front panel lifts and the dogs run out.

Mr. Color-Within-The-Lines yells, "Come, Lamar! Come on, boy!"

His slightly larger Dachshund races neck-in-neck with Mia. Both dogs focus on the goal line. The rest of their competitors lose steam partway down the course. I don't clap, yell, or wave a doggie treat. I wait until Mia reaches the halfway point, her eyes fixed on the *ball* in my hand.

I open my fingers. "Oops."

When the meatball hits the ground, I kick it a few inches away. Mia's muscles bunch and she puts on a burst of speed to hit the finish line inches ahead of Lamar. As soon as my little dog grabs the meatball, her head jerks in surprise. This isn't her usual rubber ball. She tears off a small piece of meat and swallows. Lamar pushes in, sniffing. Mia doesn't growl or grab the treat away from him. Instead, she nudges the meatball his way. He hesitates then bites off a good-sized chunk.

"Lamar! Stop that!" shouts his owner.

The dog wolfs down the rest of the meatball as the man snaps a leash onto his collar. I pick up Mia.

The judge trudges over. "Congratulations, Number Six. You're the winner."

"B-but," the Enforcer of Rules sputters. "She had a ball."

The judge winces. "Ah, man. I told you only food."

I show him the empty paper tray and foil in my hand. "It was my lunch. In all the excitement, the meatball fell on the ground."

The judge checks the grass at his feet. "Where is it?"

I point to Lamar. "He ate it."

The judge turns to the accountant. "Did that happen?"

He sighs. "Yes. Lamar ate the *ball*."

Flashing a grin between his scruffy white whiskers, the judge says, "Okay, then. We have a winner. The awarding of the ribbons and certificates will be in the pavilion in fifteen minutes."

All at once, someone grabs me from behind and strong arms envelop me and Mia in a garlicky embrace. "Congratulations! We knew you could do it," says Rudy.

When he releases us, his mother pats Mia's back. "She is such a good girl."

Rudy's wife, Rita, barks a throaty laugh. "We showed everyone who's the real winner here."

Angie hugs me. "You and Mia did it again."

I smile. "Thank you. We couldn't have won without your help."

More people approach and offer their congratulations until the circle around us doubles. When I look around, Lamar and his owner have disappeared.

CHAPTER 3

WITH MIA IN my arms, we arrive at the awards pavilion. All the other owners and dogs from the various divisions stand in place. A young girl accepts a ribbon and certificate for her paralyzed, wire-haired dachshund as the best Wheelie Weiner. The little dog rolls his contraption forward to receive a trophy-shaped dog biscuit from the announcer.

I sidle behind the other race winners to a sign on a pole that reads: Ball Park Franks, Ages 9-14. Lamar and his owner are next to me, behind Hot Dogs, Ages 5-8. The man nods and shifts left to give us more room. I place my smaller, long-haired, black and tan dog on the ground next to his larger red male. Lamar twists around and sniffs as Mia checks him out. Their bodies wiggle in concert with wagging tails.

Lamar's owner focuses on the award for the Wannabe Wieners which are small dogs of mixed breeds. Cocktail Weenies, puppies, and young dachshunds under four years of age, comprise the next presentation.

A breeze brushes against my cheeks like a light kiss, and I catch the hint of a clean and masculine scent. I lean closer to my race rival and inhale a delicate sniff. He glances over his shoulder. I plaster on a weak, if-you-think-I'm-interested-in-you-you're-wrong smile as I widen my eyes with fake innocence. With his back to me again, I study his thick, reddish-brown, styled hair. His shoulders and arms aren't bulky, skinny, or flabby. A visceral ache sweeps through me. I yearn to have a man hug me in more than a familial or friendly manner again. Then I picture the last man who embraced me that way and red-hot anger fills me followed by the icy coldness of betrayal.

Mia whines. My dog's amber eyes scan my face. She places her paws on my knees, begging to be picked up. Lifting my best friend and holding her compact body against my heart, the tightness in my chest evaporates. Mia's pink tongue pops out and swipes my chin.

The man watches us with a ghost of a smile. "They're more than our pets, aren't they?"

"Yes, much more."

When the presentation for the next winner begins, I place Mia at my feet and pay particular attention to the name of the man beside me.

"And the winner in the Hot Dog division is Park Robinson and his dog, Lamar."

Park shakes hands with both the announcer and the woman carrying the ribbons and certificates. When the announcer extends the trophy dog biscuit, Lamar snaps at the treat like a starved mongrel.

The emcee checks his fingers then lifts the microphone to his mouth. "Folks, this is the second time this particular wiener has won the title of Grand Champion. So without further ado, the winner of this year's Delray Beach Dachshund Derby is Mia and her owner, Marin McAllister."

The assistant hands me the two-foot-tall trophy with a large blue ribbon and a framed certificate. While a photographer snaps pictures, cheers and applause along with doggie barks add to the cacophony.

The announcer taps several times on the mic to quiet the crowd then he swings his arm around my shoulders. "In addition to bragging rights for another year, the champion receives a five hundred dollar check." He hands me a large piece of paper printed like a check but holds on to one end while the photographer snaps pictures. "Any words on your spectacular win today, Marin?"

I hand him the trophy and pull the microphone toward my mouth. "I would like to thank all the sponsors of this event, especially Atlantic Animal Hospital with Dr. Angelina Rosetti, the best veterinarian in Palm Beach County and my good friend."

Loud whistles, clapping, and woo-woos come from Rudy, Rita, and Mrs. R. Angie smiles and shakes her head at their enthusiastic response.

I reach into my pocket and pull out an envelope. "I'm donating today's award money and my personal check to Florida Dachshund Rescue. Mia and I appreciate all your support for our beloved wiener dogs."

After more pictures, I hand over the money to the announcer's assistant who is one of the organizers of the derby. She says, "I'll make sure the rescue group gets this. Thanks, Marin."

Family and friends of the winners climb onto the pavilion, including the Rosetti entourage. Angie takes Mia's leash. Rita tucks the certificates under her arm while I hold onto the ribbons.

Rudy lifts the trophy from the announcer's hands. "I'll carry that."

I swivel my head back and forth, but Park and Lamar are gone. I wanted to introduce him to my friends.

"Who're you looking for?" Rudy puts his hand on my back and propels me toward the steps.

Behind us, Rita pipes in. "Probably the red-haired, good looker standing next to her."

"Oh, Mom," Angie drawls.

"Hey, how do you know I wasn't talking about the dog?"

"Because I know you, that's how."

CHAPTER 4

THE FOLLOWING WEEKEND, I drive my GMC Acadia to within inches of a wrought iron gate mounted in an eight-foot-tall wall. Ivy grows on wires in a crisscross pattern across the front face. The green X's break up the gray monotony of the concrete barrier. I hit a remote above my visor and the ornate, black metal doors open. After traveling on a brick paver drive as long as a football field, I park behind a Mercedes sedan and grab the handle of a gift bag. As I step out of my car, a stiff breeze off the Atlantic ruffles my wide-legged, white linen pants. I smile at the hint of lavender-striped panties peeking through the thin fabric. At the front door, I punch a code into the keypad and the lock snicks open.

"Anybody home?" My voice echoes through the two-story marble foyer.

"We're in the living room, darling," calls out my mother with her boarding-school drawl.

Walking the width of the front entrance, the place smells of Sweet William, clean linen, orange beeswax, and earthy wool. The original fifty-foot-long reception room, which now is the family's living room, has a wood-coffered ceiling decorated with hand-painted shields. Arched doors along the far wall open to a view of Lake Worth. The tip-tap of my heels soften when I step from stone floors to inlaid mahogany and go silent on the room-sized antique rug.

My mother, Elizabeth Winslow McAllister, sits on the plush sofa facing a carved limestone fireplace. Betsy and I bear an uncanny resemblance. We're of similar height with elongated arms and legs on a compact ballet dancer's body, although neither of us was a ballerina. Unlike my ebony locks, Mumsy's hair is an artful mixture of dark cocoa and silvering highlights applied with unnatural precision. The only obvious claim I have to my father's DNA are my green eyes.

My half-sister, Katherine McAllister Coughlin, sits at the other end of the sofa, as delicate and pristine as a life-sized doll in a cellophane box. Her long gleaming mane is brushed back from a high forehead and falls around her shoulders like a butterscotch waterfall.

I bend over to embrace my smaller but older sibling. "Happy birthday, Kit. Where are the kids?"

"Where else? Up in the media room."

After placing the gift bag on the leather-topped coffee table, I turn toward the two brocade-upholstered armchairs. In one is my father, Stanford McAllister of the McAllister, Coughlin & Montgomery law firm. His tie is removed in deference to this casual family gathering, although the suit he wears costs more than most decent used cars.

In the other chair slouches my half-sister's blond upper-crust husband, Garrett Coughlin. I skirt my brother-in-law's outstretched feet without acknowledgment. My father scrutinizes my sheer white blouse under which is a skimpy lavender tank top.

He greets me in his usual annoying and overbearing manner. "You're very revealing today, Marin."

I plant a kiss on his golf-tanned cheek. "Thank you. I always strive for honesty and openness."

He winces. "I'm talking about your clothing. When are you going to invest in more appropriate attire?"

"I guess when my broker suggests it, Pops."

He heaves a sigh. "And why can't you call me Father like Kit does?"

"You're her father, but you're my Pops."

Stanford had been a widower and father to three-year-old Kit when he and Betsy married. Ten years later, I had been unexpectedly conceived. At the time, my father was in his mid-forties, and my mother on the downside of thirty-nine.

Betsy scoots over half a cushion and I squeeze in between her and the poufy sofa arm. "How are you, Mumsy?"

"I'm fine, dear. I saw you pictured in the paper last week."

In a bored drawl, my brother-in-law sneers, "What did you do this time? Help a family of ducks cross the street? Rescue a puppy from a storm drain?"

I ignore Garrett and smile at my mother. "I read the article too. The Post did a nice job of reporting the Derby. What they didn't report was how Mia and I were almost disqualified."

Betsy's plucked brows rose even higher. Her Botox injections must be wearing off. "What happened?"

"It was right before the final race to determine the champion. According to the rules, only food or treats could be used. No toys or balls. They must have changed them since we won last year, and I didn't notice. Park complained about me rolling a ball at the finish line, so the judge said I couldn't use it."

She tilts her head to the side. "How can a park complain?"

"No, Mumsy. The guy's name is Park."

"Is he Korean?" my father interjects. "We had an intern at the firm named Shin-woo Park, but he went by Sean."

"No, his first name is Park."

Stanford leans forward in his chair and puts his elbows on his knees. "So how did you circumvent the complainant?"

"Rudy and Rita were there with the food truck. I had them make a plain meatball about the size of Mia's racquetball and told the guy it was my lunch."

"Hah! Good thinking." Stanford sits back in his chair, clearly pleased with my solution to the dilemma.

Warmth slides through me with his approval. Under a lowered brow, I flash a devious smile. "Somehow in all the excitement, my *lunch* fell on the ground, and Mia shot over the finish line ahead of Park's dog to win the final heat. He still complained to the judge, but since his dog ate the evidence, Mia was declared the winner."

My sister leans forward in her seat to look past Mumsy. "Was Mrs. R cooking with Rudy in the food truck?"

"She sat outside under an umbrella and watched Mia for me between races. Rudy and Rita cooked. Angie manned the cash register."

Betsy asks, "How is Mrs. R doing? Just the other day Stanford said he hasn't had a good tiramisu since she retired."

Mrs. R cooked for the McAllister family until I turned eighteen. In the massive kitchen, she taught me, the often-ignored little girl, how to make pasta from scratch, cook authentic Italian gravy, and bake desserts. "Mrs. R isn't quite as spry as she used to be but still sharp. She's one of the foundation's best foster mothers for our dogs."

Garrett points his chin at me. "So how much did you win?"

"Five hundred dollars, but I gave the money to Florida Dachshund Rescue."

"And how much of your own money did you give away? It wasn't even a race you could bet on and win something back."

I was prepared to ignore Garrett today to maintain family civility but a retort slips out. "It was probably less than you lost at online poker last week."

The stare-down between me and Garrett lasts until Kit speaks. "Tell her what you're doing now, darling."

My brother-in-law's features crease into a scowl, and he utters his words between clenched teeth. "I'm attending Gamblers Anonymous meetings."

I look at my sister. "Are you sure that's where he's going or just where he says he's going?"

Kit's eyes become glassy with tears. "We're trying our best to overcome this."

Numerous times in Kit's ten-year marriage, she would be closeted with our parents, her crying audible through thick carved doors. Although I was never been privy to the conversations, I figured out my brother-in-law owed mountainous credit card debts at online gambling sites. Often Kit left the room with a check tucked into her pocket while offering thanks, and vowing she would never ask for help again.

But, of course, she did.

The final straw for me, where Garrett is concerned, occurred five years ago. When my Grammy Winslow died, she left me, her only biological granddaughter, a trust fund worth multiple millions. I acquired access to the money when I turned twenty-one. Somehow Garrett found out about the gift if not the exact amount.

At my party, he cornered me by the boathouse. His walk bordered on clumsy, his hand gestures were flamboyant. "There's my poor, little, rich sister-in-law all alone at her grown-up party."

Alcohol had induced a degree of recklessness which Garrett usually kept in check. My eyes shifted around. No one stood within shouting distance.

I lifted my chin in false bravado. "What do you want, Garrett?"

"I came to offer my congratulations."

"Thank you. Now I need to get back to my party." I skirted around him, but his hand shot out and latched onto my arm.

Garrett pushed me against the wall. "I know you've always had the hots for me."

For a second, I panicked then stiffened my shoulders. "You're right. But we can't do anything to hurt Kit."

"Looks like I married the wrong sister. Why couldn't *my* wife have the rich grandmother?"

When he leaned in to kiss me, I grabbed his neck as if to embrace him and drove my knee into his groin with the speed of a striking cobra, hissing through my clenched teeth. Garrett's breath whooshed out in a boozy cloud. I pushed him away with a mighty shove. He landed on the grass and curled into a ball.

My voice trembled with a combination of rage and fear." If you ever try something like that again, you *bastard*, I'll tell my parents and sister."

Now the verbal warfare we engage in baffles my family. Despite their inquiries, I have never revealed the reason for my obvious antipathy to my brother-in-law. Garrett never asked me to keep what happened between us a secret, but I choose not to hurt Kit with the revelation of what her husband said and did. Although I doubt Garrett will overcome his gambling addiction, I am certain he'll never try to kiss me again.

CHAPTER 5

THE SLAP OF shoes resounds on the marble staircase like little penguin feet. As if by tacit agreement, the tension in the room vanishes into the corners as we plaster on pleasant smiles. Craning my neck, I wait for the children's entrance through the wide doorway. A boy with shaggy blond hair races into the room followed by his younger sister.

I stand and put my hands on my hips. "Well, it's about time."

"Auntie Marin," squeals the little girl.

The five-year-old bundle of energy, in a somewhat grubby, blue Elsa dress from *Frozen,* hurtles across the room toward me. I lift Ainsley into my arms.

My nephew stops short and frowns. "When did you get here?"

In the last year, eight-year-old Trevor has become quite bratty with me. His face will shift from animated to disdainful as if I showed up to announce his bedtime.

I ignore him and address Ainsley. "How's my favorite niece?"

She cups my cheeks with her little hands. "Good."

"What's new?"

"You know what I'm going to be when I grow up?"

"A truck driver?"

"No." Ainsley giggles and brushes white-blond hair out of her eyes.

"A shepherd?"

"What's a shepherd?"

"Someone who watches over sheep."

Ainsley's brow crinkles. "Like Jesus?"

I nod.

"No, I'm going to be a princess, and marry a prince, and live in a castle."

I set the little girl on her feet. "Good luck with that."

Ainsley dances over to her mother. "Is it time for your party? I'm hungry."

In a normal family, a birthday involves fun food like pizza, presents, and cake. For the McAllisters, the celebration means a five-course meal, a hefty check or stock certificates, and lots of wine. Of course, we have cake, too. My family isn't totally clueless when it comes to birthdays.

Mrs. Nichol, the family housekeeper, enters the room. When the black woman in a spotless white uniform spies me, her face breaks into a wide, white smile. "Miss Marin. Good to see you again."

I approach the tall, Jamaican woman and give her a quick hug, certain my parents cringe behind me. "How's your husband?"

"Elvin is fine." Mrs. Nichol's smile stiffens. Either Betsy or Stanford has given her the eye. "Dinna is served."

Kit and Garrett escort their children to the dining room as the housekeeper hustles away.

I turn to my parents. "How's Mr. Nichol? Has he finished chemo?"

Betsy halts. "Chemo?"

"He's had weeks of treatment for lung cancer. The last I heard the doctors thought he was in remission."

My father strolls past. "We do not get familiar with the help."

I cock my head at Betsy. "Isn't asking about an ill man's health a common courtesy?"

"Of course, dear," my mother says over her shoulder. "But health issues are discussed in private."

Dinner is in the formal dining room where a custom-made table for fourteen stretches out under a sixteenth-century carved wood ceiling. My father sits with his back to the castle-sized marble fireplace. My sister, brother-in-law, and the children are in upholstered chairs along one side of the inlaid wood table. I count eight settings with place cards and spot mine. I don't have time to read the name of the person seated next to me before the doorbell chimes.

Betsy flashes a saccharine smile. "Marin, would you let in our guest?"

Crossing the foyer with heavy steps, I recognize the person through the etched glass of the door. My abdominal muscles tense as if doing a Pilates crunch while, at the same time, my shoulders slump. Of course, it would be him. This particular train has been barreling toward me for months, but nothing I say or do derails its advance.

I fling open the front door. "Hello, Trey."

A tall strawberry blonde, who is a near twin of England's Prince Harry, walks inside with a colorful bouquet. "Hi, Marin. These are for your mother."

I've been friends with Harrison Montgomery the Third since grade school. His father works as one of the partners in the law firm of McAllister, Coughlin & Montgomery. After Kit married Garrett Coughlin, the McAllister and Montgomery families, like royals of old, hoped to create a legal dynasty among their offspring by throwing me and Trey together at every chance.

I lift the mix of spring flowers from his hand and lean down to smell their light fragrance. In a low tone, I murmur, "How's Carmen?"

His lips curl back against his teeth. "Three months pregnant."

Carmen Arias, a beautiful professional ballroom dancer, is the daughter of the Mr. and Mrs. Montgomery's landscaper. Several years ago, Trey attended a dance competition with a date, saw Carmen's name on the program, and they have been together ever since.

I'm one of only a handful of people who know about their clandestine relationship. "What are you going to do?"

"What choice do I have? I wanted to wait until I finished law school in May and passed the bar to tell my parents. If they cut me off now, we'll have to live on Carmen's salary as long as she can work at the dance studio."

"If things get rough, let me know. I'll help out."

"We can't take your money."

"Consider it a loan then. What good is having a trust fund if you can't use it to help your friends?"

"You're the best, Marin." Trey wraps me in a tight embrace.

"Oh, excuse me. Hello, Harrison." Betsy approaches and smiles at us in each other's arms. "We wondered what was keeping you two. The vichyssoise is served."

Trey steps away from me and walks over to my mother. "Thank you for the invitation tonight, Mrs. McAllister."

Purring, Betsy loops her arm around his elbow. "What lovely flowers you brought, Harrison." They walk ahead several paces. "Are you coming, dear?"

I hand the bouquet to Mrs. Nicol who stands at attention inside the dining room doorway. My father rises from his chair and shakes Trey's hand then claps him on the back like a prodigal son. Bowls of untouched chilled soup sit atop gold-rimmed small plates at each place setting. Trey pulls out my chair and takes his card-designated spot between me and Betsy.

"Can we eat now?" Trevor whines.

Ainsley, in a booster seat, bangs her elbows on the table. "I want crackers, and I don't like cold soup."

Once the children are settled with warmer vichyssoise, water crackers, and slivers of cheese, the dinner settles into the semblance of a formal meal. Salads with mixed spring greens, yellow beets, and goat cheese are followed by Kit's favorite roast chicken, mashed potatoes, and asparagus.

Stanford and Betsy inquire about Trey and law school. Where has he applied to intern? Has he started studying for the bar yet? When does he plan to take the exam? Is he still interested in a political career?

The polite, though insistent, interrogation remains innocuous enough until Betsy changes the topic. "Harrison, will you be attending the Ross wedding?"

"Unfortunately, I can't. The date conflicts with my school schedule."

"Marin received an invitation but has said she is *absolutely* not going."

Trey turns to face me. "Why not?"

I lay down my knife and fork. "Evan and his fiancée, whoever she is, are marrying for richer and not for long. The only way he can get his hands on his grandfather's money is if he's *legally* married at the reading of the will. The old man is not expected to live much longer, but that's what Evan said months ago. So I refuse to spend my time and money on his farce of a wedding."

Trey frowns. "Are you sure about the will?"

"Yes, I'm sure. He asked me to marry him last summer and offered a quickie divorce once he inherited."

Betsy gasps. "Why didn't you say anything to us?"

"Would you have advised me to accept his proposal?"

Betsy looks aghast. "No, of course, not." Her eyes shift for a quick confirmation to her husband who nods, so my mother continues. "I just don't know why you kept it a secret."

I keep many secrets, and people trust me with them. I shoot Trey a significant glance. Two years ago, he and only a few others knew the secret of why I ended my engagement.

Betsy raises her chin as if to address a crowd who will disagree with what she is about to say. "I'm sure both you and Harrison are well aware that most of your contemporaries are either engaged or married by now."

"Or divorced," I add.

"Yes, however, you do not want to wait too long. Remember . . . tick-tock."

"Sorry, Mumsy, but I don't speak clock."

My mother ignores my snarky reply. "Harrison, I know you're anxious to finish law school and begin your career, but it's never too early to make plans. You two are perfect for each other. You know the same people and have much in common. That's a wonderful basis for a union."

I grind my teeth in frustration. "Trey and I are just friends. There is no chemistry between us."

"Darling, sometimes a couple just needs to be together more to realize their attraction. Friendship often grows into love. Being friends first is the best kind of relationship since infatuation can be fleeting."

I throw my hands in the air. "It doesn't matter how many of these little get-togethers you engineer, I'm not a bitch in heat. Do you think Trey will get a whiff and suddenly fall in love with me?"

"Marin!" Betsy slaps a hand to her throat.

Stanford scowls, his fork poised between his plate and mouth. "That's enough."

Trevor grins with malicious glee, entertained by shocked and angry adults who rarely display emotions. Ainsley puts a hand over her mouth and giggles with childish delight. Their parents bear expressions of amusement and pity.

Trey pats my arm as if to calm me. He speaks in a soothing, yet implacable tone. "Your mother means well."

Betsy closes her eyes and holds two lacquered nails to her forehead as though the stress of her obstinate and indelicate daughter is too much to bear. "Thank you, Harrison. You are so perceptive."

I scowl at him. "My parents and yours think of us an endangered species, like panda bears. If we don't procreate with each other, the Palm Beach social species in general, and McAllister Coughlin & Montgomery, in particular, may cease to exist."

Trey shifts in his chair. "That's putting it a bit strongly, don't you think?"

"No, I don't. I know you're getting the same pressure at home. We need to present a united front, so they'll stop. We have to make them understand we will not consent to an arranged marriage." I wait for his agreement, but he says nothing. "Well, at least, I won't."

Trey stares at me then turns to Stanford and Betsy with his hands outstretched, like a mediator who has tried his best but failed. "I'm sorry, Mr. and Mrs. McAllister. She's right. I love Marin as a good friend, but there will be nothing more between us. I would appreciate it if you would accept our positions and urge my parents to do the same."

Stanford pats his mouth with a white linen napkin. "I admit I find the prospect of having you as a son-in-law very appealing. We know you and your family well." The underlying message in my father's words is that they have no idea who I might marry to spite them. "My wife and your mother believe that, with persuasion and proximity, you and Marin will come to realize your attraction. I do not agree, but my protests fell on deaf ears. You are young adults and have reached an age where your decisions are determined without parental intervention or preference. Therefore, I can assure you neither Betsy nor I will, in any way, attempt to foster a relationship in the future between you and my daughter." He delivers this soliloquy matter-of-factly but ends with a stern look at his wife.

Trey nods. "Thank you, Mr. McAllister."

I smile. "Yes. Thank you, Pops."

Ainsley tugs on her mother's sleeve. "Is it time to sing Happy Birthday?"

CHAPTER 6

THE FOLLOWING WEEKEND I sit in the humid shade outside a pet supply store with Mia and a crate of dachshund puppies. Two other volunteers signed up for the mobile adoption event but canceled with excuses, so I'm on my own. Numerous shoppers stop to admire the plump, playful puppies, but no one fills out an adoption application. I check my watch and wipe a bead of sweat off my forehead. Ninety minutes to go.

A man exits a pickup truck with two small boys. "Daddy, look, puppies. Can we see 'em? Can we?"

The father grumbles then he flashes a quick leering glance in my direction. His stare lingers on my bare legs and short shorts. "Sure. We can take a look."

He saunters over as his kids run ahead. The boys squat and poke their fingers through the bars of the crate to stroke the pile of sleepy pups.

I rise from the folding chair. "Hi. Have you ever owned a dog?"

The man pushes up the brim of his camouflage ball cap. "Lots of them. We got one now."

"Well, these are the last three of a litter rescued from a puppy mill in Georgia. The mother was adopted last week. The puppies have had all their shots and are ready for good homes. If you're interested, we have an adoption application to fill out. We'll check your references and do a home inspection."

"References? An inspection? It's a dog, not a kid."

I point to the boys. "And just like one of your children, a dog is a family member."

"What if we don't like it after a while? Can we give it back?"

"Would you ever give away one of your boys?"

"There are days I get why some animals eat their young." He throws back his head and laughs.

One of his sons tries to open the crate, but it is secured with a padlock. I kneel and refasten the loosened latch. "We need to keep the puppies inside."

The boy's bottom lip pouts. "But I wanna hold one."

"I know. They're really cute, aren't they? But I'm by myself here today, so I can't let you hold a puppy and talk to your dad too. I'm sorry."

The boy cries, "I want a puppy, Daddy. Please."

I twist around, still crouching on my haunches. The boys' father stares at me like he's wearing X-Ray specs. Revulsion races through me as quick as the flash of a camera. I stand and square my shoulders.

The man licks his lips. "Maybe we can make a deal."

"What do you mean?"

He puts his hands in his back pockets and rocks on his feet. "We have a beagle at home that's about two years old. Damn thing barks all the time. The boys are tired of her. How 'bout you and me do a trade?"

I stiffen. "You want to trade your dog for a puppy?"

"You want to get rid of yours, and I want to get rid of mine."

I don't answer, unsure of how to express my outrage since I represent the foundation, and children are within earshot. I itch to tell this guy that dogs are meant to be family. If he can't love them and treat them like another kid then he doesn't deserve to have one. "Tell you what. You turn in your dog to me, and I'll find it a good home."

"What about a puppy?"

"No, I don't think a puppy would be a good idea."

"Well, you gotta give me something." He pauses with a quick scan of my legs again. "She's a purebred beagle."

"How much do you want for her?"

"Whaddaya mean? You'll buy it?"

"Right. How much do you want?"

The man's eyes narrow. "Two . . . hundred?"

"Go home and get her. I'll have your money when you get back."

He shoots a look at the kids who giggle as one puppy nibbles on their fingers. "It's like a fifteen-minute drive there then I gotta come back."

"And when was the last time you made two hundred dollars in half an hour?"

The man glances again toward his children. "The kids aren't going to be happy."

"I'll throw in an extra fifty so you can buy them toys to play with, instead of a dog that barks all the time."

"Yeah, well, I don't know if Daisy's a purebred or not. We don't have no papers or nothing."

"Three hundred. Cash. If you're back here with Daisy by . . ." I check my watch. "Two-thirty. That's when I start to pack up and leave." Behind my back, I cross my fingers.

Several seconds pass then the man jerks his head. "Get in the truck, boys. We're going back home."

The kids wail and protest until their father tells them they'll stop at Walmart later to buy toys. The pickup peels out of the parking lot with a squeal of rubber.

Mia yips and I meet her gaze. "I know, little girl. We'll be leaving with more dogs than we came with."

"Why?"

I jump. Park Robinson stands behind me, tall, devastatingly attractive, and slightly sweaty with a bag of dog food from the pet store under his arm. He wears knee-length basketball shorts and a sleeveless T-shirt. His shoulders and arms are roped with lean muscles. A ray of sunshine bounces off his reflective sunglasses like a mini lightning burst. My attractive-male-in-the-vicinity sensors spin like crazy.

He shifts the dog food into his other arm. "I saw you talking with that guy and his kids. Why are you leaving with more dogs? Aren't you here to find homes for the ones you brought?"

"Yes, I'm looking for good people to adopt, but when a dog needs rescued I do that too. Anyway, I'm paying the guy who owns Daisy to give her to me." A feeling of disgust makes me shake my head. "I have the feeling before long she'd be abandoned on the street or dumped in the Everglades."

I work with a rescue group that saves dogs and cats whose owners let them loose to fend for themselves. The animals we find in time are usually starving, full of blood-sucking ticks, and suffering from heartworms. Many others are dead or near death from disease, the elements, wildlife, or injured by vehicles. These types of rescues embody heartbreaking labors of love.

Consoling myself with a mantra, I recite it aloud to Park. "I can't save them all, but I can save some. And today, it's Daisy."

"Are you working here alone?"

I nod. "The other volunteers couldn't make it."

"How much are you paying this guy?"

"Three hundred dollars. He claims she's purebred, but I doubt it."

Park puts his head to one side, as though measuring me. His one eyebrow arches behind the Oakley sunglasses. He lowers his lenses to the tip of his nose, and his gaze drifts down to my abdomen which peeks out below my cropped tank top. "I'll be right back."

He disappears around the corner of the store. A few minutes later, he returns without the dog food and thrusts several twenties at me. "All I have with me is a hundred. If I go to an ATM, I don't know if I'll be back in time."

"In time for what?"

"You can't be here by yourself when you hand over that much cash. Who knows what the creep will do? I'll stay with you."

Here in front of a pet supply store with shoppers coming and going, my girl equipment zings with an awareness of Park's boy equipment. I will never chase a man again, but this one could definitely make me speed walk a little. "Thank you. I appreciate that."

Park stays with the dogs while I retrieve the rest of the money from a hidden compartment in my car. When I return, Mia is sprawled on her back in an undignified position. With her rear legs spread wide, she offers her pinkish-white belly, as if I never pay her any attention. Park crouches over the dog, murmuring and stroking her hairless stomach.

When he stands, I bite my lip with the awkwardness of the situation. After all, I'm the recent winner of the dachshund derby, beating him out of first place. I thrust out my hand. "We've not been formally introduced. My name is Marin McAllister. And you are . . . Park?"

"That's right. Park Robinson."

His hand is strong and warm against my palm. "Do you spell your first name with an *e* at the end?"

"No *e*."

"Is it short for Parker?"

"Just Park."

"It's an interesting name. I like it."

His voice is dry and flat. "Mom will be thrilled you approve."

And just like that, he's back to being a jerk.

Several more people stop to see the puppies, but no one completes an adoption application. Thirty minutes later, camo-cap man returns without his kids and with a dog that indeed has some beagle in her. She is a woebegone little thing with patches of brown and black on a white coat that hasn't been bathed in quite a while. I unfasten the too-small collar around her neck then drop a slip knot leash over Daisy's head.

Mia approaches the canine newcomer with caution. After the two females sniff each other to their satisfaction, tails wag. On the other hand, Park and camo-cap act like two territorial strays itching for a fight.

I stand and address the man. "What can you tell me about Daisy?"

"What's there to know? She's a dog."

A muscle pulses in Park's jaw.

"Is she up to date on vaccinations?"

"I dunno. She had some when we got her."

She hasn't been vaccinated in two years? "So she isn't licensed?"

"What's the point?"

Park's eyes have gone flat and hard. I shift back to Daisy's not-for-long owner. "Is she housebroken?"

"Probably not. We mostly keep her tied up outside or in the garage."

Park's hands ball into fists as he steps closer to the guy.

Oh no. Daisy might have heartworms. The disease commonly occurs in dogs kept outdoors in Florida and can be fatal if left untreated. I reach behind me for a clipboard with a form on it. "Before I can give you the money, you need to sign this."

The man crosses his arms and juts his chin toward the papers I hold out. "What's that?"

"The form says you agree to give Daisy to The Forever Homes Dachshund Foundation. You're welcome to read it before you sign. But I can't give you the money without the completed information and your signature." I hand him the clipboard and pen. "Here, take a seat."

With obvious reluctance, he sits. Either he's an Evelyn Wood speed reader or doesn't bother with the fine print before he fills in the lines at the bottom. When he hands it back to me, I read what he wrote. "May I see your driver's license?"

"What for?"

"Just to verify who you are. This is a binding contract between you and the foundation, so I need to confirm your identity."

The man stands and fishes his wallet out of his back pocket. The name and address on the form match his license.

He grumbles, "That it? You got the cash?"

In a low, toneless voice, Park says, "Give him the money. He needs to leave. Right now."

Without a word, I tear off a carbon copy of the signed form and hand it to the man. Then I reach into the pocket of my shorts and give him the folded bills. The guy pockets them without counting while his eyes remain locked on Park. As if facing down a predator, Daisy's former owner backs away a few feet, turns, and hustles to his vehicle.

After he drives off, Park inhales a deep breath which seems to release his tension. He squats and pets Daisy's head. "What are you going to do with her?"

"Take her home. Bathe her. Get her to the vet. Try to find her a loving family. She deserves it. Also, I'll be entering the guy's information into a database here in Palm Beach County. It'll prevent him from adopting a pet from another shelter or rescue group."

Park walks Daisy, Mia, and the three puppies around the parking lot while I pack up. After helping me get all the dogs into my SUV, he closes the hatchback. "Can you handle everything on your own, or do you want me to follow you home?"

"Thanks, but I got it."

"Are you working at any other adoptions?"

"I have one in Wellington next Saturday. Why?"

He pulls out his phone. "Give me the address and time. I'll help out. And what's your phone number, in case I need to get in touch with you?"

When he finishes adding the information into his phone, he waves and jogs off.

I study his muscled legs and backside as he heads across the parking lot. "We'll see if you do show up, Park, with no e, Robinson."

CHAPTER 7

THE FOLLOWING SATURDAY, I arrive early at the farmer's market for the mobile adoption. The Forever Homes Dachshund Foundation is co-sponsoring the event with the local Humane Society. The March temperature is cooler than the previous weekend which will be easier on the volunteers and the animals. Because of the weather, I expect more potential adopters to come.

Sandy Hanna and her husband, Ray, sit in two chairs under a pop-up canopy. I became friends with the couple when I volunteered at my first mobile adoption. A variety of recent health issues now slows the older woman who single-handedly started the county's Trap-Neuter-Vaccinate-Release, or T-N-V-R, program, for feral cats. Sandy waves as I struggle with one hand to pull a wagon stacked with supplies over the bumpy ground. In my other hand, I hold three leashes, one for Mia, Daisy, and another foundation rescue named Angel.

Sandy rises from her seat. "Don't you look cute?"

That morning, I pulled from the back of my closet a turquoise, flamingo-printed sundress. I added a hot-pink cropped cardigan to ward off the morning's coolness. The outfit had been a birthday present from my sister who probably has an identical dress in her size. I have never worn mine until today. In this outfit, I resemble a 1950s housewife—except for my purple ponytail.

Sandy rounds the long table covered with a skirt imprinted with the name of the county shelter. "Why did you have to bring everything in one trip? Weren't you allowed to park close? Those idiot kids directing traffic tried to make me park halfway to West Palm. I nearly had to run one over to get him to move out of the way. Ray, grab those leashes."

I have never seen Sandy's husband in anything but T-shirts and sweatpants. Today is no exception. He heaves himself out of the folding chair and inhales like he has to psych himself up for a hundred-meter Olympic final. He lumbers half a dozen steps forward, his jowls and belly jiggling.

I hand off the three dogs. "Hi, Ray."

He nods his greeting. The man rarely speaks, as if being married to the garrulous Sandy has atrophied his vocal cords.

After he attaches the leashes to a tent leg, Sandy bends and pets the dogs. "Hello, sweet Angel. Maybe we'll find you a home today. Well, Miss Mia, is this your new friend, Daisy? She seems like a nice girl." Sandy braces a hand on her knee, groans, and raises herself upright. "Purebred, my ass. Daisy's got about as much beagle in her as I have good manners. I can't believe you gave the guy three hundred dollars. I would have gone off on that poor-excuse-for-an-orgasm until he paid *me*."

Daisy wags her tail and appears excited, rather than fearful, with the new people and environment. I smile down at my latest foster. "You should have seen how pitiful she looked. I was worried she might have heartworms, but Dr. Rosetti gave her a clean bill of health. She is so pretty now after a bath and regular meals." I stop and stare open-mouthed at Sandy. "Wait a minute. How do you know about Daisy?"

"I told her."

For the third time, I whirl at the unexpected sound of Park's deep baritone behind me. "Stop sneaking up on me."

He shakes his head at me like I'm as crazy as a bag of wet cats. A folding table is under his one arm and two chairs under the other. In pristine jeans and a cotton Henley shirt with the sleeves pushed up to his elbows, he looks like a catalog model. After setting up the table and chairs where Sandy tells him, he asks her, "Do you want me to bring the cooler now?"

"Yeah, that'd be great." As Park walks away, Sandy's eyes remain glued on him. "He is one fine piece of man. I hope he's not married. I didn't see a ring, but that don't mean nothing nowadays. If he's not, you two should go out."

I duck my head with a secret smile and describe to Sandy my two previous encounters with Park. "All I really know about him is he volunteered to help out today and loves dogs. He can be a pain in the ass, though."

"Two out of three ain't bad." Sandy drops her Sponge Bob square body with its stick-thin arms and legs into a chair. "He was waiting for us when we got here. Sure is nice to have some young muscle around to fetch and carry. His good looks might get some Wellington mamas to stop and look at the dogs. Why don't you ask him to take off his shirt to draw them in?" Sandy does a wink-wink with one eye with an accompanying nudge-nudge with her elbow.

"I can't ask Park to do that."

"Do what?"

I spin around and drop the clipboards onto the tabletop. "You did it again."

He puts the cooler down. "Are you always this tense?"

"I am *not* tense," I say in a too-loud voice.

The vendor in the next tent frowns in my direction.

Park places his hands on his hips. "What can't you ask me?"

I focus on rearranging the clipboards and forms. "Tell him, Sandy, it was *your* idea."

The older woman leans back in the canvas chair and folds her arms beneath her expansive bosom. "You seem like a nice guy and really care about dogs, like Marin here. So how about having dinner tonight? Do you have plans? Maybe brunch tomorrow would be better?"

As Sandy speaks, my horror grows. This is like the time my mother asked a friend's son to escort me to the debutante ball—and she did it right in front of me. I wanted to disappear. And just like that time, I stand frozen in place as a flush of heat burns my neck and face.

Sandy's inexorable voice continues. "Whaddaya say? You interested?"

Park stares at the ground. "Uh, I guess. I, um—"

Oh no. He has a girlfriend, or is gay, or is just not interested. How humiliating.

Sandy blows out an exasperated breath. "Come on, what's so hard? You need to use a lifeline? Maybe phone a friend? Do you want to go out with Marin or not?"

He emits a shaky laugh. "You're talking about her? I thought *you* were asking me out."

"Sorry, bud. I don't think my hunka-hunka burning love over there would be too happy about me dating you." Sandy points to Ray, who has fallen asleep in the chair, his hands clasped across his ample abdomen, chin tilted forward as if resting on an invisible pillow.

Park glances my way. "Sure. I'll take her to dinner."

Sandy studies him with narrowed eyes. "You're not wearing a ring. You married?"

"Never been."

"How old are you?"

"Twenty-nine."

"Do you have a steady job?"

"Nine to five."

"What else should we know about you?"

Park's expression remains deadpan. "I'm a Gemini. Love to run on the beach. I'm a lousy golfer. My pet peeve is people who insult their dogs by saying they're human."

Sandy bobs her head once and brushes her palms together. "My job here is done. We wrap up around two o'clock. That should give you enough time to go home, get ready, and pick Marin up."

"Works for me." Park pulls his cell phone out of his pocket.

"You better make a reservation since it's the season when all the shithole snowbirds litter the place. She loves seafood, by the way, but doesn't care for hoity-toity restaurants. Still, you gotta do better than Red Lobster."

"I'll need her address, so I can plan how long it'll take me to drive from my house to hers."

Sandy reaches into her voluminous shorts. "I have it on my phone. Let me get it for you."

"Hell-o." I wave my hands. "Did you two forget I'm standing right here?"

Sandy scans each end of the aisle in front of the tent. "Okay, you guys work out the details later. It looks like the market's opening up. Wake up, Ray. You and Park need to bring the shelter dogs from the RV."

When the two men leave, I round on her. "I could have gotten my own date."

Sandy sits back in her chair with a self-satisfied grin. "Yeah, but I did it quicker and easier. You can thank me later. Name one of the kids after me."

When all the dogs are under the tent and everything set up, Sandy positions Park out front with a puppy in his arms. He turns out to be a chick magnet. Women approach and strike up a conversation while petting the little mixed-breed terrier. Their hands often brush against his firm chest. He directs them to the table of adoption applications where Sandy and I interview those who express an interest.

After a time, Sandy calls for Park to bring the puppy back to the crate. "Let's give him a rest." She hands me a leash. "You're up. Stand out there with Angel."

Some people ask if the tan-coated dog is a Pit Bull then shy away. I can't believe their ignorance. The abusers, who mistreated the breed for decades, are the ones who have given the dogs a negative reputation. This young pit bull behaves like her angel name while I, a woman wearing a dress covered in pink flamingos, holds the leash with two fingers.

How can that be scary?

Several young men inquire about Angel who is not as large as many of the breed. One Hispanic teenager with his sideways ball cap sneers. "I need me a more macho dog, so my homies respect me."

I study the short teenager with coarse-grained skin in an over-sized T-shirt, baggy jeans, and pricey sneakers. "They'll respect you because of your dog?"

"Yeah, man. That's right."

"In your case, you might need a wolf."

He eyes me with a set jaw, but I keep my expression neutral. The guy flashes gold-capped teeth and bobs his head. "Yeah, that's what I need. A wolf. You got any?"

"Sorry. Only dogs. But good luck finding one."

He swaggers off as a baritone voice behind me says, "What are you doing?"

This time I don't jump, even though he still startles me. I look over my shoulder. "Why do you always sneak up on me?"

"I'm practicing my stalking technique. What were you doing with those homeboys?"

"Just drumming up adopters."

"By making fun of them? By the way, Sandy told me Angel's story." He kneels and strokes the dog's square head. "Was she really close to death when you rescued her?"

"As close as I've ever seen. She was skin and bones and had a terrible wound on her neck. I prayed the whole way to the veterinary hospital. Even after we got there, it was touch-and-go for days."

Park scratched Angel's chest where two white splotches resemble wings. "Did you pay her owner like you did with Daisy's?"

"Yes. I find many animal abusers are motivated by money to relinquish their pets. Later, I testified against the guy in court."

He stands with a ferocious scowl marring his classic features. "Was he punished?"

Before I can answer, two women and a child approach. Angel jumps to her feet with her tail wagging, as if she spots a long-lost friend. The younger woman holds the hand of a darling boy who is about five-years-old. His towhead tilts at an odd angle, and he stares trance-like at his flicking fingers. Angel whines. The boy's eyes snap up, and he shudders. In the next second, he stills as if an internal switch has turned off. He becomes as fixated on Angel as he was on his fingers.

The curly-haired blond woman jiggles his hand in hers. "Don't worry, Dylan. She's a nice dog, like grandma's dog, Barney."

Angel strains forward to get closer to the boy and whines again. I give a slight sideways tug on the leash. "Sit."

The dog does as I command but quivers in place.

As the boy's mother meets my eyes, her lips quirk into a sad smile. "I'm afraid Dylan isn't very interested in animals."

The other woman, an older but smaller version of the young mother, says, "Nor people."

Without warning, Dylan slips loose and rushes to Angel. He drops to his knees and wraps his arms around her neck. She licks his hair, cheek, or wherever her pink tongue can reach.

The two women stand frozen. Dylan giggles and sits back. He and Angel look at each other. Some form of primal nonverbal communication seems to pass between them. Then the dog slides her front paws out and lays flat on the ground. The boy straddles her back and puts his cheek on top of her head. They both close their eyes. Dylan smiles, and it seems Angel does too.

"Oh, my God! Do you see that, Mom?" The younger woman's eyes fill with tears.

Her mother nods, a hand covering her mouth. For several seconds, no one speaks or moves. The sights and sounds of the farmer's market disappear as I focus on the survivor dog and the little boy.

The spell breaks when Dylan raises his head with a beatific smile and, in a robotic voice, says, "Fend."

His mother's knees buckle slightly. "He said friend. I heard him say friend."

The older woman wraps her in an embrace. "It's a miracle."

Thirty minutes later, we complete the adoption paperwork. Dylan sits with his arm over Angel's back. Every few minutes he rubs his cheek against her. In turn, she sniffs him or licks his face. The boy babbles nonsensically to the dog, but every so often a clear word or two emerges.

"A-gel."

"Love."

I agree to bend the rules and allow Kerry Kowalski and her mother, India, to take Angel without checking references or a conducting a home inspection. My only other option is to take Dylan home with me because he and Angel are now inseparable. I tell the two women about the dog's history.

Kerry's lips tightened. "I'm sorry such a terrible thing happened to such a sweet dog, but because of it, she's here today. I've been praying for something to help Dylan, but I didn't expect God's answer would have four legs."

Before they leave, India reaches into her purse. "Can I write you a check?"

I hold up a hand. "You can do that after the home visit on Monday. We ask for a sixty dollar donation if you can afford it."

India extracts her checkbook, opens it, and writes. "If you only knew how much has been spent to help Dylan. I can't believe this dog got him talking." She hands the check to me. The amount is two hundred dollars. "Thank you so much."

Kerry takes the leash in one hand. "It's time to take Angel home. Say goodbye, Dylan."

The boy turns, his dog beside him, and waves. Angel never looks back.

Park leans down close to my ear. "Now I see why you do this."

I wipe a tear from under my eye.

CHAPTER 8

ON THE WAY home from the farmer's market, I stop at the Rosetti's house. I have to explain Angel's absence. I open the door from the garage into the kitchen. "Anybody home?"

Rudy calls out. "On the patio."

When I step onto the raised wood deck I find Rudy, Rita, Angie, and Mrs. R sipping Pellegrino and playing cards. "Hi. Who's winning?"

Rudy stands to kiss my cheek. "Mama is, as usual." He motions for me to take his seat and pulls another chair over for himself.

I unclip the leashes from Daisy and Mia to allow them to wander the fenced-in backyard.

Mrs. R looks around. "Where's my girl?"

Unable to meet the older woman's gaze, I say, "I found Angel a home."

Rita slaps her cards on the table. "Don't tell me you let somebody take her without an inspection."

"Let me explain."

After telling the story, Rudy blinks dampness from his eyes, and Rita knuckles tears off her cheeks while Angie beams.

Mrs. R sits immobile with a stoic expression. "I will miss my Angel, but that little boy is why she lived when there was no reason on Earth she should have."

Angie reaches over and puts an arm around her grandmother's narrow shoulders. "Nonni, you're the reason Angel survived. None of the medicine I gave her was as powerful as your love."

After her rescue and with a dire prognosis for survival, Rudy's mother decided the pit bull puppy should not die alone. For five days, she spent almost every minute with Angel in her arms and willed her to fight. At night, she slept on a cot in Angie's office with the dog next to her. Since then, Angel has lived with Mrs. R.

I swallow a lump in my throat. "I'm doing a home inspection on Monday. Do you want to come with me?"

Mrs. R shakes her white-haired head. "No. Angel is where she should be. I don't want to confuse her, but my house will seem so empty." She watches Daisy and Mia play tug of war with a toy. "How about I take Daisy?"

"That would be great. She's housebroken now and pretty good on a leash. She'll come when called, sits, and stays. She needs to work on separation training. I can't leave her alone more than two or three minutes before she starts howling and won't stop."

Mrs. R calls Daisy over and tells her to sit. She holds the dog's muzzle in her two arthritic hands and stares into the beagle's amber-colored eyes. "You and I are going to be working and living together. You're going to learn people who love you will come and go, but you'll never be alone again. Understand?"

It appears Daisy agrees with a quick head bob. Mia comes over to the group with a ball in her mouth. She nudges it toward Rudy's foot and scampers back. My dachshund looks at the man then at the ball. Rudy picks it up and holds it above his head while Mia, taut and trembling, is ready to spring into action. She sprints before his arm completes the grenade-throwing arc.

I smile at Rudy's mother. "I came here to tell you about Angel and ask if one of you will keep Daisy tonight. Thanks, Mrs. R, for letting her stay with you until she's adopted."

"Why were you going to ask one of us to keep her?" Rita frowns at me. "Where are *you* going?"

"Mom," Angie scolds. "That's her business, not yours."

"Someone should know where she'll be." Rita faces me with her arms crossed like a skeptical parent ready to hear a flimsy excuse. "So, what's up?"

"I have a date."

"With who?"

Angie's head jerks in my mother's direction. "*Mom.*"

She ignores her daughter. "Who is this guy? Did you meet him today? Why haven't we heard about him before this?"

Although Rita's intrusiveness irks her daughter, I don't mind. It comforts me to know someone worries about me and is stricter than my parents ever were. My mother's nosiness is like a weapon flashing from a hidden compartment, sudden and unexpected. Often her cloying concern involves a social expectation or societal nicety, not my safety.

"It's the guy who complained about me using a ball at the dachshund derby."

"You're going out with *him*?" Rita rears back with a shell-shocked expression like my date is a recent parolee from prison.

I tell my friends about meeting Park the day of Daisy's rescue and today at the farmer's market. "He loves dogs and is kind of hot."

Rita is still doubtful. "Well, if he gives you any trouble, call us, and we'll come to get you."

CHAPTER 9

AS A RESULT of the time I spent with my friends, I have to hustle to get ready for this date. In my bra and panties, I throw another outfit across the bed and sit on the edge of the mattress in frustration. My fashion style leans toward quirky and eclectic as I thumb my nose at the snobbery of the Palm Beach elite. I rail against the anodyne of their pastel colors and staid traditional apparel. I've made a career of flouting society's conventions, but tonight I don't want to embarrass or alienate Park with an outfit that is too outré.

At last, I choose a pair of charcoal, slim-fit ankle pants, a low-cut pink blouse, and a vintage Lillie Rubin jacket covered in white ribbon flowers with pearls and sequins. The doorbell rings as I fasten the last strap on my high heels. I take a quick peek in the full-length mirror and head to the front door.

As I pass the living room window, I spot a small car parked in the driveway but it's not a sports car. Is that a Prius? I'm surprised Park drives a fuel-efficient hybrid. He seems more like a Lexus-Cadillac-Lincoln kind of guy; staid with a little bit of traditional flash.

I open the door and gesture Park inside. He wears a sports coat over a pressed T-shirt and black slacks. "Come in."

"You look very nice. I hope you don't mind I'm a few minutes late. You're a lot farther west than I thought."

"Did you have any trouble finding the place?"

"No. My GPS brought me right here." He looks around the living room. "Where's Mia and Daisy?"

"Daisy is now being fostered by a friend of mine who had been taking care of Angel, so I left both dogs with her for tonight. Do you want to see my little house?"

My 1960s bungalow is original to the thirty acres I own between two main roads. We do a quick tour of the basic two bedrooms and one bath. I remodeled every room before I moved in. The kitchen has modern appliances, quartz countertops, and sleek white cabinetry. All the floors throughout the house are long ceramic tiles that mimic weathered gray wood planks. The bathroom has a walk-in shower, tiled in cool colors of silver and white.

Park shows the most interest in the ramp I had constructed for Mia to get up and down from the couch. In the bathroom, he points to the doggie entry cut into the bottom of the door leading to the patio. "Does she use that?"

"Only when I'm away. Let me show the outside." I lead him to my elaborate canine-designed backyard.

He stands with his hands fisted on his hips. "Wow. What all is here?"

I walk to a long rectangle of unnaturally green grass. "This area is covered with synthetic turf specially designed for dogs to do their business. It has a flow-through mesh backing and is a lot easier to maintain than real grass. Also, the droppings seem to harden faster than usual, so cleanup is easy. I found gravel to be too hard on little dogs' feet and mulch was just too messy."

"I see you have a doggie pool."

"Shouldn't every Florida house?"

Mine is a large plastic kiddie pool sunk into the ground. A small aluminum ramp leads from the water up to the brick pavers which surround it like a mini-deck.

He squats to examine the depth of the water. "I like it. You don't have to worry about drowning."

"I've always taught my dogs where the stairs are in a regular pool, but you never know what they'll do if they panic. This way I don't always have to be supervising them whenever they're outside."

He points to a mound at the back of the yard. "What's that?"

"A dachshund tunnel."

Park peers inside. "What a great idea."

I used a large, black plastic pipe and buried half of its interior in the ground and the rest above. Both the top of the pipe and the dirt inside the tunnel are covered with artificial turf. "This appeals to their burrowing instinct and is a dark, cool place for them to hang out on a hot day."

Next to the house, I installed an automatic waterer and a pet shower. By the patio door which leads to the kitchen are a basket of rubber balls and a round, white plastic device.

"Is this a ball thrower?" Park asks.

"I got tired of being yipped at by my OCD dog to throw the ball, throw it again, over and over. I bought this and taught Mia how to drop a ball into the chute at the top. There's a delay of a few seconds before it's launched out this opening. She loves it. Well, you've seen everything. Let's go inside, and I'll get my purse." I lock up, and we head out into the balmy but breezy evening.

Before Park starts the car, he says, "I made a reservation at a place along the water. I figure the drive and a quiet dinner would give us a chance to talk. Since I know almost nothing about you, I'm looking forward to peeling back your layers."

I shiver with unexpected prickles. I imagine him stripping one piece of clothing off me at a time and kissing the exposed skin. I suddenly freeze with a new interpretation of his words. What will his reaction be if, or when, he finds out about my family's status and wealth? In my experience, lazy men are the ones most impressed. My mother was almost thirty years old when she married Stanford, the first man more attracted to her than her money. Will Park be genuine or just another player like other men I dated?

He stares straight ahead as he drives. "You were about to tell me today about Angel's former owner when Dylan came by. What happened to the asshole who abused her?"

"He was charged and convicted of a third-degree felony."

"What kind of sentence did he receive?"

"It was several months in jail and a thousand-dollar fine. His probation requires him to not have any animals for three years."

"That's it?" Park's voice has a whip-lash tone. "He should have been starved like she was, so he'd know how it feels. What good is having laws to protect the innocent if the punishment doesn't fit the crime? I'm sick and tired of human felons having more rights than their canine victims."

"We have a great state attorney who's a rescue dog owner and fights for animal rights. He's prosecuted a number of abuse and neglect cases. Angel's was one of them. Like you, he would like the sentences to be tougher. The problem is, by law, animals are considered property and have no legal rights."

Park's hands grip the steering wheel until his knuckles whiten. "If they're considered legally worthless, why do the courts allow them to inherit money or be the subjects of custody battles? It pisses me off. They are the most beloved members of the family but not equal in the eyes of the law."

Anticruelty laws require owners to provide only the most minimal necessities of food, water, and shelter, regardless of the suffering it causes. But the laws don't apply to animals in industries such as agriculture or scientific research. Those creatures suffer unimaginable horrors justified as necessary.

I need to change the subject or doom this date to an evening of sad hopelessness, so I ask, "How did you like working at the mobile adoption today?"

On the remainder of the drive, we converse about the farmer's market, Sandy and Ray, and The Forever Homes Dachshund Foundation. We are seated within minutes of our arrival at the waterfront restaurant by a hostess who looks like she just graduated from middle school. Our table abuts a wide picture window looking onto the Intracoastal Waterway.

The teenage worker gives Park a shy smile. "Do you want to order a drink?"

Park looks to me. "What would you like?"

"A glass of white wine would be nice."

The young hostess stares at him as if he embodies Justin Bieber singing her a love song. Park holds up two fingers. "We'll each have a glass of Riesling."

"Uh? Oh, yeah." The girl claps a hand to her chest. "Riesling. What kind?"

"What do you have on hand?"

A tiny perplexed frown creases her features. "I think we have Castle Rock."

"Okay, let's go with that." As the girl scurries away, Park moves his linen-wrapped silverware off to the side. "Now tell me about you."

I run through a quick checklist of information to share and details I shouldn't divulge at this time. "I'm a Scorpio. I love to sit on the beach. I'm a so-so golfer. My pet peeve is people who dress their dogs in costumes or make them do stupid tricks."

"You remember my bio from this morning. When I asked what you did at the dachshund derby, you said you were a free spirit. What did you mean? *Do* you have a job?"

Here we go. "I'm a professional fundraiser."

"I didn't realize it's something you get paid to do?"

"There are some who earn six-figure incomes."

"Geez, I'm in the wrong line of work. What else should I know about you?"

Before I can launch into the more sanitized aspects of my biography, a young waiter approaches. The emaciated man-child has a hairstyle where half his head is shaved close. He acts like he is not here to wait on us but came to admire the view from the window. He says, "Are you ready to order?"

"We don't have menus yet," Park says with a hint of irritation in his voice. "And what about our drinks? We ordered two glasses of wine from the hostess when we were seated."

The waiter looks at the linen tablecloth then to our left and right, as if the menus and drinks may have been given to other diners. "You haven't gotten your wine yet?"

"No." Park waves a hand over the empty tabletop. "See?"

I offer a possible answer. "Maybe the hostess forgot to tell you."

Park spits out, "Can you go check?"

"Right. It was two glasses of . . " The waiter cocks his head toward Park as if the answer will be whispered to him.

I jump in. "Castle Rock Riesling."

When the waiter heads toward the bar, Park shakes his head. "When did nice restaurants start hiring not particularly bright children to wait tables?" He doesn't wait for me to answer his rhetorical question. "Before the interruption, you were about to tell me your life story."

"Well, I grew up a little farther north in Palm Beach County. My mother and father still live in the house built by my grandfather. I have an older half-sister and a niece and nephew. What about you? Do you have family in the area?"

Park seems to mull over his response. "Right now they're staying in Broward County."

"Where?"

"Coconut Creek."

"That's not too far away. Do you get to see them much?"

A strange little hitch of time occurs before he answers. "Our schedules don't mesh. They have more free time during the week while I'm working. We can only get together on Sunday evenings. Let's talk about you now."

Let's not. I'm afraid the half-truths I tell him tonight might come back to bite me later.

CHAPTER 10

"HERE ARE YOUR drinks. Two Castle Creek Chardonnays." The waiter has wine glasses crisscrossed at the stems in one hand and a bottle of opened wine in the other. He sets the glasses down, folds one arm behind his waist, bends forward, pours, and steps back.

I wait for Park to complain that we ordered Castle Rock Riesling. After all, he seems to be a man who expects everyone to toe the same narrow line he does. To my surprise, he doesn't say a word.

The waiter tucks the bottle in the crook of his arm. "Anything else?"

"We'd like to see menus," Park reminds him.

After receiving them, we study the selections and place our orders the next time the waiter cruises past the table. The appetizers arrive after only a few minutes of small talk. While Park bites into one of his colossal shrimp, I sip a spoonful of Manhattan clam chowder.

To avoid talking about my background, I say, "Tell me more about your family in Coconut Creek."

He chews for a while before answering. "My parents, brother, and sister come to south Florida every year for about six weeks in an RV. They head back north, stopping at various places along the way."

"Are your siblings younger than you?"

"River is three years my junior, and Meadow just turned twenty-one."

I pause with the soup spoon halfway to my mouth. "Wait a minute. I just realized you're named Park, and your brother and sister are River and Meadow."

A flush creeps across his cheeks. "My parents are nature enthusiasts."

I pick up on his curious embarrassment and change the subject. "So, what do you like doing in your spare time other than running on the beach and being lousy at golf?"

"I don't have a lot of free time and even less with tax season coming soon. In fact, volunteering today at the farmer's market was out of the norm for me. Usually, on weekends I'm running errands and working out."

"What about dating? You're doing that this weekend too."

"I haven't done much lately."

My last relationship with a closet homosexual flits through my mind. "Have you known many women?"

Park raises his eyebrows. "Quite a few."

"I mean, in the biblical sense."

He flashes a lopsided grin, and my insides melt. "I do too. What about you? Have you *dated* much lately?"

"Are you asking how long since I've had sex?"

He shrugs. "Take it any way you want."

"It's been a while." He waits, and I roll my eyes. "Okay. It's been over two years."

"Were you in a relationship?"

"I was engaged."

"What happened?"

I stir my soup. "I was instrumental in confirming his desire for men."

"Before or after you had sex?"

"Thank God, it wasn't after. Actually, we never slept together. I thought he was being gentlemanly."

Park's brown eyes are steady behind the lenses which make him look scholarly as well as damn sexy. "Trust me. Gentlemanly is the last thing a real man would want to be with you."

I clamp my thighs together to still the quivering between them. By the time we receive our dinners, eat the delicious food, and Park pays the bill, my watch reads ten p.m. I skated around revealing too much personal information to him this evening, and it seems like he did the same. At times, our conversation was as generic as elevator music. Despite this obvious keep-away ploy by both of us, a definite underlying sexual current pulses through me with the warmth of his smile, his cool appraising gaze, and his low, seductive voice. It's been a long time since a man attracts me as much as Park does. At his car, he unlocks the door using his smart key.

When he doesn't open it, I turn to face him. "Is something wrong?"

"I have a favor to ask. I didn't expect we would finish this late. Would you mind if we stopped at my condo, so I could let Lamar out?"

"Not at all. I totally understand."

"I guess if anyone would, it'd be you." We stare at each other for several seconds until he puts his hand on my arm. "If you don't say anything, I'm going to kiss you."

I use my thumb and finger in a pantomimed zip. Park's warm mouth covers mine. His arms wrap around my back, and I lift mine to his shoulders. The kiss is gentle at first. I soon become accustomed to his height, the firmness of his chest, the strength of his embrace. His tongue slides past my lips, and I brush my fingertips through the hair at his nape. Park's hands drift downward, but he stops at my waist and presses, so the space between us disappears.

When the kiss ends, he murmurs, "Lamar's waiting."

CHAPTER 11

PARK'S CONDO IS in a six-story building of fairly new construction and only a ten-minute drive from the restaurant. He parks in a ground-level garage. "I can go up and get him. Lamar is pretty quick about taking care of business. Then we can be on our way, or you can wait in the condo until I bring him back."

I'm curious about Park's home. Is the place neat like him or bachelor pad messy? Does he have nice furnishings or mismatched castoffs and DIY assembled pieces? "You've seen my place. I want to see yours."

At the elevator, he pushes the number six button on the panel after glancing at my stilettos. "Usually I take the stairs."

"Does Lamar go up and down them?" I ask since stairs, as well as jumping on and off furniture, can be hard on dachshunds' backs. For this breed especially, I advocate for ramps.

"He can, but I carry him to be safe."

"Did you have trouble finding a building where you can have a pet?"

"The by-laws allow one dog under twenty-five pounds or two cats. Some tenants and homeowners have tried to skirt the rules, but the management is pretty strict about enforcement."

The elevator doors ping open. On the sixth floor, he unlocks a nondescript door halfway down the carpeted hallway. Lamar runs out, his tail wagging. He whines and jumps onto our legs. Park tells him to sit, but Lamar continues his song and dance of canine excitement. At last, the dog plops his behind on the hallway carpet. Park grabs a leash from a hook beside the door and snaps it onto his collar. "Look around inside. We'll be back shortly."

I cross the threshold and close the door behind me. Park's condo reflects what I know about him so far. The rooms have an uncluttered neutral color palette highlighted with splashes of reds and dark browns in artwork and decorations. There's a definite masculine vibe here. The condo is so neat and clean it looks like it's been detailed. A nubby grayish-brown sectional with an extended lounger at one end anchors the living room. A flat-screen TV hangs on the opposite wall. The entrance to a small galley-style kitchen opens on one side of the TV. On the other side, the doorway leads to an area with a light fixture hanging in the middle of the ceiling. This must be the dining room. Instead of a table and chairs, a desk and credenza fill the area to functions as Park's home office.

I head toward a hallway off the living room. Straight ahead, the master bedroom contains a queen-sized bed with a white duvet. Another flat-screen TV is attached to a wall mount above a low dresser. All the furniture is stained with a dark charcoal finish. The bedroom has a walk-in closet and a bathroom with a shower. Everything in here is also obsessively tidy.

I exit the master suite. On one side of the hall, is a second bathroom with a shower-tub combination. In a second bedroom, I flip the wall switch and peek inside. Two cube-shaped upholstered chairs are placed against the far wall with a small cabinet between them; but in the middle of the room, sits a strange-looking, cream-colored lounger. I walk around the unusual piece of furniture as my hand trails a path along its buttery leather upholstery. The chaise doesn't resemble any I've ever seen before. It has a curvy shape like the letter S on its side, with wood legs, decorative nails, and fine stitching.

Why is this placed in the middle of the room?

I sit down on it. The dipped seat pushes me against the backrest, so I swing my feet up. The chair cradles my body in the bottom of the big depression. The design supports my entire back as well as my neck, waist, and knees. The lack of armrests and the narrowness of the seat seem to be the only deficiencies.

"Do you like my Tantra chair?"

I bolt upright.

Park leans against the door jamb, legs crossed at the ankle. Lamar is next to him, panting, with his pink tongue protruding. The dachshund seems to be grinning at me, just like his owner.

I rub my palms on the seat. "What kind of chair did you say this was?"

Park uncrosses his legs and steps into the room. "It's called a Tantra chair."

"I've never heard of a manufacturer with that name."

"Tantra is a design."

"Can you get it with armrests? It would be more comfortable with them when you're reading."

"That's not what the chair is intended for."

I hold up my arms to simulate them on invisible armrests. "Even relaxing, it would be nice to have the support."

"Marin, a Tantra chair is used to enhance positions in the Kama Sutra."

"Kama—" My eyes open wide. "This is used for sex?"

Park nods.

CHAPTER 12

I JUMP TO my feet as fast as my tight pants allow and brush my bottom as if I had sat in a wet spot.

He laughs. "Don't worry. It's clean."

"Why do you have it here?"

Park cocks his head and raises his eyebrows.

I sputter. "I mean . . . I know, of course, why you have it. Why do you have it in the guest room?"

"Three years ago I lived here with a woman. When we broke up, she took everything but the Tantra and Lamar. As far as I'm concerned, I won." He points to the other furniture. "Those two chairs pull out to single beds for guests, like my family."

"Can you use the Tantra as a bed?"

"Not really. You can only sleep in a sitting position. I don't have it in the living room because, like I'm doing with you, I don't want to explain its purpose to everyone, and it takes up too much space in my bedroom."

I rub my palms against my thighs. "Well, I've learned something new tonight. I'll have to look online to find out more about Tantra chairs."

An easy smile plays at the corners of his mouth. "If you go to the website, there are films to view."

"What kind of films?"

"They show couples demonstrating the various positions."

"Do you mean . . . like, real people having sex?"

He nods.

Heat floods my body. I grab the front edges of my jacket to shrug out of it then stop. Will Park see it as a signal to undress? "The rest of your condo is very neat and clean. I like your style of decorating."

"I went to one furniture store and told the designer what I wanted, and she picked everything out."

My voice squeaks. "Did she know about the Tantra chair?"

"No." Park steps closer. "Listen, if you ever want to try it out just let me know, but nothing will happen until you say the word."

"And . . . uh . . . what word would that be?"

In his velvet-edged voice, he murmurs, "Any word you want, but *Tantra* would work. I promise you'll love how it changes your lovemaking. The design benefits the woman more than the man."

I study the chair. "How?"

"The geometry of the arcs and the width of the seat allow you to maximize your muscle movements."

I inhale a shaky breath. "It does?"

"You can easily change the angle of your pelvis during lovemaking because your body is supported, unlike on a bed or the floor."

My heart beats in double time. "Really?"

"The chair displaces my body weight, so you can guide me to give you the most pleasure. The result is you have more frequent and intense orgasms."

I can't seem to draw enough air into my lungs. His right eyebrow lifts above the tortoiseshell frame of his glasses as his chocolate-brown eyes linger on my displayed cleavage.

When he leans down to kiss me, I place my index finger on his mouth. "I need to tell you something about me."

He has a calculating look like he might need to reassess how my revelation will impact his designs on my body. "What?"

I take a deep breath. "I, uh, I'm not very experienced with . . . lovemaking."

Park gives me an incredulous stare. "Are you a virgin?"

"No. I had a boyfriend in high school, but we were both pretty clueless about what we were doing. In college, I dated another guy who thought he was a good lover, but he didn't . . . he wasn't . . ."

"He couldn't bring you to orgasm?"

"That's right."

"Have you ever had one? Do you know what it feels like?"

"I've had orgasms." Heat floods my cheeks. "Just . . . not with another human being."

Park flashes an indulgent smile like I said something unintentionally cute. "Are you issuing me a challenge?"

"No. I mean . . . I just thought you should know. That's all."

"Are you also telling me you're not on birth control?"

I nod, unable to voice the confirmation.

"I appreciate your candor."

From Park's grim expression, it appears I just blew any chance for a second date, let alone an opportunity to try out the Tantra chair. I head for the door.

He extends his hand to stop me. "Where are you going?"

"To get my phone and call for a ride home."

"Why? I can take you."

"After what I just told you, you probably don't want to see me again, and it's okay. I understand. There's no reason you should drive across the county to take me home. I'll just call Uber."

"You're wrong, Marin. I very much want to see you again."

"You do?" With a slow, cautious movement he comes closer, which gives me time to stop him if I want, but I don't.

"Let's just take things slow and see where this goes."

Grateful, not only for his understanding but also for not writing me off as a bad first date, I gave him a tiny smile. "Thank you."

His countenance is serious. "I do have a recommendation. If you want our relationship to become intimate, sometime in the future, you might consider birth control. I have no problem using condoms, but they're not always convenient."

"Okay," I say in a soft and shy voice, like a little girl too embarrassed to say she has to pee.

Park hugs me then leads me from the room. Lamar camps out in his dog bed in the living room, huffing in his sleep, unaware and uninterested in the awkward human encounter in the guest room. I reach over the sleeping dog and lift my purse off the end table.

Has Lamar watched Park using the Tantra? I smile to myself. If Park's last relationship ended several years ago, maybe he's been *walking his dog by himself* for a while. On the drive to my house, neither of us has much to say.

At my front door, Park gives me a gentle goodnight kiss. "You have my number. If you want to go out again, give me a call."

He walks to his car, and I wave goodbye then enter my empty house. I lean against the closed door. Delicious anticipation fills me, like the feeling of growing hunger held in check until deciding whether or not to have a scrumptious meal.

CHAPTER 13

ON MONDAY, I finish the home inspection at the Kowalski residence. The grandmother, a middle school art teacher, and kindergartner, Dylan, are not at home. I instruct Kerry in the hand signals and voice commands taught to the dog. Angel and Barney, the family's elderly greyhound, seem to have formed a bond with both sharing an elevated platform bed.

Kerry pets the blocky head of the pit bull. "Angel has had an amazing effect on Dylan already. He says the words *sit* and *come* then laughs when she does it. In just two days, she has done more to teach him the power of language than all the speech therapy he's had to date."

We tour her photography studio in a remodeled barn on the property. She volunteers to take appealing photographs of the foundation's dogs to post on our website. In place of payment, I offer to have Kerry's business featured with the photos and given to potential adopters. As a result of the wonderful home visit, I arrive late for my lunch appointment at the sushi restaurant on Southern Boulevard. I spot my sister in a booth near the back.

Kit waves me over, and I throw my purse across the bench seat then slide in. "Hi, how was kitty day?"

My sister sighs. "I gave extra special care to those I suspect won't find homes, like the pure-black kittens. When I don't see one that I cared for on my last visit, I can't ask if they were adopted because my heart breaks when I learn the kitty was euthanized."

I shake my head. "It's a shame we don't have a no-kill facility for kittens in this county. I've been thinking we should."

Kit brightens. "Would you start one?"

"Maybe, but right now it's all I can do to handle the dog rescue. We should compile a list of shelters across the country and keep in touch with them through phone calls or emails. If they're low on kittens and we're overrun, maybe we can find a way to get ours to them."

"I think that's a great idea. I can look into it this week when I'm at the foundation."

In unison, Kit and I recite, "We can't save them all, but we can save at least some."

My love for canines is stronger than for other animals, while my sister adores cats, which is ironic considering her nickname. Kit can't keep a feline inside the house because of Garrett's allergies, so she receives her kitty fix by volunteering at the shelter one day a week. She also works two days a week at The Forever Homes Dachshund Foundation while her children are in school.

A tiny Asian waitress appears at our table with two filled glasses. "Two unsweet ice tea for you. You want shrimp tempura Bento box. Mushroom soup. Salad with ginger dressing. Eel sauce."

We hand over our unopened menus. As the waitress bustles away, I laugh. "If the food here wasn't so good and the location so convenient, I'd say it's time we find another restaurant. So, tell me what else is new?"

Kit unfolds the napkin and places it on her lap. "I saw an article in the paper this morning about the Guardian Angels in New York City. They're the group who patrols subways to keep passengers safe, but now they're taking on the city's rats. It's what our local T-N-V-R group is doing by placing fixed feral kitties in vermin-infested areas. After neutering the adult cats, the Guardian Angels also feed and provide shelters to the colonies to keep them healthy and active."

"But wouldn't feeding make them not want to hunt?"

"I feed the ones in the boathouse. They kill for fun, not food. You know there hasn't been a single live water rat in the place since I brought those two kitties home from the shelter. Father wasn't too happy finding cats asleep in his boat, but I asked him if he would rather have disease-carrying rats running all over the place. When will people realize cats are so much cheaper and better for the environment than exterminators and toxic chemicals?"

Our soups and salads arrive. I spear a forkful of orange-coated iceberg lettuce and hold it aloft. "I love this ginger dressing. I've tried to make it several times using different recipes, but none of them tastes exactly like this."

"It's so great you can cook. I don't know what I'd do if we ever left the estate and didn't have meals prepared for us. Garrett and the kids would get nothing but peanut butter sandwiches and frozen dinners."

Kit and her husband moved into a wing of the mansion when Trevor was a baby. I still think it was a mistake for Pops and Mumsy to allow the Coughlin family to live there. Now Garrett can continue his gambling addiction without worrying about providing a home for his wife and children.

"You know, Kit, you can't always depend on living at Del Lago Al Mar. Mumsy will never sell the place, but there is no way I need or want a house that size. I don't anticipate anything happening for years, but you should prepare for the day to come eventually. Have you and Garrett been able to save any money to buy your own place?"

"It's been hard."

"Bento box here." The waitress places two lacquered compartmentalized containers in front of us. "I come back with eel sauce."

Kit stares at the food. Ever since money woes began shortly after her marriage, my sister has a habit of floating off somewhere whenever the subject of money is introduced. Her face becomes slack and expressionless, like a recent stroke victim.

I use my chopsticks to lift a piece of fried sweet potato. "Have you thought any more about my offer for you to work full-time at the foundation?"

My sister jolts and scans the restaurant as if realizing where she is. "What did you say?"

"I asked about you working more than two days a week at the foundation. Once my plans for Forever Homes Village get underway, I'm going to need the extra help. I can pay you, and the money can be saved for a down payment on a house or your kids' college fund."

"I'll think about it, but Garrett wants me to be available for the children." We eat several items in the Bento boxes in silence then Kit's eyes meet mine. Her sugary tone belies her obvious curiosity. "Have you talked to Trey since he came to my birthday dinner?"

"No. Why?"

"His parents asked what happened at dinner that night. Mr. Montgomery questioned Father at work. A few days later, Mrs. Montgomery called Mother. They want to know what Trey said but wouldn't say why. Do you have any idea what's going on?"

Maybe he finally told his parents about Carmen and her pregnancy. "No, but I hope he's convinced them I'm only his friend and nothing more."

Kit clicks her tongue. "I knew it was a mistake for Mother to bring up the subject of marriage. You've never responded well to coercion. It wouldn't matter how many eligible bachelors they presented. You haven't been interested in a relationship since your engagement to Blaine ended."

"As a matter of fact, I had a date Saturday night."

Kit chews and swallows a mouthful of dumpling with speed. "With a man?"

I roll my eyes. "No, with a biker chick I picked up in a gay bar. Of course, with a man."

"How did you meet?"

"Remember the guy I told you about at the Dachshund Derby who threatened to have Mia disqualified if I used a ball?"

Kit's face works through expressions of disbelief and surprise. "You went out with *him*? Why?"

I lean back in the booth with calculated nonchalance. "Well, he loves dachshunds. He's very good-looking. And he asked me out." With Sandy's help, of course.

Kit studies me with bright, interested eyes. "You must really like this guy to have said yes."

"Call me crazy, but I only date men I like."

"Are you going to see him this weekend?"

"Yes, I am," I say with my decision to see Park again finalized.

CHAPTER 14

WHEN I RETURN to the foundation, I phone my gynecologist's office. With a serendipitous cancellation for Friday morning, an appointment is scheduled. I call Park but get his voice mailbox. "Hi, this is Marin. You told me to contact you if I want to go out again. If you're not too busy this weekend, I'd like to spend part of it with you. Bye."

For two days, I wait but receive no return call from him, and my happy mood sours. I guess he decided I wasn't worth a second date after all. On Wednesday evening, my phone rings when I return home from the foundation with a new pair of dachshunds named, Brewster and Lili. My heart skips a beat when Park's name appears on the screen, but I'm unable to answer at that moment.

Mia waits by my side while I unlock the front door, but skittish Brewster has wrapped his leash around my ankles and quivers with nervousness. Tiny Lili pulls me forward and off-balance. This new miniature female is demonstrating the dominant posturing of an alpha dog. She wants to lead the pack into the house. After untangling the leashes then instructing the two new canines to wait, I open the door and step inside. It takes several minutes until they learn to wait for my signal to enter. By the time the lesson is completed, Park's phone call has long ago been routed to voice mail.

Before I can call him back, there's more work to do with my new foster dogs. The next lesson involves learning that everything in the house, including food and toys, belongs to me as the leader of the pack. Lili futilely attempts to usurp power, but I remain firm. Feeding the dogs their supper is another exercise in establishing dominance. Time passes as Brewster and Lili have to wait until given the signal to eat. I struggle to not let my weariness or frustration show, despite being as tired and hungry as they are.

An hour after entering the house, the three dogs are finally fed. I sigh. We'll be repeating the exercise tomorrow at the morning and evening meals and every day until they learn. Later, on the sofa with Mia in my lap, Brewster on one side, and Lili on the other, I listen to Park's voice message.

"Hi, Marin. I'm sorry it's taken a couple of days to get back to you. I'm glad you'd like to go out again. I'll be working at home this evening, so give me a call." I tap *Call Back* on the screen, and Park answers after two rings. "Did you get my message?"

"I did. I wasn't able to answer because I was wrapped up in leashes."

"I hope it was with dogs and not some fetish you have."

"No fetish. I picked up two new dachshund fosters today. The female and I have been engaging in a battle of wills. She insists on being the alpha in this house."

"What about the other one?"

"Brewster is a sweetheart, but he's not very bright and scared of everything. I turned on the vent fan over the stove, and he hid under my bed."

"Sounds like you have your work cut out for you."

"They just need to learn the rules around here. I don't think their previous owners set many boundaries with them."

"Why were they surrendered?" Park's voice hardens. "Were they mistreated?"

"Not at all. The woman's fiancé is allergic to them, but he loves the dogs and took medication. However, they recently had a baby who has the same allergy. After the child's third hospitalization with breathing problems, the couple had no choice but to give up their pets. It was heartbreaking for them."

"I can't imagine how difficult that would be. I'd be devastated without Lamar. I try not to think about a day when I won't have him around anymore."

"I feel the same about Mia."

"What else did you do today?"

I deleted a document I spent two hours writing and thought about you. I lost my sunglasses which were on my head and thought about you. I forgot to lock a kennel and ended up with a dog strolling into the office area while I thought about you. "Not much," I say.

"Well, I'm glad you want to go out again. What did you have in mind?"

"Since you bought me dinner last week, how about I prepare a meal for you?"

"You can cook?" His voice sparks with a note of incredulity, like no woman he ever dated could perform this domestic skill.

"I welcome the opportunity to prepare food for someone other than me."

"Sounds great. What can I bring?"

"Wine?"

"Okay. What kind?"

I chuckle. "How about some of the Castle Rock we were supposed to have at the restaurant?"

Park's voice rumbles with quiet laughter. "Red or white?"

"Bring one of each. I haven't decided what I'm going to make. Do you have any food restrictions?"

"Just liver and onions. What time do you want me to come?"

"Six-thirty is fine. Oh, there is something else you can bring."

"Sorry, but the Tantra won't fit in my car."

My heart races with the thought of Park's chair. I viewed the films on the website several times. Although graphic, they didn't come across as pornographic. With my limited sexual experience, watching the couples seemed like studying the mating rituals of an unknown tribe. More than turning me on, it was like a Margaret-Mead-Sex-in-the-South-Pacific kind of fascination. "I was going to say you could bring Lamar. Mia would be happy to have another dog play with Lili and Brewster. Besides, I'm sure he'll enjoy my backyard playground."

A pregnant pause occurs before Park responds. He sounds as if he is at a loss for words. "Thank you for inviting him. It means a lot to me."

"Then we'll see you on Saturday. Bye."

CHAPTER 15

AT THE APPOINTED time on Saturday evening, my doorbell rings. All three dogs bark twice then stop. When I walk out of the kitchen, Mia, Lili, and Brewster sit on a throw rug positioned six feet away from the front door.

I bend over and rub their ears. "Good dogs."

The doorbell rings a second time. The dogs rush forward, bark, and run back to the rug.

As a reminder, I hold up my hand like a school crossing guard. "Stay."

I open the door. Park is on the front step with two bottles in a divided wine bag, five pounds of dog food, and Lamar on a leash. He wears pressed jeans and a starched white dress shirt. His dachshund rushes over the threshold and into the house, jerking Park forward.

"Whoa." I block Lamar with my legs, backing him up until he's outside on the front step. "I have an ironclad rule here. Humans always enter first."

Park's eyes widen. "Really?"

"The pack leaders go in before the followers."

"But he's my buddy."

"Does he help with the mortgage? Buy groceries? If not, he's the follower, and you're the leader."

"You are one tough lady." Park eyes the three dogs on the throw rug. "Why are they sitting over there?"

I move my hands in a wide half-circle. "This is no dog's land in front of the door. They are allowed to bark to alert me then they have to wait. The rug helps them know how far back they need to be."

"What are you? A dog whisperer?" Park sports an expression of awe, as though I've morphed into the Animal Planet TV star.

"I actually learned a lot from watching Cesar Milan. Every pack needs a leader, and dogs prefer their humans take the role. The exception to the rule is Lili." I point to the little black and white dachshund.

"How do you want us to come inside?"

"Have Lamar wait until you're over the threshold then signal him to follow you." As soon as Park takes a step forward, Lamar surges ahead. I reach for bags. "Here, let me take the wine and dog food from you."

With my directions and encouragement, Park finally enters the house while his dog waits on the step. Once both are inside, I shut the door. Lamar tugs on the leash to get closer to the other dogs.

"Is it okay to let him loose?" Park asks.

"To be safe let's have him sit right there and I'll bring each dog forward to meet him. Mia will be fine, but I'm not sure about the other two."

Mia and Lili greet Lamar with butt sniffs and tail wags. To my surprise, Brewster is the problem dog. He runs forward, barks and retreats, again and again.

I set the wine and dog food on a nearby credenza, grab Brewster, and hold him with his rear end facing forward. "It's fear aggression. He's too stupid to know his behavior will cause him more problems than if he just acts friendly or ignores other dogs." I kneel and allow Lamar to sniff Brewster's butt.

"Why are you doing that?" Park says with a slightly scandalized expression.

"So Lamar can greet him." After a couple of seconds, I stand again, still holding Brewster. "Okay. You can release him from the leash once everyone's outside."

We troop to the backyard, and Park unclips the leash. Lamar runs after the two girls, and soon they race around, chasing each other. Brewster watches from his safe position cradled against my side. After a few minutes, he whines, and I place him on the ground. He shakes from head to tail, releasing his pent-up anxiety then tentatively joins the pack.

"They should be fine now, but we'll watch them for a few minutes."

Soon all four dachshunds race through and over the tunnel, catch balls and jump into the kiddie pool which contains only a couple inches of water. The females tug on a knotted rope with head shakes and growls. Brewster and Lamar lay side-by-side in the coolness of the tunnel.

Park laughs. "The guys think those girls are crazy."

"They are. Let's go inside and open the wine."

Park picks up the bottles from the credenza while I lift the white *Science Diet* bag. "Thank you for the dog food."

"That's Lamar's contribution. If it's not the kind you use, maybe you can donate it."

"I do use this brand." I call out to the backyard, "Thank you, Lamar."

In the kitchen, Park raises a bottle in each hand. "Red or white?"

"I've made spaghetti, so let's start with red." I stir a pot of simmering sauce and gesture with my chin toward the counter where two goblets and a corkscrew sit. "Will you open it, please?"

He pops the cork and half-fills the glasses. I reach for one, but he steps in front of me. "There's something I need to do first."

Park wraps his arms around me. He touches my lips with his, pulls me tighter into his embrace then deepens the kiss. A tingling in the pit of my stomach makes me warm all over. Like with the kiss in the restaurant parking lot, his hand drifts down my back. His citrusy aftershave emits a clean fresh scent. I ache for him to hold me tighter, undress me, and touch me all over. Instead, I break off the kiss and step away.

If Park is aware of my discomfort, he doesn't let on. "I meant to tell you how nice you look."

Pleasure flows through me with the sincerity of his unsolicited compliment. In contrast to his preppy jeans and shirt, I'm wearing harem trousers in gold paisley silk, strappy jeweled high-heeled sandals, and a black, puffy-sleeved crop top that bares my midriff. "Thank you."

He hands me a wineglass and watches me take a sip. "How is it?"

"Good." My voice quivers with jumpiness overlaid with desire. Feeling like soaring Icarus in wings of wax and feathers, I'm giddy with a new adventure of getting to know Park. Overshadowing the excitement, warnings echo in my head to make sure I don't fly too close to the sun. I set the wineglass on the countertop. "Are you hungry for some antipasto?"

Without waiting for his reply, I step around him and head to the refrigerator. I withdraw a platter-sized square dish and bump the door closed with my hip. Shaved prosciutto wraps around slivers of cantaloupe. Marinated artichoke hearts nestle next to marble-sized balls of fresh mozzarella. A variety of black, green, and purple olives are heaped in one corner with dried and fresh figs. In the center of the platter, a small bowl overflows with triangles of focaccia. Cocktail forks dot the rolling landscape of appetizers like miniature trees.

I grab a handful of napkins and nod to Park. "Can you bring my wine and those two small plates? Let's sit outside and watch the dogs while the gravy cooks a little more."

"Gravy? For spaghetti?"

"I was taught to make it by an Italian cook. She called it gravy instead of sauce."

We set everything on a glass-topped patio table and pull out chairs facing the backyard.

Park picks up his wineglass. "Have you ever made pasta from scratch?"

"All the time. I have my own pasta maker and made some for dinner tonight."

He touches his glass to mine with a soft clink. "You are one surprising woman, Marin McAllister."

"Thank you."

To my surprise, the doorbell rings. Four dachshunds race through the open patio door into the house, barking all the way.

Park pauses with his glass halfway to his mouth. "Are you expecting someone?"

"No." I shoot him an apologetic and concerned glance. "Excuse me."

By the time I reach the front door, Mia, Brewster, and Lili sit in silence on their rug. Only Lamar sniffs at the threshold.

I call out to my unseen visitor. "Hang on."

Using my feet, I back up Lamar until he is beside the other dogs. When he gets to his feet and follows me to the door again, Mia yips at him. Whatever she says works because he turns around and plops down next to her. I look over my shoulder to ensure the canine lineup remains in place. Park waits inside the patio door. He smiles and shakes his head at the dogs lined up like soldiers for inspection.

When I open the door, I find Rudy, Rita, Mrs. R, and Daisy on the doorstep.

Rita steps forward. "There's a strange car in your driveway. Are you okay?"

CHAPTER 16

I OPEN THE door wider. "I'm fine."

Rita kisses my cheek and moves inside. "Mama said Daisy would enjoy seeing Mia again, so we stopped by."

From the rear, Mrs. R speaks up. "I said that before we saw you had company."

Rudy sidesteps around his wife with his hand extended out toward Park. "Hi, I'm Rudy Rosetti."

Rita stares at the tall man inside the open patio door and whispers, "He's the no-balls guy, right?"

Introductions are made all around, including Lamar, Lili, and Brewster to Daisy. The dachshunds head to the backyard and Daisy's leash slips from Mrs. R's hand. Before she can pick it up again, the little beagle follows the other hounds outside.

"I'm sorry." No hint of apology tinges Rudy's mother's voice. "I'll go get her, so you two can have dinner in peace."

Park says, "Why don't you stay and have a glass of wine with us?"

Rita links her arm through his. "That would be lovely. I'll help you serve."

Rudy walks through the patio door. "I'll keep an eye on the dogs."

Mrs. R follows Rita and Park into the kitchen. "I smell gravy. Let me check on it."

Left alone in the foyer, I throw my hands into the air. What just happened to my evening with Park? Then an awful idea pops into my head. He doesn't know Mrs. R was the cook at our family's estate. I need to make sure nobody inadvertently tells him. While Mrs. R, Rita, and Park remain in the kitchen, I creep into the backyard. Rudy sits on one of the patio chairs.

He twists around when I step through the doorway. "I'm sorry we butted in. Rita said she wanted to check on you, but you know she was just being nosy. We'll get outta your hair as soon as we have a glass of vino."

"It's fine. Listen, Park doesn't know about my family background. I'll tell him when the time is right."

Rudy raises his thumb in the air. "Gotcha."

"I better get inside to warn Rita and your mom."

As soon as I enter the kitchen, Park asks Mrs. R, "Are you the woman who taught Marin how to cook?"

I blurt out, "Yes, the Rosetti's are friends of my family. I was interested in cooking, so Mrs. R graciously became my instructor."

Rita frowns when I say *friends of my family*. There is no way she, Rudy, and Mrs. R would ever be friends of Stanford and Betsy McAllister.

Mrs. R winks at me. "She was a very good pupil, but this gravy needs some more spices and a little bit of vino."

When Rita and Park head outside with the wine and glasses, I lean in close to Mrs. R as she stirs and tastes. "Park doesn't know you worked for my parents. I haven't told him yet about . . . you know."

"I knew what you were trying to say. I hope Rita does too."

Everyone gathers around the patio table after Mrs. R corrects the gravy.

Rita forks the stem of her glass between two fingers and spins the base in tiny circles. She sniffs then sips, closing her eyes for a second to savor the taste. "Park, what is it you do?" Beneath her breezy tone is the unmistakable interrogation of a male suitor.

"I'm a certified public accountant. I have a small firm in Delray Beach."

"Really?" Rita sits straighter in her chair. "The Forever Homes Dachshund Foundation is going to need a new accountant soon because my nephew, who's been doing the books, is getting married and moving to Atlanta."

I freeze.

Rudy gives his wife a hard-eyed look. "Rita, the foundation's director knows Matteo is quitting soon. Maybe *she* already has someone lined up. You need to talk to *her* first."

Rita catches the panic in my eyes. "Uh, yeah, that's right. I'm not the person in charge."

Park studies Rita before he speaks. "I'd be willing to volunteer my services and help out the organization. How do I get in contact with the director?"

Rita's eyes dart around the table, looking at everyone except Park. "Uh, I guess Marin can let you know."

I smile at him, hoping my expression does not convey deception. "I'll check on that and get back to you."

Mrs. R says to Park, "Your dachshund is a beauty. What's his name?"

The talk shifts to the dogs, a safe topic in which everyone can ask and answer questions with ease. Fifteen minutes later, I escort my friends to the door. Upon my return, I find Park in the kitchen rinsing out the used wine glasses.

He dries his hands on a dishtowel. "I recognize your friends from the Dachshund Derby."

"I wanted to introduce them to you after the awards presentation, but you and Lamar disappeared."

"He started whining and squatting. I left before he took a dump on the stage with all those people walking around."

So, he hadn't hustled away from the ceremony like a poor loser. "Are you ready for dinner? I see Mrs. R started the water for the pasta."

"What do you want me to do?"

"You can set the table."

It's a pleasant, temperate evening for south Florida. Burning citronella candles keep flying critters away. During dinner, the four dachshunds jockey for position around the table to catch any crumbs that might fall. When Lili whines and Lamar growls, I send them to wait on the grass and off the patio which, by my decree, now designates another no-dog zone.

When I sit down again, Park asks, "Have you ever thought of becoming a professional trainer?"

"Considering all my foster dogs and the ones at the foundation, I'm training several every month."

"But you don't get paid for it. I guess you'd have to get some kind of certification, but it seems like you wouldn't have any trouble qualifying. It could supplement your fundraising income." He looks at my small bungalow.

"The problem is the dog wouldn't be the one paying me. They're easy to train, humans aren't. I'd rather work with the animals than get paid by people."

Park puts his arm along the back of my chair and pulls me toward him. "Was I a difficult owner to train?"

"No, but are you going to keep up the exercise at home? If not, the next time you're here with Lamar, we'll be starting at step one again."

He leans closer and nuzzles my ear. "I may not know much about dog training, but there are a few things I'm looking forward to teaching *you*."

His lips descend on my neck. A soft whimper passes my lips when a shiver runs through me. He locates a spot with the tip of his tongue that makes my bones soften and melt. I grip the arm of the patio chair to hold myself earthbound.

Park scoots his chair away from the table and rises to his feet. He hauls me up and kisses me again. His hands rove up and down my spine, leaving a trail of goosebumps in their wake. He furrows his fingertips through my hair and tilts my head back, opening my mouth wider for his plundering tongue.

I bunch his shirt in my fists, holding on to the only stable part of this world. We stand as close as two fully-clothed, upright people on a patio can be. Although no one can see us, I break contact with Park's mouth and inhale a deep, cleansing breath. Our faces are inches apart as we look into each other's eyes.

"You okay?" he asks.

I brush a strand of ebony hair from my cheek. "Yeah, I'm fine." I teeter for a moment in my too-high heels.

Park grabs my arm. "You sure?"

"I'm not used to wearing these shoes. That's all."

He tips his head sideways to look at my footwear. "I don't know how you can walk in those things."

I shrug; grateful we can discuss something other than my reaction to him. "I don't wear them if I'm going to walk very far or stand on my feet for a long time."

"They're very sexy." He gives me a smoldering look, one that strips me of everything but the shoes.

I swallow hard. "Are you ready for dessert?"

After brewing espresso, we eat tiramisu made from Mrs. R's recipe. When we finish, the dogs follow us inside to lick the plates. Park loads the dishwasher while I put away the food.

After tidying up the kitchen, he looks around like he misplaced something. "Where did the dogs go?"

I shut the refrigerator door. "I don't know. They've been awfully quiet."

We find all four dachshunds sacked out on the living room sofa. Park leans over to view the pile of fur. "Well, that's never happened before. My dog got more tired on a date than I did."

"It is after their bedtime."

"You know, if I didn't have to leave, we could let sleeping dogs lie."

I snort with wry laughter. Soon I'll ask him to stay but not tonight.

Park lays his hand on Lamar's head. His gentle strokes cause the dog to open his eyes and yawn. "C'mon, buddy. The lady is kicking us out."

Park snaps the leash on his dog's collar and leads him down the ramp from the sofa to the floor. I follow as the other three dogs slumber on.

After I unlock the front door, he says, "What are you doing next Saturday?"

"I'm going with a friend to a Renaissance fair." When a flash of revulsion flits across Park's face, I ask, "What's wrong?"

"Nothing."

"If you've never been to a Renaissance fair, it's good . . . fun." I stumble with the omission of the word *clean*. Considering the corsets, boobs, leather, whips, and chains at the event, the definition of clean fun is different for some people. Once again, Park is unable to hide a sour expression. I say, "The performers are dressed in costumes, but the attendees don't have to. There are demonstrations, shows, and people selling handmade crafts."

"Believe me, I know what they do," he mumbles. "I'm just not into that kind of thing. Will *you* be wearing a costume?"

I spread my arms out and point my foot to showcase my current harem-like outfit. "According to my mother, most of my clothes *are* costumes."

"What time will you be there?"

"I'm supposed to meet my friend, Angie, at noon. She has to work in the morning. Then we'll get dressed and drive to the park in Broward County."

"You'll arrive around one-thirty?"

"That sounds about right. I can tell Angie I need to get home rather than stay until closing if you want to go out later." For some reason, I have the uncomfortable feeling Park is a puzzle with missing pieces.

He smiles for the first time since the subject of the Renaissance fair comes up. "I would like to see you next weekend. I can't reciprocate with a fabulous home-cooked meal like tonight. Also, no other dogs can be at my condo, even for a short visit. How about we do dinner and a movie?"

"I'll look forward to that."

He reaches out with his index finger. It trails from just under my ear, along the column of my neck, across my shoulder to the elastic neckline of my crop top. His fingertip meanders to the midline of my chest then traces a path to the pulsing hollow at the base of my throat. He raises the point of my chin as his lips descend toward mine.

After a minute, Lamar whines and tugs on the leash, pulling Park's mouth off mine. He frowns at his dachshund. "Buddy, you've got lousy timing. I better let him out before he has an accident in your house. I'll pick you up next Saturday at seven."

CHAPTER 17

ANGIE CALLS ME the day before our visit the Renaissance fair. "I have good news. I found another vet who'll cover for me tomorrow morning. Now we can be there when the gate opens at ten."

"Good. I have a date with Park in the evening."

"Mom told me about meeting him at your house last weekend. She likes him. So does Dad and Nonni. When are you going to tell him about your family?"

The need becomes more pressing the longer he and I see each other. "I plan to tell him soon. Are we dressing up tomorrow?"

"Of course, but the problem is we haven't planned any great new outfits, and I don't want to wear what we did last year."

"Why not?"

"People have already seen us as fairies."

"What people?" I ask.

"You don't know them. Anyway, I was looking online for ideas. Why don't we go as archers? I'm going to send you a picture I found on Pinterest. I think we can put together costumes with clothes we have. When we get there, let's hit the tent of the guy who sells handmade weapons. We'll each buy a bow and arrows, and we're all set."

The next morning, I dress in a white off-the-shoulder, hip-length blouse. Around my midsection, I lace a steel-boned black corset which is part of a steampunk outfit I wore to one of my mother's dinner parties.

Betsy insisted my attire be an LBD, a little black dress. So I ordered the entire outfit off the Internet including the high-low tiered skirt, tall, lace-up boots, striped stockings, a sheer blouse, and a mini top hat, called a fascinator.

When my mother saw me, she gasped with a hand to her throat. "Oh my, you look like a chorus girl from the Moulin Rouge."

My father scanned me from head to toe. "Were this a Halloween party, I would have found your clothes amusing."

As it turned out, several women at the party admired my outfit and asked where to purchase it. An older gentleman couldn't take his eyes off me until his wife elbowed his flabby midsection.

For today's archer's costume, I'm wearing black leggings, the steampunk boots, and heavy black eye makeup. Angie has on olive green leggings and brown boots. Unlike me, she isn't wearing a blouse but sports a lace-up leather vest that barely contains her boobs. She tied a shoelace from a work boot around her head to hold back her flaming-red hair and a multitude of skinny belts encircle her waist and cross her rounded chest.

She pirouettes. "What do you think?"

"I like it. You better hope the knot on your vest doesn't come loose and spill out the girls."

Angie studies me with a critical eye. "I think you look too plain."

"Nobody's ever said that to me before."

"What you need is more accessories."

By the time we leave for the fair, black bracers cover my forearms and a low-slung belt rests on my hips and threads through the loops of a suede pouch. Pointy pixie ears peek through the strands of my midnight and violet hair.

We arrive a little after ten, but already a snaky line of cars waits to park. After being directed to a grassy area to leave our vehicle, we head to the main gate with paper tickets Angie purchased online.

Once inside, she grabs my elbow. "C'mon. Let's get our bows. We would look silly walking around without them."

I roll my eyes and touch one of my pointy ears. "You're right. We wouldn't want that."

While Angie chooses which weaponry we need to buy, I chat with the proprietor. His grayish-blonde hair hangs past his shoulders. Both he and his wife are dressed in costumes of medieval workers; nothing flashy, fancy, or paranormal, although their designer-framed eyeglasses contradict their historical costumes.

Once Angie and I are properly equipped, we review the map provided at the gate and check the schedule of events. With two fingers and some difficulty, Angie pulls her cell phone from where it is tucked between her leather-bound breasts. "It's ten-thirty. There's a high wire show straight ahead at the Pirate's Cove. Let's go there first."

Shortly before noon, we stop in the food area and each of us buys a fried turkey leg. Like many attendees, we gnaw on the greasy meat and stroll along the dirt pathways taking in the sights. All of a sudden several fair workers hustle away from us.

Angie throws her bone into the nearest trashcan. "We have to hurry! The parade is about to start."

Blaring and thumping music leads us to a wide dirt pathway. Drummers and bagpipe players lead the cavalcade, followed by a motley crew from the various venues. There are ambassadors from the Ottoman Embassy, nuns from The Sisters of Perpetual Inebriation, and actors from the Play-Along Players. Village dancers and characters surround the king, queen, knights, and ladies-in-waiting of the royal court.

One pirate, inspired by Johnny Depp's Jack Sparrow character, steps out of the procession, grabs Angie around the waist, bends her over his arm, and plants a kiss on her lips. My breath catches with the man's audacity.

He returns to her to an upright position, tips his tricorn hat, and bows. "Thee hast stolen mine own heart, fair mistress." He runs to rejoin the parade.

I gape at Angie. "I can't believe that guy—"

"Isn't he wonderful?" My friend's gaze remains on the pirate until he disappears into the crowd.

"You know him?"

She nods as if in a trance. "That's Brent."

Any additional questioning is halted by a cacophony of trumpeters leading jesters, performers on horseback, and woodsmen carrying pooper-scoopers. When the parade ends and the spectators disperse, I grab Angie's arm. "Who's Brent, and why haven't I heard about him?"

"He's a guy I met here last year, but he had a girlfriend at the time. We've hooked up now that he's single again."

"You're dating him?"

"We've been going out for the last couple of weeks."

"But what's going to happen when the fair ends? You're not going to see him until next year."

"Brent only volunteers at this event. He lives and works in Boca Raton." Angie takes hold of my sleeve. "C'mon, I told him that after the parade we'd meet up at the carousel. Let's go."

Brent waits for us next to a booth selling miniature plastic dragons. "Hi. You must be Marin."

"It's nice to meet you . . . finally."

Angie squeezes his arm against her breast. "Do you have some time to spend with us?"

Brent retrieves his cellphone from a pocket of his baggy pantaloons. "If we walk around together, I can keep performing until my break."

He links arms with us, and every few minutes, he approaches a child or an interested adult and launches into his Jack Sparrow impression. He is clever, inventive, and stays in character, although to me he seems a little more menacing than Johnny Depp was in the movies. Near the archway which doubles as both the entrance and exit to the fair, he thrills and intimidates a pair of pre-teen boys also dressed in pirate attire.

Angie hisses into my ear. "Look to your right. There's a guy over there who looks like the one you're dating."

About thirty feet away, stands Park with members of the royal court. What is he doing here? His jeans and T-shirt contrast sharply with the opulent attire of the king and queen. A young man around Park's age, who is dressed as a knight, gives him a one-armed, chain-mail-covered man-hug. A young woman wearing a tall, cone-shaped headdress and an ornate gown flings her arms around his neck.

And kisses him.

CHAPTER 18

A RESERVOIR OF flammable fuel ignites within me. How dare he act like a Renaissance fair is the equivalent of a swingers' party or a dog fight. First, he made me feel self-conscious about attending this event then he shows up and is kissed by another woman. All my life people have belittled my interests and choices as inappropriate or unacceptable, and later I find out they have far worse predilections.

After stomping over to Park's back, I say, "I thought you didn't like Renaissance fairs."

He turns to face me, eyes wide behind his glasses. "Marin? What are you doing here?"

"I told you I was coming."

Park checks his watch. "But it's only twelve-thirty. Why are you here so early?"

"Maybe I wanted to catch you with your other girlfriend."

The young woman smirks and waggles her fingers at me. Park shoots the costumed princess an icy glare. "Listen, I—"

"If you haven't figured it out already, we won't be going out tonight. . . or ever again."

I head back to Angie and Brent, but Park grabs my elbow and draws me to a halt. "Hold on a minute."

I wiggle against his grip. "Let me go."

"Not until I've explained." As I continue to struggle, his other arm encircles my waist and his mouth closes in on my pointy ear. "My so-called girlfriend is my sister. Do you want to meet her?"

I go still, and he releases me. We turn to face the amused royal court as I give the elegantly dressed group a weak wave. "Hi."

His sister lowers her head in acknowledgment. The pointed hat tips forward as her dark hair floats over her shoulders. "Valorous day, mistress. I am Princess Katerina of the court of Valencia."

Park's breath tickles my cheek. "Meet my sister, Meadow."

The knight steps forward, removes his leather glove, bows, and extends his hand. "I am thoust cad's brother, Don Alonzo de Aragon, attendant to the royal family."

I put out a hand and his reddish beard tickles my skin when he plants a kiss on the back. I say, "Hello."

Park sighs. "His real name is River. Mom, Dad, this is Marin McAllister."

The older woman, with dark hair turning silver, comes forward, her chin at a regal angle. She draws herself up into a haughty posture and places lace-gloved hands on my shoulders. "I am Queen Juana of Aragon. Mine eyes doth taketh interest in thee. Thou art a beauteous archer."

In a dry voice, Park says, "That's my mom, Nancy Robinson."

The queen looks over her shoulder at the King. "Doth thee not concur, thy majesty? Isn't the lady a quite quaint wench, King Ferdinand?"

The Spanish monarch smiles behind a chest-long auburn beard shot with gray. "Yond the lady is so, mine own valorous queen. Ye hast chosen well, son."

Park scowls. "Cut it out, guys."

The King shakes a finger at his modern-day offspring. "Thee knoweth we might not but beest true to ourselves in the midst of the valorous people of our realm."

"Yeah, I know you have to stay in character. We still need to talk about the situation here. I'll get back to you after I speak with Marin." He cups my elbow and leads me several feet away. "By the way, my dad's real name is Bob. I'm sorry my family can't greet you like normal people when they're dressed like that."

"Did you forget you're talking to someone wearing pointy ears?"

Park retreats half a step and eyes me up and down. "You look pretty good. Not too wenchy at all."

"Why did you act like a Renaissance fair is so terrible? Your family obviously enjoys it."

"It's silly for grown people to be playacting like this."

"Then why are you here?"

Behind Park's back, his family watches us and whispers among themselves. "This is my parents' business. They've been putting on these fairs for the last fifteen years. I participated when I was younger. Actually, I didn't have much choice, but now I do their accounting."

"You're here on business?"

Park glances around, but no one is within ten feet of us. "I came today to tell my parents the receipts aren't adding up. Someone is skimming money. It wasn't a lot at first, which is why I didn't catch on earlier. But it's now adding up to almost a thousand dollars every weekend."

"Do you know who's doing it?"

"No. I need to conduct a more in-depth forensic audit. I suspect ticket sales, rather than food, beverages, or souvenirs. There are only a few more weekends left, so I need to uncover the thief before the place closes down and moves on." His eyes become hard and flinty. "I hate when people think the hard-earned money of others is theirs for the taking. Maybe the Renaissance had it right when it came to crime and punishment. If someone stole money and didn't put anyone's life in danger, a brand was burned into their left hand to mark them as a thief."

I shiver. "That's a little harsh, don't you think?"

"Maybe, but it certainly would make them think twice about stealing again." He points. "Do you know the woman with Jack Sparrow?"

To my left, Angie and Brent are staring at us and whispering. "That's my friend. You met her parents and grandmother last week. Do you have time for me to introduce you?"

"Sure."

With my hand in his, I bring him closer. "Angie, this is Park Robinson. Park, this is my friend, Angelina Rosetti."

Angie beams at him. "I saw you at the Dachshund Derby. You have a wonderful little dog. He really gave Mia a run for her money."

"You were there?"

"I was helping out in my dad's food truck. He makes the world's best meatball subs."

Park's mouth stretches into a crooked smile. "Meatballs, huh?"

I jump in. "Angie is the doctor at Atlantic Veterinary Hospital and helps take care of the dogs for The Forever Homes Dachshund Foundation." I gesture at Brent. "And you already know this guy."

Jack Sparrow removes his tricorn hat. "We've never met before." He holds out his hand. "Brent Hoover. This is the fifth year I've volunteered at Ren-Faire."

Park shakes the shorter, but more muscular man's hand. "And how long have you known Marin?"

"I met her for the first time today."

"Brent and Angie are dating," I add.

Park relaxes, and the two men release their grip on each other.

Angie frowns. "Marin said you don't like Renaissance fairs. She was surprised to see you here *kissing* another woman."

Before I can tell Angie there's a reasonable explanation, Park says, "I'm the accountant for Ren-Faire which is my family's business."

My friend looks at the royal personages greeting and speaking to fairgoers. "Those are your parents?"

"Yes, and the knight is my brother and the lady is my sister." He takes my hand. "It was a pleasure meeting you. Please excuse me while I talk with Marin." He stops just off the pathway and several feet shy of the royals. "Are we still on for tonight? I made reservations at a restaurant and bought movie tickets online."

"I'll be ready."

"Good." Once again, he scans our surroundings. "I would love to kiss you, but not in front of all these people, including my family. I don't have time for an interrogation." He views me again from head to toe with eyes dark, insolent, and seductive in their intensity.

I lick my lips. "Stop it."

His low and throaty voice rumbles, "Stop what, sexy wench?"

"You look like you're measuring me for a bed."

He chuckles. "Not a bed. A chair."

CHAPTER 19

THAT EVENING, PARK arrives at my house wearing jeans, sneakers, and a white button-down shirt. Without intention, my outfit matches his, except my jeans have strategic tears in the knees, my sneakers have wedge heels, and my ruffle-sleeved blouse is sheer cream-colored silk. I pick up my large Louis Vuitton handbag which contains fresh underwear, a T-shirt, and my toothbrush. Depending on how the date goes tonight, I might say the Tantra word.

Park drives to the Cinemark Palace Theater near the Boca Raton airport. "I thought we'd have dinner upstairs."

We ride the steep escalator to the upper-level restaurant. After an artichoke appetizer, we each order the bacon burger topped with a fried egg and barbecue sauce. I swallow the last bite and wipe my gooey fingers on a wad of napkins.

Park checks his watch. "The movie starts in ten minutes."

My wineglass is still half-full wineglass. It seems a shame to waste it.

Park catches the waitress's attention, points to his empty glass, and holds up a finger. "I'm going to order another one for myself. We can bring our wine into the theater."

After paying the tab, we stop at a counter for free bags of popcorn, compliments of our premier level tickets. I juggle my large purse, the wine, and popcorn as we walk down the carpeted hallway.

I squint at the marquee signs outside the viewing loges. "Which one are we seeing?"

"This one. It's got action for me, and the tomb raider is a kick-ass female for you."

Inside the theater, the previews of coming attractions play on the screen. Park chooses a loveseat on the upper-tier centered in a row. We chat as more people enter. By the time the lights darken, only a couple dozen patrons occupy the seats in the room.

Halfway through the movie, with my popcorn and wine consumed, I shift closer to Park. Without moving his eyes from the screen, he lifts his arm and puts it around me. After tucking myself against him, I lay my hand just above his belt buckle. His abdominal muscles constrict, and he kisses my temple.

I wait a few seconds then turn my face toward him. With excruciating slowness, Park brings his mouth closer. His tongue teases my lips then opens them for a long but undemanding kiss. Minutes later, the message becomes one of agonizing persuasion. Sliding my arm across his body, I press my breasts against him. The firmness and heat of his chest penetrate the thin fabric of my blouse. My nipples harden. His arm tightens and pulls me closer. He twists at the waist and enfolds me in his embrace.

I've never been kissed with such skill and passion. Every flicking movement, every tantalizing tease, every hot contact melts my spine one vertebra at a time. I moan against his lips. For the first time, I feel like I'm being tasted, not devoured; savored with a sensuality that liquefies my body. We kiss for minutes or hours until a loud, roaring reverberation hits me like a blast from a jet engine. The crashing tsunami of an onscreen explosion rolls over the rows of seats. I break contact with Park's mouth and gasp for breath. My arm slips down and bumps against his burgeoning erection.

With an awkward flail, Park lifts his arm from behind me, catching strands of my hair in his watchband. I smooth the back of my head, uncross my legs, and sit up straight. Park fidgets in his seat to adjust his jeans. I turn toward the screen to give him privacy.

I have no clue what's happening in the movie but watch as if fascinated. After a few minutes, Park enfolds my hand in his and rests them both on his thigh. We stay in this position until the final credits roll.

When the theater lights come on, I open my mouth to apologize, but he speaks first. "Are you okay?"

"Me? I'm fine. What about you?"

Park releases my hand and fiddles with the cuffs on his shirt. "I have to admit that hasn't happened to me since high school."

"You haven't had a woody since then?"

"You are a funny lady. I meant I haven't made out in public since I was a teenager." Park stands up. "You ready to go?"

I rise to my feet, and he follows me to the end of the row. I stop, check my watch, and turn to face him. "It's almost eleven. Do you need to let Lamar out?"

"I took him for a long walk before I picked you up. He should be okay."

"I don't think he should wait. Let's stop at your place. At least, I can walk with you in these shoes. Wouldn't you like some company tonight?" I smirk. "And maybe your Tantra chair will get a workout too."

The drive to his condo takes less than twenty minutes. He pulls into his parking spot and shuts off the engine. "Do you want to wait here while I get Lamar?"

"I'll come upstairs with you, so I can leave my purse inside."

We enter the rear foyer of the building. He presses the call button for the elevator, and the doors slide open at once. When we reach his floor, Park clasps my hand with his long, cool fingers as we walk down the hallway.

He unlocks the door and steps aside. "You open it. There's something I want you to see."

Did he move the Tantra chair into the living room? My already rapid heartbeat accelerates. Am I ready for this? I push down on the lever and swing the door wide. It takes me a moment to grasp the situation. "You've been practicing."

Lamar isn't whining at the door or racing out into the hall. Instead, he sits in his dog bed next to the sofa.

Park bends at the waist and pats his knees. "Good boy. Come, Lamar." The dachshund leaps from his bed, runs to his human and sits again. Park snaps on the leash. "He now knows the area in front of the door is . . . What did you call it? *No-dog's land.*"

A feeling of satisfaction and pride fills me. Park doesn't think of me as a crazy lady who insists a pet be courteous and well-behaved. "I'm impressed."

"I've always worried about his barking when I came home or when someone knocks on the door. I was afraid one of the neighbors would complain. Now I don't have to thanks to your training advice."

I lay my bag on the floor, Park locks up, and we head to the elevator. I slow my pace. "Do you always let him walk ahead of you?"

Park frowns. "Is this another leader-follower issue?"

"Yes. He should either walk beside you or slightly behind."

"Show me what to do."

I inspect Lamar's collar and leash. "I'm glad to see you're not using a harness. That cues the dog to pull, not follow. You want the collar high on his neck. Just like with a horse, if you control the head, the rest of the animal will follow. Does he ever lunge ahead when you're walking?"

"He only does it if he sees another dog he wants to meet."

"Actually, as the walk leader, he's lunging to get a sense of friend or foe before *you*, the follower, get any closer. May I?" I hold out my hand for the leash and shortened the tether, so Lamar has only enough leeway to stay beside me.

With a decisive step forward and a slight tug, I say, "Come." Walking up and down the hall, I demonstrate how I keep my arm relaxed. "The leash is a conduit and sends a message to him. If you're stressed or anxious, he's going to know and take over as the leader."

After Park practices a few times, we head to the elevator. Outside, the warm but breezy weather makes for a beautiful night in South Florida. Near Park's condo, several restaurants are still serving patrons seated in bistro chairs under striped table umbrellas. Music mixes with conversations. The smell of fried food mingles with the salty breeze. We stroll up the street for several blocks. People thin out, noises deaden, and the sidewalk darkens between haloes of light from widely-spaced street lamps. The empty eeriness causes me to peer into black doorways and alleys. As I open my mouth to suggest we turn back, Park heads for home.

In the elevator, he presses the button for his floor. With the closing of the steel doors, the atmosphere within the enclosed space changes. An electrical charge zips through me. Park growls, drops the leash, and pushes me against the rear wall. His lips land on mine, and his hips pin me. When the elevator stops and the doors open, Park steps away, breathing hard. I blink, lightheaded and giddy. Lamar stares at us, cocking his head side to side, with the quizzical expression some dogs use when trying to figure out strange human behavior.

I say in a breathless voice, "He didn't run out of the elevator."

Park picks up the leash. "We've been working on that too." Taking my hand, he says, "Now let's see what I can teach you."

Lamar and I scurry to keep up with his long strides down the hall.

CHAPTER 20

INSIDE THE CONDO, Park locks the door with a quiet click. After unsnapping Lamar's leash, the dog scampers to the kitchen. The tinkling of his tags against a metal bowl accompanies the slurping sounds of water. I swallow a knot of nervousness and ignore the swarm of rabid butterflies in my stomach.

Park hasn't moved from his position by the door. As if I'm seeing him for the first time, I'm taken aback by his good looks in the soft lamplight. His chestnut hair is mussed by the breeze during our walk. My fingers itch to run through the disarray, to make him even less perfect. His eyes appear almost black behind his glasses. His above-average height, broad shoulders, and flat abdomen epitomize a sexual male. I breathe a silent prayer of thanks because he appears to want me as much as I want him.

Park raises one eyebrow. "Do I meet with your approval?"

"Yes. You do."

His hot gaze roves over my face. "You are the most beautiful woman I've ever been with."

"I am?"

"The others were pretty or cute but not beautiful like you."

Unsure what to say, *thank you* comes to my lips but stalls there. "I, um . . ."

"We had discussed protection at one time. Have you done anything about that?" Park takes a step toward me.

His question acts as an effective ice bucket of reality. I reach down, lift my purse from the floor, and pull two papers from my bag. I extend the documents to Park. "I went to my doctor. The form on top is the result of my blood work. I'm clean. The yellow sheet confirms I'm now using an IUD for birth control."

He makes no move to take them. "I trust you." He walks over to a stack of mail on his kitchen counter, picks up an envelope, and removes a folded paper. "I also went to a clinic and was tested. I'm clean too."

I reach for the report and read everything, including confirmation of his age, his birthday in June, and his O negative blood type. I place the papers on the counter. Park moves a quick step nearer, puts a hand on my waist, and tugs. The proof of his desire presses against my abdomen. When I relax with a shy smile, he rests his other hand on my opposite hip. Park's kiss is softer and gentler than I expected. He waits until I fold against him then wraps his arms around my waist. His hands drift lower and squeeze.

His lips meander away and cross my cheek. "Any time you want to stop, just tell me. Promise?"

With his deep baritone voice so close to my ear, the vibrations ignite triggers that race down my body to the spot between my thighs. I draw in a deep breath, nod, and press my lower body tight against his.

His arm around my waist becomes a steel band, keeping my crotch notched to the rigidness of his erection. "I get hard just looking at you. Whether I'm with you in public or private, I'm at half-staff most of the time. Thank God you wanted to come back here with me. I almost suggested we skip the movie after dinner."

With the intense way Park stares into my eyes, my body tingles all over. What will my response be when we're naked? Or on the Tantra chair? I quiver with the same excitement and terror as being at the top of a roller coaster. Finally, my curiosity and anticipation win out. Bunching his shirt, I lift the fabric until my palms rest on his warm, bare waist.

Park maneuvers me backward, one careful step at a time as he kisses and touches me. We execute the *pas de deux* through the bedroom doorway with grace and precision despite not breaking contact. He hits a switch on the wall, and the table lamp between the two armchairs illuminates the room with low light.

I reach with shaking fingers for the top button on his shirt. Park strips his glasses off with a quick sideways movement and tosses them onto the cushion of one of the side chairs. His warm fingertips arch my spine as he pulls my blouse from the waistband of my jeans. With his shirt unbuttoned, he is all toned slabs of muscle with a light dusting of russet-colored hair across the center of his chest.

I take a step back and haul him with me until stopped by the low-slung Tantra chair. Park has my blouse unbuttoned. I shrug the fabric off my shoulders and the soft silk puddles on the floor. Park toes off his shoes then he drops to one knee. He places his face between my thighs and inhales. I close my eyes, willing myself to remain upright. After loosening my shoelaces, he cups the heel, freeing one foot then the other. His tongue blazes a searing path up my abdomen and between my breasts to the base of my throat. Reaching behind me, he unfastens my white lacy bra with ease. The scrap of lingerie ends up tossed onto the nearby chair. I raise my forearms to cover myself.

Park stops me with gentle hands. "No. I want to look at you." He cups the undersides of my breasts as his thumbs skim over the peaks as if mesmerized by his hands on me. Encouraged by his rapt state, I unfasten and lower his jeans. My breath catches with a moment of uncertainty. My two previous lovers were boys compared to him.

"You're doing great." He smiles at me. "I'm kind of nervous too."

I glance at his erection tenting the silky boxer shorts. "You are?"

When he kisses me again, my tension eases and is replaced by boldness. I skim the boxers down his hips. Without breaking contact with my lips, he steps free of his jeans and shorts. I undo my pants and wiggle them along with my lacy panties down my legs and off my feet.

Park kisses me while using his body to guide me onto the chair. My bottom comes in contact with the hump of the seat. The leather cools my skin and contrasts with the heat of his body. His kisses are like white noise for me, blocking out my nervousness and awkwardness.

He breaks away and shrugs off his shirt. "Let's have you sit back." Holding onto my ankles, he swings my legs up.

As soon as my feet come off the floor, I slide down the hump and settle into the valley of the seat. Park sits on the edge of the chair, facing me. He runs the tip of his tongue around my nipple.

Combing my fingers through his thick hair as he suckles, I bite back a moan. His hand strokes the top of my thigh. Little lightning bolts of pleasure spark between my legs. I'm torn between squeezing my knees tight or opening them wide. Soon I grant access to his gentle explorations. His fingertip flutters against my clitoris.

Oh. My. God.

His forearm on my leg keeps me from flying off the chair. One of his long fingers slips inside as his thumb rubs tiny circles. My body trembles, and a helpless sound escapes my lips. His gentle lips on my breasts contrast with his relentless hand. Without warning, I jolt with a shuddering climax and a throaty cry of surprise.

As I descend back to earth, my eyes focus, and my fingers unclench. Park slows his pace which keeps me from becoming hypersensitive. I open my mouth to tell him—What? Keep doing what you're doing. Stop. Don't stop. I want more.

At last, I choke out, "Please . . . inside."

His fondling slows but doesn't cease as his hand withdraws by inches. He lifts his head and sits upright. "Let's move you a bit." He stands, slips his forearm under my knees, and lifts my legs. Park straddles the chair facing me and places each of my thighs over his. The natural curve of the seat cradles us together in a V position.

I clasp the back of his neck and drag him forward for a kiss. My tongue slips past his lips as he presses the tip of himself against my entrance. A momentary panic flutters through me. He proceeds no further. We kiss, touch, and stroke. Every time I relax or become distracted, he moves another inch forward.

I expect he might have to work to enter my unused body. I expect discomfort; maybe pain since it's been so long. I expect to have a chance to change my mind. I did not expect he would enter so easily or fit so well. He waits then withdraws and moves deeper.

My head spins. He thrusts into me, deeper and harder, triggering a shower of sparks. Before I can recover, he drives inside again and again. I whimper, dig my fingers into his biceps, and hold onto him.

He pants. "Too hard?"

"No. No. I'm okay." At least, I think I am.

He touches and ignites some perfect place inside, a spot I never knew existed. Park wraps his arm around my waist, arching my hips toward him. My position on the Tantra shifts the angle of his entry, and I'm so close to the feeling I've never achieved before with a man inside me. Park seems to sense my teetering and his speed increases.

The first tremor slams into me, making me gasp. The next shockwave produces an involuntary scream of pleasure. Then the dam breaks sending me tumbling into intense sensation and heart-stopping ecstasy. Over my ragged breathing, the only sounds are Park's low groans as he follows me into orgasmic bliss. He collapses against me, his arm still wrapped around my waist. I cross my arms over his back and hug him tight.

When our breathing slows, I murmur against his neck, "You did it."

He sits up and chuckles. "Are you sure it was me? Maybe it was the chair."

"I think the chair helped."

"You're not so bad yourself if I just go by all the sounds you made."

I lower my eyes, and my face heats. "Oh, God."

"You said that a lot too." He lifts my chin with his finger. "Don't be embarrassed. It drove me wild." He squints at the large decorative clock on the wall. "I guess I better get you home. It's late."

A wave of regret swells through me. Oh no. He's a slam-bam-thank-you-ma'am kind of guy. He isn't a post-coital cuddler or a man who sleeps with a woman after sex.

"Or can you stay until morning?" he asks.

I jerk my head up. "What?"

"I'd love to wake up with you beside me, but I know you have dogs to take care of."

"Actually, they're all at Angie's house for the night. I packed my toothbrush and some clothes in my purse, just in case."

Park gives me a quick kiss. "That means we can sleep late. There's more I want to teach you about this chair tonight. Just let me know if you get too tired or sore."

A shiver runs down my spine. "Okay."

"I'll be back with a washcloth."

The clock reads one o'clock in the morning. I'm not sleepy or tired. Instead, I'm invigorated and curious about the new position. I review my favorites from the Tantra chair website. I hope I have the nerve to tell him what I'd like to try next.

CHAPTER 21

I AWAKE TO the wonderfully acrid smell of coffee brewing, stretch, and open my eyes. Sunlight filters through slatted blinds. The sheet drags against my skin. It's not as silky as my Egyptian cotton linens. A door closes in another room. A dog yips.

I'm in Park's bed. Images of the night before flood my senses. His energy and commitment to my pleasure still astound me. I lost track of my orgasms, although Park only came twice.

I rise on one elbow. The nightstand clock reads eight-thirty. I fall back onto the pillow and lace my fingers behind my head. It was close to three when we finally left the Tantra chair. My legs had been a little rubbery when I walked to the bathroom and stared at myself in the mirror. Whisker burn reddened the side of my neck, but my face was radiant with an inner glow. Once in bed, with his goodnight kiss lingering on my lips, I fell asleep in minutes, wrapped in his arms.

So that's what a night with Park Robinson is like.

The experience feels different this time, even though it is nothing more than unemotional sex. With my previous partners, I pretended to take pleasure in the act to stroke their egos. With Park, I have the freedom to enjoy the ride or not since he knows about my past lack of response.

But sex with him is far from clinical or unfeeling. Maybe the lack of pressure, along with the Tantra chair, and his inventive stamina contributed to my enjoyment. I never considered myself capable of what he wrung out of me. I clawed at his shoulders; screamed *more, harder* numerous times. He had been so deep and at just the right angle and speed. I wonder if he and the Tantra will become my addiction.

"You're awake."

I jerk to a sitting position, and the sheet falls to my waist.

Park stands in the doorway, wearing a pair of shorts and a sleeveless tank top. "Did I sneak up on you again?"

I pull the sheet over my naked breasts. "I, uh, was thinking and I, um—"

"Forgot I was here?" He grins and comes forward to his side of the bed. "I took Lamar out and gave him his breakfast. How do you feel this morning?"

"Good."

"Just good?"

My cheeks burn. "Okay, I feel great. I'm not frigid."

"No, you're far from it." He pulls the shirt over his head and skims the shorts down his legs. Throwing back the sheet, Park climbs in naked beside me. "I'm curious. What did you think of the Tantra chair during the second part of last night?"

I lie on my side and prop my head on my hand. "That is a phenomenal piece of furniture design. It should be shouted from the rooftops." He laughs and I smack his chest. "I'm serious. Why don't more couples know about it? Think of how many marriages and relationships could benefit, maybe even be saved. Furniture stores should have a special Tantra section in their bedroom department. I mentioned the chair to Angie, and she had no idea what I was talking about."

After my first visit to Park's condo and my introduction to his Tantra, I told my friend about the chair one day at lunch. After loading the website onto my phone and muting the volume, Angie's eyes grew wide as the first film played. I hit the end button when our entrees arrived.

The handsome young waiter asked, "Is there anything else I can get you?"

Angie stared at him with hungry eyes, but before she asked him to father her children, I said, "No. I think we're good here."

Park lays his hand on the curve of my waist and interrupts my reverie. "Are you up for a little romp in the sack?" He trails a finger along my ribs to my breast. I tense. "What's wrong?"

I stare at the white sheet between us. "What if the chair is the only thing that . . . does it for me?"

He murmurs against the pulse in my neck. "I know I can make you come in a bed somehow, some way." He rolls me onto my back. "And I'm going to do my damnedest to find out how."

CHAPTER 22

PARK AND I stay in the condo until close to noon. We stop for breakfast at an old-fashioned, twenty-four-hour diner since both of us proclaim our starvation. The restaurant can be described as a working-class place designed to swap calories for money as fast as possible. We slide into a red vinyl booth and grab laminated menus anchored between the wall and napkin holder. A matronly waitress in jeans and a black T-shirt comes to the table.

She juts out her hip as if weighed down with the half-full carafe she carries. "Coffee?"

"As long as it's not decaf."

"Honey, does this look like a decaf place to you? You want any of those fancy latte drinks then you best head to Starbucks. You're lucky we have Lipton tea bags." After filling our cups, she says, "I'll be back in a minute for your orders. You better be ready."

Park laughs. "She's not kidding. Do you know what you want?"

I order and eat the biggest breakfast I've ever had. My two eggs, bacon, sausage, tomatoes, hash brown potatoes, and rye toast disappear in record time. I lean back in the booth with a hand on my abdomen. "I guess I was hungry."

Park glances up from mopping egg yolk with his last piece of bagel. He flashes his signature sexy smile. "We certainly did enough to work up an appetite. I think I got a little . . . *dehydrated.*"

I run my tongue over my lips and return his smile with a sultry one, I hope. "You've become my favorite form of exercise."

He leans across the table and speaks in a hushed tone. "If hard-ons burn calories, you'll have me down to skin and bones in no time."

His blatant words make my cheeks flush. "Park!"

The waitress cruises by with a full pot of coffee. Without asking, she tops off our mugs. "You ready for the check?" Without a response from Park, she sets the carafe on the table and fishes in the pocket of her apron for a notepad. She licks her thumb and flips through the papers, tears a page off, and slaps it onto the tabletop.

After she leaves, Park nods toward my coffee. "Drink up. We're being kicked out." Thirty minutes later at my house, we walk to my front door. Park holds my shoulders. "I need to ask you something."

"What?"

"My parents would like to have dinner with us. Since they know we've been seeing each other, they asked to meet you before heading north in two weeks."

"When do you want to do this?"

"That's the thing. Fridays, Saturdays, and Sundays are out for my family because of Ren-Faire. I'm busy every evening this week except Thursday."

I do a mental calculation of my schedule for the upcoming week. "I can do Thursday."

"We might as well get this over with. Otherwise, they'll bug me every day. I'll call you and let you know the plan." He hugs and kisses me.

I wait on the front step until Park beeps his horn in farewell. Instead of entering the house, I head to the garage door, flip open a box anchored to the wall, and punch in my code. Once inside my car, I drive to Angie's house.

My friend flings open the door. "Get in here, and tell me about the chair. I can't believe you didn't call before this." She subjects me to a thorough scrutiny. "Look at you. I can tell you're satisfied."

It's true, but is Angie seeing the result of great sex last night or the gargantuan breakfast I ate this morning? Five dachshunds line up on a runner six feet inside the door. Mia thumps her tail in welcome. Lili holds a ball in her mouth as her body wiggles from head to toe in expectation.

Brewster shakes in quivering nervousness and whimpers. Angie's red standard male dachshund named Jamie, who weighs in at twenty-five pounds, yawns. Her slightly smaller black and tan female, Claire, waits with bright eyes for the signal to leave the rug. Both of Angie's dogs tower over my three like professional linebackers on a junior high varsity team.

I lean forward. "Come." All five dogs race to me for welcome pats, and in Lili's case, a toss of the ball.

Angie takes me by the hand. "Let's go into the kitchen. I want to hear all the erotic details. I made coffee. Want some?"

"I just had two cups at breakfast. Ice water is fine."

The dogs are sent outside, and we settle at the kitchen table. Angie assumes a pouty expression. "I've been on pins and needles waiting to hear from you. I drove Brent crazy last night wondering how you were doing."

I slosh water from my glass onto the tabletop. "You told Brent about me and Park?"

"I said you were going to spend the night at his place for the first time, and he had a Tantra chair."

"Ang!"

"It's okay. Brent knows about the chair. He's never tried one, but it got us talking. You'll never believe what he told me. There is this whole subculture of BDSM among Renaissance fair workers and some of the people who attend."

I frown. "At the one Park's family runs?"

"Not necessarily. It turns out the fair circuit is like Disney Land for kinksters. It's where a lot of people first discover the lifestyle."

"You're kidding."

"No. Think about it. You have staff and visitors in costumes and doing role play all day, and often it carries over to the bedroom after dark. Brent said some people use codes on their costumes to advertise their sexual preferences to find new partners."

I shake my head. "That can't be. Renaissance fairs are family-friendly and educational. Yeah, there's a lot of leather, corsets, and boobs, but it's the style of dress from the period. It doesn't have anything to do with that other lifestyle."

"Brent said that's how the fairs started, but some have evolved into events for those who have fetishes and like BDSM."

I picture the Robinson family dressed in their regal costumes. Is this another reason Park doesn't want anything to do with Renaissance fairs? Maybe he doesn't agree with the alternative sexual preferences of the attendees and participants.

Angie puts out her hand. "I'm not saying it happens at Ren-Faire, but there are others around the country with that express purpose."

"So . . . is Brent involved in this sex-fest?"

Angie wiggles in her seat and fiddles with her coffee cup. "I don't think so."

"Does he dress up as Jack Sparrow because he has a pirate fetish?"

"Nooo." Angie rolls the word around her mouth but it doesn't sound convincing.

"What you're telling me is . . . a Renaissance fair is basically about sex?"

"Absolutely not." This time Angie responds with more emphasis. "People find it liberating to dress up, drink lots of beer, and walk around speaking with a British accent. Besides, who cares if some people use it to find new sexual partners? It's like Vegas. What happens at a Renaissance fair stays at a Renaissance fair."

"I wish I had known this before I attended with you. I might have viewed things differently."

"The kinky stuff is kept very private, and people are careful. Trust is crucial when it comes to things like that. But we're done talking about fairs." Angie's hand slices through the air. "I want to hear about you and Park. How was it?"

A memory of the events of last night flickers through me like an X-rated movie. "Pretty amazing."

"Was the chair everything the website claims it is?"

"More. I may have spoken in tongues last night."

Angie leans forward like a lottery ticket holder with four numbers, waiting to hear the fifth. "How many times did he make you come?"

"It was four, no five times. There was this morning in bed."

With Gestapo-like insistence, Angie wrings out more details from me. At the end of the recounting, she jumps up and heads out of the kitchen.

I twist around in my chair. "Where are you going?"

"I'm getting my laptop to order a Tantra chair."

"What are you going to tell your parents when they ask about it?"

Angie returns with her Mac under her arm. "Well, I'm not going to do what Park did. My chair will go in the living room, right in front of the TV. When my mom asks, *and* you know she will, I'll tell her it's the latest thing in furniture. Unlike most recliners that men use, I'll say this one is built especially for a woman. And the best part is . . . I won't be lying."

Chapter 23

PARK CALLS ME two days later. "I talked with my parents. We're meeting at the Cheesecake Factory in Boca at six. Would you be able to drive there? I won't have time to pick you up."

"I'll be glad to." The information Angie told me about the simmering sexuality of Renaissance fairs bounces around inside my head. "Um, is there anything I should be aware of before meeting your parents again?"

"Like what?"

How do I ask a guy if his parents are kinky sadists? "Like . . . are they teetotalers or alcoholics? Are they vegans or meat-eaters?"

"I guess they're your average, run-of-the-mill family who travels around in an RV doing Renaissance fairs."

"Is there a topic I should avoid? Or questions I shouldn't ask?"

"Don't ask my mother how she likes having a CPA in the family."

"Why not?"

"When I announced my college major, Mom threatened to have a heart attack," Park says in a dry voice. "She eventually consoled herself that I was going through a phase. I know she thought I would come to my senses and change my major to theater or some other useless field."

"She must be thrilled now that you're doing the books for Ren-Faire."

"Mom would only be thrilled if I would wear a jester's costume and speak with a fake Shakespearean accent while filing their tax returns."

On Thursday, my phone beeps with an incoming text while I park my car in the Cheesecake Factory lot. The screen reads: *We're here.*

Upon entering the foyer, I discover that, in addition to his parents, Park's brother and sister wait on a bench next to the hostess stand. I wave at the Robinson contingent. "Hi, everyone."

Park strides over from the glass-fronted cheesecake display. He wears a lightweight gray suit with a white dress shirt and a knotted maroon striped tie. He's breathtaking in a civilized and ubersexual way.

In contrast, his family and I look like a lost caravan of gypsies. His mother, sister, and I are all dressed in long, flowing skirts of gauzy fabrics printed with vibrant colors. Nancy Robinson wears a linen tunic. Meadow and I sport midriff-baring peasant tops. Park's female relatives elevate their bohemian look to a higher level with headscarves over their shoulder-length dark hair, hooped earrings large enough to hang shower curtains, multiple bangle bracelets, and beaded necklaces. Even Mr. Robinson and Park's brother, River, dress unconventionally in boots, jeans, and white T-shirts under leather vests. The men wear wristbands and medallion necklaces in place of the watch and tie Park has on. The one commonality among the males is their red hair, although Mr. Robinson's is paler with age.

When I'm out in public with my family, I never care when surreptitious glances or outright stares flash at me, but this time I inwardly cringe for Park who appears as the square peg in this party of round holes.

His mother steps forward and kisses me on both cheeks. "I'm so happy to see you again. Marin, isn't it?"

"Yes, Mrs. Robinson."

"Please call me Nancy. Mrs. Robinson reminds me of my mother-in-law, and she was a bitch with a capital B."

Mr. Robinson says, "Mother was a federal judge, which was highly unusual in her day. She had strong opinions about women. You can call me Bob."

Park's mother snorts. "Do you know on our wedding day, his mother told me I was a bubble-headed idiot for taking her son's name? Barbara disapproved of wives who were housekeepers or stay-at-home moms."

His sister joins us. "Stop it, you two. We just met Park's new girlfriend. Don't scare her off with horror stories about our crazy family. She's the first one who doesn't look and act like him." Meadow studies me from head to toe. "I love your outfit."

"Thank you."

She darts behind me and tugs at the waistband of my skirt. "Just as I thought, this is an Emilio Pucci. I recognize the skirt and top from a *Vogue* article about his spring collection a few years ago. Did you buy it at Saks or Neiman Marcus?"

"I-I'm not sure."

Meadow casts appraising looks at my 18K gold choker, Tiffany mesh earrings, and Badgley Mischka jeweled sandals. She seems to add up their costs with a mental calculator.

River Robinson muscles his way forward. "I have a question for you. Where's your seeing-eye dog?"

I frown at him. Did Park tell his family I'm involved in animal rescue, and they think I train service dogs?

Park speaks first. "What are you talking about?"

His brother shrugs. "I figured she couldn't see shit to be interested in you, bro."

The Robinson parents gasp. "River!"

He hunches his shoulders and raises one palm toward me and one toward Park. "Can't you see it? She belongs with us more than he does. What could've attracted her to *him?* The suit and tie?"

Park opens his mouth, but this time I beat him to it. "I'm sure you've heard the adage, opposites attract. I think that's part of it, but Park has many qualities I find very appealing. He loves dogs." Especially dachshunds. "He's very handsome." And has a killer body. "He's always concerned about my safety and well-being." With strangers and during sex. "And I appreciate his good sense and style." Particularly when it comes to furniture.

A hostess approaches with a stack of menus cradled in her arm and leads us to a large round table. I end up seated between Park and his brother. A white-shirted server with the obligatory red tie and black pants approaches, introduces herself, and takes our drink orders.

River flips through the menu. "There are twenty goddamn pages in this thing. It's longer than most books I've read. How are you supposed to decide what to eat?"

Meadow smacks her brother's arm. "It doesn't matter. You're going to order a burger and fries anyway."

Nancy casts a pained gaze at her youngest son. "I wish you would order something healthy. Why not try a salad instead of beef and grease?" She launches into a spirited dissertation on the benefits of vegetables and whole grains.

River holds up his two hands like he's trying to stop a rampage. "Cool it, Mom. I eat all that healthy shit when we're at home. At a restaurant, I want red meat."

"Then order a side salad instead of fries and eat it first."

"In Paris, they eat their salads last."

"Well, when you go to France, you can do that."

River snaps the menu shut. "Fine. Since we're out to dinner and my brother, the CPA, is paying, maybe I'll get a salad . . . and a steak."

Nancy winces.

I wonder if her pained expression is because of River's meal choice or is it because of Park's career choice. The server returns with the beverages and takes our food orders. We pass the breadbasket. Nancy eats a slice without butter and frowns when the rest of her family lathers spread onto theirs. Meadow and River argue over who has the right to the last slice until Park reminds them they can get bread refills.

Nancy turns her attention to me. "When I learned you and my son are dating, I was very surprised."

Park halts in buttering his bread. "Why?"

His father strokes his beard and says, "Because your lady friend didn't come to Ren-Faire dressed as a mundane."

I tilt my head to the side. "I haven't heard of that medieval person before."

Bob says, "A mundane is someone who doesn't wear a costume to a Renaissance fair."

Park puts his hand on my arm. "Yeah, if you're a mundane you get the whole fake voices routine and the hard-sell to buy dragon hearts, magic wands, and Ye Olde Honey Wine."

"And if you *are* in costume?"

Park's brother touches my other arm to direct my attention his way. "Then we'll share our flask with you and try to get you into bed."

Mr. and Mrs. Robinson gasp. "River!"

Before our food arrives, I skirt around questions about my family and background. Park and I tell about how we met. When I'm asked a personal question, I offer a vague or incomplete answer then ask one of the Robinsons a similar question to deflect the interrogation.

"How did you and Mr. Robinson meet?"

Park's mother tells the story of being fixed up on a blind date by friends. At first, she and Bob couldn't tolerate each other, but when Mr. Robinson saw Nancy dancing in a musical he asked her out again.

"She had great legs," he says by way of an explanation.

I fiddle with my glass of ice tea. "When did you start traveling the fair circuit?"

Mr. Robinson tells about his mother dying twelve years into their marriage. With the money from her estate, he and his wife decided to pursue their dream of operating a Renaissance fair rather than continue in their careers as an electrical engineer and a dance teacher.

"Best decision we ever made," Park's father says with a satisfied smile, and his wife nods in agreement.

"Where are you from originally?"

Park's mother says they were born and raised in the Philadelphia area, but their three children had been born up and down the eastern seaboard.

"I asked Park about the origin of his name. He said you guys were very into nature."

River chokes on a mouthful of Coke. Meadow covers her mouth with her hand and laughs. Mr. Robinson feigns an interest in rearranging his silverware. His wife blushes. Park sits statue-still and stares straight ahead.

"Well, in a sense, that's true," Nancy says in slow, measured tones as if I might be recording her. "We decided to name our children after the places they were conceived."

Without looking at anyone, Park mutters, "I was almost called Central."

River scowls. "Not as bad as me being named Mississippi."

Meadow levels a glare at her parents. "I'm lucky I wasn't saddled with Cow Pasture."

"Stop exaggerating," Nancy reprimands them then catches my eye. "We would have never given them those names. It's only a family joke."

Our entrees arrive. During the meal, the Robinsons share stories about the people they know and places they have been during their years on the fair circuit.

Mr. Robinson lays down his fork and levels a look at Park and me. "If you two don't have plans for next Thursday, we're doing a vaudeville show for RESCU in the Coconut Creek High School auditorium. The tickets are twenty-five dollars apiece."

I ask, "What's rescue?"

"It stands for Renaissance Entertainers Services Crafters United. It's a nonprofit offering financial assistance and medical advocacy to fair folks who are sick or injured. Many of our full-time workers can't afford health insurance, so that's where the foundation helps out. We would really appreciate your support."

Park looks up from his dinner. "I didn't tell you this before, but Marin is a professional fundraiser."

Oh no!

Bob's eyes light up. "Really? We would be grateful for any advice or services you can provide. Of course, we can't pay you, but your help would be very welcome."

I smooth the napkin in my lap. "Um, well, the date of your fundraiser doesn't give me much time to plan anything, but I'll make a few phone calls and see what I can do."

Park's parents ask me questions about my *job*. I cull my memory for information I learned while working with my grandmother and mother in planning and staffing charity events. "The most important thing is how many people you ask to help rather than how much money you raise. If they don't contribute this year, they may the next time."

River wrinkles his nose like he's caught a whiff of an unpleasant odor. "I know it's for a good cause, but fundraising seems just one step above panhandling."

"My grandmother told me if the organization is doing good work I should be willing to raise money for it. Someone did a survey at one time and asked people why they donated to charity and other fundraising causes. The majority said it was because they were asked."

River asks, "Don't people get pissed off when you're always hitting them up for money?"

"They do if you treat them like ATMs. I have the advantage of working with dogs, so we appeal to animal lovers. The people who enjoy Renaissance fairs are not just your donors but your ambassadors too. They should be treated like they have other gifts to offer besides money."

Bob crosses his arms on the tabletop and laser-focuses on me. "Such as?"

"They might recommend RESCU to another service club or professional association. Or maybe they'll forward your e-mails to others interested in the fairs. We get donations of dog food, office equipment, bedding, and towels from sources we never contacted. What's important is to thank them, individually and personally. When The Forever Homes Dachshund Foundation receives any kind of donation, the first thing I do is write a thank you note by hand. It's old-fashioned but still appreciated by those who have written a check to support your cause."

My eyes circle the table. The five Robinsons seem to view me in a new and different light. I'm not just Park's less-than-traditional new girlfriend. I bask in the glow for a few seconds until an awful thought intrudes. Will the Robinsons' opinion of me change when they find out I don't work for a living like they do? How will Park react to my lies?

All of a sudden a high-pitched childish squeal sounds from across the room. "Look, there's Auntie Marin!"

CHAPTER 24

A SUDDEN CHILL freezes me in place until a little hand touches my arm. I turn my head and look down into the smiling face of my niece, Ainsley.

The little girl squeezes between my chair and River's then struggles to climb onto my lap. "Hi, Auntie Marin."

Without looking at anyone except the child, I lift her. "What are you doing here?"

"Grandmama needs new shoes."

Oh no. That means Mumsy is here with Kit and Ainsley.

The hairs on the back of my neck stand on end, waiting for the ax to fall. I twist around in my seat. Kit is behind me, wide-eyed, with a tentative smile as she views the spectacle of the Robinsons. My mother is a half-pace back, wearing a polite artificial smile like she's about to make contact with the members of a cult who abducted her daughter.

"I'm surprised to see you here." It's also surprising how calm my voice sounds.

My sister doesn't respond, but Betsy comes to her long-held etiquette good senses. "Marin, aren't you going to introduce us to your friends?"

"Of course. These are the Robinsons." My mother smiles and nods across the table to Park's parents. "That's Nancy and Bob." I point to my right. "These are their children, Meadow and River."

Ainsley motions over my shoulder. "What about him?"

"He's also their son . . . Park."

His name sparks Kit and Betsy's attention. My mother's smile widens at the man dressed in a business suit. "How do you do? I'm Betsy McAllister, Marin's mother. She mentioned you when she told us about the Dachshund Derby." Mumsy never forgets a name, even one spoken in passing. This useful trait stands her well in many social circles.

My niece says, "My name is Ainsley." She points to Kit. "That's my mommy."

I give a weak smile. "Sorry. This is my niece and my sister, Katherine Coughlin."

Kit raises her hand in a general wave. After Betsy shakes Park's hand, she circles the table to do the same with Bob and Nancy.

By then, I recover some of my equilibrium. "What's this about shoes?"

Betsy returns to stand between me and Park. She lays a hand on my shoulder. "I found a pair that would be perfect with my gown for the Black Tie Ball. I wanted to try them on before I bought them. The Saks at Town Center had my size in stock, so we drove down here."

Ainsley announces, "I got hungry. But not for cheesecake."

Kit licks her lips with fleeting eye contact for those seated at the table. I recognize my sister's fidgeting behavior as a symptom of the situation's awkwardness and her nervous anticipation for the inquisition she'll get on the drive home. Meanwhile, Betsy makes tiny adjustments to my blouse, raising the elastic neckline higher.

"You have a lovely daughter, Betsy," Nancy says in the sugary tone mothers use when complimenting each other's children. "We're thrilled she and Park are dating."

Betsy speaks in a tone of polite disbelief, similar to when the caterer told her fresh stone crabs are available only from September to April. "I'll admit I was surprised to see her here today with Park. It was quite unexpected." She laid a manicured hand on Park's shoulder. "Now that we've been introduced, I'll insist she bring you to dinner, so you can meet her father."

Park flashes Betsy his drop-dead smile. "Thank you for the invitation, Mrs. McAllister. I'd like to meet the rest of Marin's family."

I'm sure Park's blatant masculine appeal affects most young women, just as it had me. But when my mother responds also, I stifle a giggle. His urban handsomeness and bedroom baritone breaks through Betsy's defenses with ease and melts them away.

My mother stares trance-like into his chocolate-brown eyes behind the classy glasses. "Then I will get in touch with Marin to set a date. It's wonderful to meet you and your family. We won't keep you from your dinner any longer."

Ainsley slides off my lap after a boa-constricting neck hug. "Bye, Auntie. Come see me and bring Mia."

Kit waves and takes her daughter's hand. "Goodbye."

Betsy leans down, kisses my cheek, and whisper-hisses into my ear. "Call me as soon as you get home."

Nancy watches my family leave before she speaks. "You are, without a doubt, your mother's daughter. The resemblance is obvious. However, your sister doesn't look like either of you."

All the Robinson eyes are on me now. "Kit is my half-sister. My father was a widower when he and Mumsy married."

River snorted. "*Mumsy*? Sounds like you're rich and famous."

In a somewhat strained voice, I say, "It's what mothers in my family are called."

Meadow smacks his arm. "Not every mother is called Mom."

I slide a glance at Park. He pushes his glasses up his nose and studies me with his head tilted to one side. The time to tell him about my family has come, but I dodge the dreaded conversation that night.

After dinner, his family drives away as Park and I stand outside the restaurant. He touches my arm. "I'm going to follow my parents back to the park. I've uncovered who the thief is. I need to advise them about how they should handle the situation. Do you want to get together this weekend?"

"Why don't you and Lamar come to my place? I'll cook dinner again."

He lifts my hand and kisses the center of my palm. "Should I bring my toothbrush?"

"And a change of clothes, unless you don't mind a walk of shame the next morning."

"Where I live that's a badge of honor if anyone would even notice or care."

On the drive back to my house, I review the possible reactions that may occur when he learns about my family and wealth. Most involve dark thoughts of worst-case scenarios. Will Park storm out of my house because I didn't tell him before now? Or will there be a spark of greed in his eyes when he says my money doesn't matter to him?

After I arrive home, my cell phone rings as I open the patio door for the dogs. "Hi, Mumsy. I'm just letting the dogs out. I was about to call you."

"Why didn't you tell me about dating Park?"

"We've only gone out a couple of times."

"Yet, you went to dinner with *his* family tonight." The implicit emphasis falls somewhere between hurt and disbelief.

"We ran into them at a Renaissance fair. They'll be heading north soon and invited us to the restaurant."

"Is that why all of you, except Park, were dressed in costume?"

"Uh . . . yes."

"Why was Park in a suit?"

"He's the accountant for Ren-Faire and had a business meeting with the owners after dinner." I rub my forehead with the effort to construct deliberate omissions rather than outright lies.

"Well, I have to say I was pleasantly surprised to find you interested in a young man like Park. I'm sure your father would welcome a chance to meet him. I'll find out if Stanford has plans for next weekend. Perhaps you two can come to dinner on either Saturday or Sunday evening."

"Don't say anything to Pops yet."

"Why not?"

I heave a mighty sigh. "It's just that I haven't told him about . . . *us.*"

"Us?"

"He doesn't know about the Winslow money."

"I see. When *are* you going to tell him?"

"I plan to do it this weekend."

My mother hesitates. "You would like to continue the relationship?"

"Yes. I like him a lot. I just don't know what his reaction will be to finding out about me."

Betsy's voice softens. "Don't worry, darling. If your young man genuinely cares about you, regardless of your wealth, you'll know."

"I'll call you after I talk with him."

CHAPTER 25

FOR SATURDAY'S DINNER, I decide to bait the steak and potato trap and pray Park will fall headlong into it. I stop at a meat market and buy two large T-bones as well as colossal shrimp. At a farm stand, I select good-sized baking potatoes, the ingredients for a Caesar salad, and fresh berries. Park said he doesn't care about sweets, but for dessert, I plan to make a Pavlova.

When the doorbell rings on Saturday, a shrimp cocktail and salad are chilling in the refrigerator, the potatoes are baking in the oven, the steak is marinating on the kitchen counter, and the mini-meringue cakes are ready for a topping of berries and fresh whipped cream. I strip off my apron, wiping damp palms on my red tea-length full skirt, and follow the barking dogs to the door. I adjust my off-the-shoulder lace top in the same way my mother had at the restaurant so less of my cleavage shows.

When I open the door, Park has a bouquet of spring flowers in one hand and his dog's leash in the other. He steps inside while Lamar waits for the signal to follow. Once in the house, Park unclips the leash. My group of dachshunds greets Lamar then all the dogs race to the backyard.

He extends the bouquet toward me then pulls it back. "I forgot to ask about wine to bring, so I decided to give you flowers. You aren't allergic, are you?"

"No, and thank you." I sniff the fragrance of roses, dahlias, and peonies.

Placing my free hand behind Park's neck, I lift my lips to kiss him. He pulls me close. The rapid-fire of nails clicking on tile gives warning as Brewster races into the house with Lamar in pursuit. Both dogs bump against my legs in a state of manic excitement. The jostling breaks apart our kiss.

Using the bouquet, I point to the door. "Out, you two." The dogs run a circuit around the sofa and through the open patio door with Lamar now in the lead. "Come into the kitchen while I get a vase."

Park pours some decanted red wine while I arrange the flowers. After handing me a glass, he nods at the T-bones. "Are you cooking those on the grill?"

"The coals should be about ready."

"I can handle that while you get everything else."

Park barbecues while I set the table on the patio. When the aroma of the searing meat wafts through the air, interested canines sniff around the grill and whine.

I exit the kitchen with the shrimp cocktail. "If the dogs get too pushy, set your boundaries."

Park waves the extended tongs in acknowledgment. The March temperatures are warmer as spring slides closer to summer, but tonight it's still pleasant enough for *al fresco* dining. Mild breezes ruffle the palm fronds and lift the corners of the linen cloth spread over the patio table. I switch on strings of lights stretching under the pergola and light four pillar candles inside a Pottery Barn glass lantern which doubles as a centerpiece.

Fifteen minutes later, all the food is ready. Park holds out my chair. Before sitting, he tops off our wine glasses with the open bottle on the table. "Check your steak. I'm pretty sure I cooked it to medium."

I slice into the meat. "It's perfect. Do you barbecue at your condo?"

"No. There's a communal grill by the outdoor pool, but I don't think it's ever been cleaned. God only knows how much bacteria is growing on it. If I had a balcony, I would buy a little one for myself. The only time I barbecue is if I'm visiting my parents at their RV. I'm the designated grill master because I did so much of it when I traveled with them."

"River and your dad don't do it?"

"Not as well as me."

"How did your meeting with the family go on Thursday?"

Park's gaze goes flinty hard as a muscle pulsates in his jaw. "In the end, I told my parents they should just open up the till and tell their workers to take what they want. I spent hours figuring out where the losses occurred, how much was stolen, and who was responsible. When I showed Mom and Dad, instead of being angry and reporting the theft to the police, they blew it off like it was no big deal." With white knuckles, Park clutches the steak knife in one hand and the fork in the other. He leans across the table toward me like he's ready to pounce. "They feel sorry for the sonofabitch because he's addicted to painkillers as a result of a motorcycle accident. Like his reckless behavior and poor choices are their problems to handle."

"What *are* they going to do?"

"Get this. They're trying to find him a good treatment center. They decided to dedicate a portion of the proceeds from the RESCU performance to help pay for it." Park cuts off a hunk of steak, jams it into his mouth, and chews with savage jaw movements.

Uh-oh.

After Thursday's dinner, I sent a rather large check to the RESCU group through an anonymous account I have. I designated it as a contribution solicited through Bob and Nancy Robinson. If Park finds out, he might not be pleased the money will help the Ren-Faire thief. As the meal progresses, I become more nervous about revealing my secret. His mood lightens, but an undercurrent of tension still emanates from him, like an angry dog on a tight leash.

"Is something wrong?" His voice is gentle but insistent.

"W-what? No. Why are you asking?"

He points at my plate with his fork. "You've been pushing your food around for the last five minutes."

I had cut my steak into tiny, bite-sized pieces and arranged them in neat rows. The baked potato is also dissected, and the cubes mounded together. Only the shrimp cocktail and Caesar salad show any signs of real consumption.

I lay down my knife and fork. "There's something I need to tell you." My heart constricts as old fears sweep through me. "I'm not a professional fundraiser."

CHAPTER 26

PARK SITS STONY-STILL and studies me with narrowed eyes. I wipe my lips with the linen napkin and lay it back in my lap to give myself precious seconds. "I *do* donate quite a bit of money to The Forever Homes Dachshund Foundation and other charitable organizations. But it's my money."

"What do you mean *your money*? What did you do to earn it?" He looks at me like I might make a sleazy living sliding down brass poles wearing nothing but a G-string stuffed with dollar bills.

I raise my chin. "I was born into the Winslow family."

"They're the wealthy ones?"

"And so am I."

His eyes shift to the rear wall of my modest home. A thought bubble seems to materialize above his head which says: *It doesn't look like you're rich.*

"Unlike the rest of my family, I prefer to live simply and use my money to support causes I believe in."

"So your parents give you an allowance?"

"No. My maternal grandmother set up a trust fund for me. When I turned twenty-one I received access to it."

"I know better than to ask how much is in it."

"You're right. Not even my family knows the exact amount. Are you upset I didn't tell you before now?"

Park's brow furrows. "No. I understand why you need to be cautious when getting involved with someone new. I have a number of wealthy clients who I wish lived a more discreet, restrained lifestyle. It would keep them and their bank accounts a lot healthier."

His responses seem genuine and he doesn't act slighted or angry with me. "Does it bother you that I'm what they call . . . " My fingers make hooks in the air. "A trust fund baby and that I don't work a regular nine-to-five job?"

"No. Does it bother you that my family travels around in an RV putting on Renaissance fairs?"

"You know it doesn't."

He sits back, more relaxed. "It's interesting. We're both reluctant to explain our family to outsiders. I'm not embarrassed by mine. It's just that most people don't understand them. They either think they're old hippies or gypsy con artists."

I nod in understanding. "Despite my family's wealth, I've learned they're like anyone else's parents, even yours. They deal with the same problems, except theirs usually end up costing thousands in legal fees."

Park picks up his wine glass. "Where did the Winslow wealth come from?"

"My great-grandfather was fairly well-to-do at the turn of the century and owned several successful mines. He had three children, but my grandmother remained the only one still alive when he passed away. She married my grandfather who was a brilliant mechanical engineer. His company started out building mining equipment and later went into machines to move large amounts of earth. He did very well, but it was my grandmother who accumulated the most money. She took her inheritance and turned about a million dollars into hundreds of millions."

"From the stock market?"

"Some. She told me her most successful investments were in people. Many of them made her proud and very rich."

"Did she lend them money for startups?"

"Grammy never told me the details. I was twelve and heartbroken when she died. My mother is her only child. Mumsy was never interested in the business aspects of Grammy's wealth."

The fingers of Park's right hand play with the edge of the tablecloth. "Did you know about the trust fund while you growing up?"

"I had no idea. On my twenty-first birthday, I went to my father's law firm and signed paperwork for the transfer. Then I met with the financial managers who had been overseeing the trust. I've been working with them for the last five years."

"What was the first thing you did when you got your hands on the money?"

"I had a house built for Mrs. R."

Park's eyes widen. "Rudy's mother? Why did you build her a house?"

"She worked as my grandmother's cook and housekeeper until her death. She used the money Grammy left her to buy Rudy a new house. Mrs. R continued working for my family when Mumsy inherited the estate. About ten years ago, she retired and moved in with Rudy, Rita, and Angie. Grammy and Mrs. R were the two most important people in my childhood. I felt it only right for her to have her own place. I had one built that's accessible for either an older person or for dogs with short legs."

"You said the Rosetti's were *friends of your family*. That isn't really true, is it?"

I lift one shoulder in a shrug. "They're not my parents' friends, they're mine. I actually consider them part of *my* family."

Park asks more financial questions. I tell him about starting The Forever Homes Dachshund Foundation, as well as paying off Angie's medical school loans in exchange for helping out the rescue group, and giving the newly graduated doctor a no-interest loan to build Atlantic Veterinary Hospital.

Park leans forward in his chair. "Do you have any future plans for your money?"

I look out past my backyard fence. "I've been buying up land around here as it becomes available. I have this idea of creating a rescue village."

"For dogs?"

"And people too."

Park's forehead creases with his puzzled expression. "What do you mean?"

"I want the dogs we rescue to live in foster homes rather than kennels until they're adopted. For those animals too sick or too old, I want them to stay with a family until they pass away. There are a lot of good people out there who, for whatever reason, don't have a house of their own. I thought I could get the two together. I'm working out the details and legalities with professionals, but I'm hoping to create a community to provide homes for both people and animals in need."

After I finish laying out my plans, Park doesn't speak. It seems that any of his residual anger from the discussion about the Ren-Faire thief has vanished. A deep smile lifts the corners of his mouth. "You are an amazing woman, Marin McAllister."

I look at him with naked humility. "I'm just different than most people in my tax bracket because I like to spend my money on animals and others, rather than myself and material things."

"Does this mean *you're* the director of the dachshund foundation?"

"I started it, keep it funded, and run it with help, of course."

"Do you still need a new accountant?"

I smile at him from under lowered lashes. "Are you offering your services?"

"I am."

"How much do you charge?"

"No charge." He puts his elbows on the table. "Since it's a not-for-profit that I appreciate and respect, I'll do it pro bono."

"Even though I can afford to pay you?"

"Use the money to rescue more dogs."

I rise from my chair, lean across the table, and kiss him. "Your services are accepted."

After dinner, we clean up the kitchen and head to the living room with two wine glasses. Four dachshunds lay in a line across the sofa cushions like sausage links, snoring and snuffling in slumber. I set down my wine, lift Mia, and place the sleepy dog on my lap. Park squeezes in at the other end and we face each other.

I sip my drink. "My mother wants to invite you to dinner, especially after meeting you at the Cheesecake Factory."

"Sounds good. When?"

"I'll have to check with her. Would you be available next weekend?"

"Saturday evening will work."

We discuss the foundation and the financial records Park will need for the accounting he will provide. When he finishes his wine, he puts the empty glass on the coffee table and eyes the line of dachshunds between us. "Do you sleep with the dogs in your bed?"

"Mia has never liked sleeping with me, which is surprising considering how much she loves people. Since I foster so many dogs, I don't want them sleeping in a people bed, then have their new family not want them in theirs. So I have them sleep in a doggie bed or a crate. Later, if their forever family wants them in bed, they'll readily adapt. Why?"

Park raises his arms over his head and stretches, then waggles his eyebrows at me "If we head to your bedroom now, we won't have an entourage or a bunch of spectators."

"Except we need to let them out one more time tonight."

"What about the doggie door you have? Don't they use it?"

"Mia and Lili do. It scares Brewster, and Lamar won't fit."

We wake the dogs who jump up in eagerness to go outside. Upon their return, Lili and Brewster head into their crate for the night which is their usual routine. Mia marches to her dog bed in my bedroom. Lamar is our bedtime problem. He sits on the folded comforter I place on the floor for him, but he hops off and follows Park as soon as he walks toward the bed. I suggest moving his temporary bed outside the closed bedroom door, but Lamar scratches, whines, and barks to be let inside.

"I should have brought his dog bed." Park gazes down at his pet as he sits on the edge of the mattress. "Buddy, you're killing the mood here."

"Let's ignore him until he goes to sleep."

Park points to the comforter on the floor. "Go." Lamar follows his master's order with his head and tail down.

Park climbs into bed with me. After I click off the table lamp, both of us wait like stiff corpses, holding our breaths. Seconds later, the sound of dog nails clawing at the mattress accompanies soft cries. Park turns toward Lamar, but I place a hand on his arm to make him lie still.

I curl against him, with his arm under my head, and watch the slow flip of numbers on the bedside clock. Twenty minutes later, Lamar pads over to Mia's dog bed and is met with a low growl and the snap of teeth. His nails skitter on the tile. He emits one soft whine from Park's side of the bed. When we humans don't respond, he settles down somewhere in the room.

I put my lips next to Park's ear. "He finally gave up."

No answer. I lift my head. Park's eyes are closed, and he breathes in the slow, regular pattern of deep sleep.

Thanks a lot, Lamar.

CHAPTER 27

THE NEXT SATURDAY, I drive east and pick up Park at his condo. He enters my car with an over-sized bouquet of spring flowers wrapped in paper. "I bought these for your mom. Are they okay?" When I don't answer, he touches my arm. "What's wrong?"

I slept poorly the night before. Without a doubt, it was my worst night's sleep since grade school sleepovers, college all-nighters, and my last transoceanic flight. While caring for the dogs and doing paperwork during the day, I fretted about this evening. Over the years, I brought only two boyfriends home to meet my family. Each time had been a disaster. Neither young man measured up to my parents' expectations as a potential in-law at worst or a temporary hook-up at best. I can only hope that this time with Park the outcome will be different.

"I don't know which one of us is dreading this meet-the-parents dinner more, you or me."

"Don't worry. Everything will be fine." He kisses my cheek, then sits back, and fastens his seat belt. "You look nice."

As I readied myself for this event, I encountered another clothing dilemma. My choice of dress for dinners at my parents' house has become a competition of sorts. How outrageous can I be, yet remain within certain unwritten guidelines? For the first time, I'm worried about offending Park rather than my family. Over the years for birthdays and Christmases, my mother and sister gifted me with what they consider to be suitable clothing.

Most remain boxed or relegated to the recesses of my closet. This afternoon, I discover a long-forgotten jumpsuit my mother gave me.

The vibrant fabric in a tribal print runs in a horizontal pattern on the strapless bodice and vertically through the wide legs to the floor. To appease my quirky sense of style, I add a fringed black leather belt resembling a cat 'o nine tails and a studded leather neckband. My toenails are painted a lustrous black and my stilettos have thin, break-neck heels. I flat-ironed my ebony hair from a center part for a more bohemian look.

On the other hand, Park looks as if my father chose his clothes. He wears a pair of black dress pants, a white Oxford shirt with no tie, and a gray herringbone suit jacket. With his polished mahogany loafers, neatly trimmed hair, and tortoiseshell specs, he looks ready for a casual business luncheon at the Everglades Club. My father is going to fall in love with him at first sight.

"What should I know before we get there?" Park asks in a casual tone.

I exhale a sigh and cast him a quick glance. "We have a thirty-minute drive. That's not nearly long enough to fill you in on everything."

"I don't need to know your family's life story, just enough so I don't put my foot in my mouth."

"Well, the most important thing is to not be surprised if my parents beg you, or possibly bribe you, to marry me."

"Why?"

"Because you're the first guy I've brought home without shoulder-length hair, leather pants, and covered in tattoos."

"You dated bikers in the past?"

"More like rocker wannabees. One guy had a bar code inked on his neck. Mumsy asked if I had picked him up in a grocery store."

Park laughs. "Do your parents expect you to marry someone who is heir to a fortune or with a famous last name?"

"Like a Hilton? Or a Kennedy?"

"Or the son of someone they know."

"Of course, that would be their dream comes true." Like me marrying Trey Montgomery. "They thought I had come to my senses when I became engaged to Blaine."

"Was he the guy who didn't want to have sex until after the wedding?"

"Yes. I never told them why I broke it off, but later he was spotted around town with his boyfriend, so I think they figured it out. Now they just want me to end up with someone who's worn a suit since his First Communion."

"Who will be at this dinner?"

"I couldn't pin down my mother on who else is coming. Once she saw you at the restaurant, everyone she knows may be invited to prove I'm not the lost cause they all think I am."

"C'mon," he drawls. "Your mother seemed like a perfectly nice lady."

"You say that like it's a good thing."

"She was happy to see you at The Cheesecake Factory."

"No. She was happy to see *me* with *you*."

"And she was pleasant when she met my family."

Who she thought were all dressed in costumes.

He repeats, "Well, who *is* likely to be there?"

"My father, of course."

"The lawyer, right?"

"Yes. My sister, Kit, and my niece, Ainsley. My nephew, Trevor, and probably my brother-in-law, Garrett."

"What does he do?"

Gambles away most of the money he makes and then some. "Garrett works for the law firm owned by my father and his."

"You don't like him, do you?"

I shoot Park a sharp look. "Why do you say that?"

"The tone of your voice changed. What did he do to you?"

"Nothing. He's just a jerk. Listen, my family is just like yours, except more uptight and rule-conscious." I stare fixedly at the ribbon of asphalt ahead of the car. "All my life, I've felt like an outsider, so I've cultivated a lone wolf persona. I wasn't interested in their social scene, living luxuriously, driving flashy cars, or one-upping my frenemies. I love working with dogs and don't spend much of my money on me. My mother still believes my work in dog rescue is a fad like Zumba, and I'll one day become bored with it. Can you believe she once told me I was selfish because what I did with rescue groups reflected poorly on the McAllister and Winslow names? I told her I didn't care what anyone thought of me, except for the dogs. I wanted them to like me, not the people she thought were important."

"What about your friends?"

"Most of the girls I grew up with dreamed about marrying well, hosting a charity ball, or never having to hold a job. My dream was to get arrested."

"You're kidding. Did it ever happen?"

"Once. In college. I was arrested for trespassing and theft after breaking into a house being used as a puppy mill and videotaping the horrendous conditions. The problem was I stole several dogs because I couldn't bear to leave them behind."

"Good for you. What happened afterward?"

"It took the authorities more than a month to get their act together after I showed them the video. At first, they couldn't do anything because I obtained the evidence illegally. They called it *fruit of the poisonous tree*. In the end, another source also provided corroboration. The place was finally raided. When the owner of the mill found out who broke in, he insisted I be arrested too. Eventually, my dad got the charges dropped, so my record is clean."

After several more miles driven in silence, Park says, "Marin, our families aren't that different. Mine wants me to be more like them and yours want the same thing for you. We're both outsiders. Maybe that's what drew us together."

He's right. This was obvious the night I had dinner with the Robinsons. Park looked like the hostess had seated him at the wrong table, but he was too polite to point out her error. Even his brother commented on my similarity and Park's difference to the Robinson family. Tonight he'll likely fit in better with the McAllisters than I ever did.

A short time later, we arrive at the estate. I stop outside the eight-foot-high, wrought iron gates and hit the remote switch on my visor. As the massive barrier swings slowly outward, Park leans forward to peer through the windshield at the verdant lawn, the elegant trees, and the sculptures anchored at intervals around the property.

When I stop the car on the brick-paved driveway in front of the house, he sits back, his eyes wide, and his mouth slightly open like someone slapped him across the cheek. "Holy shit! This is where you grew up?"

CHAPTER 28

I EXIT AND meet Park in front of my vehicle. "Welcome to Del Lago Al Mar."

He stares at the gargantuan, winged structure. "Tell me about the place."

"The main house is about twenty-thousand square feet and sits on almost six acres. There are ten bedrooms and sixteen bathrooms. Also on the property are a caretaker's cottage, a boathouse, and a stable used for storage now. My grandfather built the estate in the nineteen-thirties and my mother inherited it when Grammy died. Mumsy will never sell, but I can't see myself living here. C'mon, let's go inside. I'm sure the firing squad is waiting for us."

We enter the foyer where I am correct. My family stands in a receiving line. Mumsy steps forward with a smile. "Darling, we're so happy you could come." Betsy executes an almost surreptitious up-down scan of me then Park. Her smile widens. "You both look wonderful."

She likely feared seeing Park dressed in a suit at the restaurant had been a fluke. Maybe his court-appointed attorney had suggested he wear one for his hearing, and he still had it on at dinner. She, no doubt, told my father how traditional and normal their daughter's new boyfriend appeared then worried he'd show up dressed like his family.

After air-kissing my cheek, Betsy gestures toward the others. "Park, I'd like you to meet Marin's father."

Stanford steps forward with a beaming smile and shakes Park's hand. "Stanford McAllister. Welcome. Welcome."

I'm right. Pops is in love.

Park says, "Nice to meet you, sir."

Betsy places her hand on his arm once her husband releases his hand and directs him to the next person in line. "This is our son-in-law, Garrett Coughlin, and our grandson, Trevor."

My brother-in-law nods at Park with a modest and friendly smile. Trevor glares with his usual mistrust of anyone associated with me. Kit holds her daughter in her arms.

Betsy places her hand on Ainsley's back. "Do you remember meeting Marin's sister and this little girl at the restaurant?"

Park bends forward and smiles at my niece. She's wearing a yellow Belle dress from the Beauty and the Beast movie. "You're Ainsley, right?"

"And you're my auntie's boyfriend."

"I am."

"Are you gonna put a baby in her tummy?"

Betsy gasps.

"Ainsley! That is not polite." Kit's cheeks flood with pink as she jostles her daughter. "I apologize, Park."

He chuckles and turns to my mother. "You have a beautiful home, Mrs. McAllister. Oh, and these are for you." He hands her the bouquet.

"Thank you." Betsy gives the flowers to my father. "Instruct Mrs. Nichol to put Park's lovely blooms on the table."

"Which one?"

"Why the dining room table, of course." She flashes a wide toothy smile as if Park might be offended if his flowers are not prominently displayed at dinner. "Perhaps Marin can take you on a quick tour of the house then you can join us for drinks on the veranda."

Soon we are alone as my family hustles away. I set my purse on a marble-topped credenza. "Let me show you around."

We make a left into a hallway with a barrel-vaulted ceiling and enter an oak-paneled library. The walls are lined with floor-to-ceiling shelves, heavy with volumes bound in jewel-toned covers containing titles etched into the spines with worn gold lettering. Despite the climate-controlled air, the room is redolent of old leather and dry paper. A massive Persian rug in muted browns, oranges, and blues covers the wooden parquet floor.

I remain in the doorway, holding the heavy wood-paneled door open. "This was my grandfather's study."

Park walks around, staring at the bookshelves. "Looks like a library."

I scan the many volumes, artfully shelved by color and size. "I don't know if anyone has ever read these books. Pops uses this as his at-home office."

Over the fireplace hangs a life-sized painting of a bearded man dressed in a starched white shirt, a red brocade vest, and a severe black suit. He holds an open pocket watch in his hand and its attached gold chain drapes across his ample middle.

Park points to the portrait. "Is this your grandfather?"

"That's my great-grandfather, the mine owner. Over between the French doors is my grandfather, Jock Winslow, the man who built this house."

The second painting is not as large or formal. A man with steel-gray hair and a bushy mustache sits on a chair in front of a window, dressed in casual attire with an old-fashioned, leather golf bag in the background.

Next, I lead Park down the hallway to a vast room with a highly-polished walnut floor. The cavernous space, though empty of furniture, has matching marble fireplaces anchored at each end. Two mammoth lead-crystal chandeliers are suspended from ornate plaster ceiling medallions.

I spread my arms wide and twirl across the floor. "This waste of space is the ballroom. Mumsy uses it as a large party room."

We proceed back across the foyer to the reception room which now serves as the formal living room. I direct his attention to life-size portraits of two women. "That one's my Grammy Winslow right before she married my grandfather." The second painting is more modern as evidenced by the hairstyle and dress. "And there's my mother."

Park examines the oil rendering with his hands clasped behind his back. "I recognize her. She hasn't changed much except her hair isn't as dark."

In the drawing room where I take him next, Park runs his hand along the top of a high-backed leather chair. "This place looks like a den or family room. Why do you call it a drawing room?"

"In the day, the ladies would retire here while the men smoked cigars and drank brandy after dinner. But you're right about it being a den now. Behind the panel above the fireplace is a flat-screen TV. Mumsy insisted on it being hidden from view."

The tour continues to the dining room where the table has been set with gold-rimmed fine china, lead crystal glasses, and silverware so heavy diners receive a workout from using a knife and fork. In the kitchen, I introduce Park to Mrs. Nichol and the McAllister's chef, Michel. We return to the foyer.

"Do you want to see my old bedroom?" I place my foot on the bottom step of the white marble staircase.

"Sure."

I turn to the right when they reach the second floor. "It's in this wing." I open doors for quick peeks into my niece and nephew's bedrooms as well as several guest rooms until we reached the one at the end of one hall. "Here it is."

In my bedroom hangs a portrait of me as a child. I'm wearing a white sundress and I'm sitting on a wrought iron bench under a tree. My back faces the viewer as ebony hair cascades to my waist. My head is in profile.

Park moves closer to the picture which is above a white marble fireplace. "Is this you?"

"Yes. As you can see, I come from a family who immortalizes themselves and their children with commissioned portraits."

"How old were you?"

"I think I was twelve. I hated sitting for the artist. He had to paint me posed like this, so he could do my face last. I kept sticking my tongue out and scrunching my eyes to look ugly." I give Park a sheepish grin. "I was a bit of a brat back then."

He laughs and looks around the room decorated in shades of ivory and lime green, including the canopied double bed. "This is nice."

"Mumsy wasted no time in removing my posters and other teenage crap after I moved out." I step close and wrap my arms around his neck. "You're the first boy I've ever brought into this room. Wanna have a quickie on the bed before we join my family downstairs?"

Park widens his eyes behind his glasses. "You're kidding, right?"

I am, but I'm also disappointed he doesn't flirt and play along for a minute. Has seeing this house and meeting my family made him even more conservative? I drop my arms from around his neck. "Of course, I'm joking. Let's go outside."

We exit from a set of French doors at the end of the hall and walk along a second-floor balcony girdling the rear of the house. Park stops to take in the spectacular view of the Atlantic Ocean. Then we descend the stone steps to a flagstone patio where three members of the family await us.

Only my mother, father, and sister are seated on the ornate patio furniture with sky-blue cushions that could easily grace the living rooms in most people's homes. On the wall, a marble fountain bubbles like the patter of water on a stony riverbed.

"What can I get you to drink, Park?" Stanford stands and heads to the outdoor kitchen.

Park's eyes flick to the glasses held by Betsy and Kit. "A glass of wine would be great."

My father pours from an open bottle chilling in a silver bucket. He heads back when I say, "I'll have one too, Pops." Or did you forget I was here?

Stanford shudders to a halt like a semi at a sudden stoplight, the wine sloshing in the goblet. "Of course. Let me give this to Park first."

Betsy indicates the vacant two-person loveseat which faces her. "You two may sit there."

I look around. "Where are the kids?"

"Garrett and the children are in the media room. Mrs. Nichol will notify them when dinner is ready."

My father returns and places a wineglass for me on a nearby table then lowers himself onto the sofa next to his wife. Kit sits like a little girl in church with hands clasped in her lap and trim ankles crossed.

I steel myself. Let the interrogation begin. Good luck, Park.

Chapter 29

As expected, the first question comes from my father, the lawyer. "I hear you're a CPA. At what firm do you work?"

"I run my own. It's a small five-person operation, but we specialize in boutique accounting."

Betsy chimes in. "You do dress shops?"

Stanford places his hand on her knee. "That's not what boutique accounting is, my dear."

"He's right, Mrs. McAllister. What makes my firm a boutique is that I limit clients to those who align with my specialty, so I can provide them with a more personal experience. I don't send their work off to be done in India or hand it over to someone still learning."

Stanford leans forward, his elbows on his knees. "Isn't boutique accounting just the latest financial flavor of the month? I've heard some less than stellar companies are claiming they're boutiques but only provide mediocre services at inflated prices."

"Pops!" I glare at him.

Park speaks in a calm voice and pats the top of my leg. "I have to admit it does happen, sir. However, before I started Robinson Account Management, I held a senior position at a mid-tier firm. I debated working at one of the Big Six but decided to take a risk and start my own instead. I already had the best training and quite a bit of practical experience."

"You're mighty young to be running your own company."

"But I'm smart and a hard worker."

"What's your specialty?"

"We handle tax returns mostly. But, of course, we do them incredibly well."

Stanford nods. "I see." My father likes confident people.

I glance at Park, but his attention remains on my parents. "Our other focus is compliance needs. We don't want any unexpected tax or fraud surprises creeping up on our clients."

My father turns his focus to me. "I'm assuming my daughter has informed you of her and the family's financial status."

"She was very discreet about any specifics."

"Has she asked you to take over her trust account?"

Park shoots a significant look my way. "No. However, I've agreed to provide pro bono accounting for The Forever Homes Dachshund Foundation."

Kit jerks to attention, as if one of my children shrieked and startled her. "When?"

"I'll take over from the current accountant at the end of April." He twists to face me and extends his hand with the palm up. "I admire the work she does and will do what I can to help."

I stare at his hand for a moment then lay mine in it. The warmth of his skin, its new familiarity, and the way his fingers enfold mine fills me with a depth of emotion. This man is very different from the others I've been attracted to in the past. Park raises my hand to his mouth and kisses the back of it.

Is this a sign he cares for me as more than just a girlfriend? My heart says yes, but my head does not. Although, old feelings of rejection rear their nasty heads, I can't drag my eyes away from our clasped palms.

Betsy clears her throat with a delicate cough. "Marin said you also provide your services to the Renaissance fair."

He faces my mother. "I do the books to help out my family's business."

"I'm s-sorry," Betsy sputters, "but I don't understand. After I met your people at the restaurant, Marin said they had just come from . . . " She trails off, two fingers on her chin with a reflective expression. "What did you call it, darling? Ren-something?"

"Ren-Faire," I say. "Park's family organizes and runs the event."

My mother's permanently darkened and perfectly arched brows squish together, but no creases appear in her Botox-injected forehead. "They work there?"

Park nods. "My parents have been staging fairs for more than fifteen years. They started out small but now run some of the largest outdoor events."

Stanford sets down his wine glass, cocks his head, and raises his eyebrows. "How does one get started doing this?"

"My father has an engineering degree and my mother is a former singer, dancer, and actress. After my paternal grandmother died, they used their inheritance to organize medieval festivals. It has become their passion."

Betsy and Stanford stare at Park with slack expressions. My father recovers first. "What is involved in producing a Renaissance fair?"

"It's an almost heroic endeavor since the purpose is to bring medieval life to the modern world. Some fairs only last a weekend while Ren-Faire runs for a month or more at each venue. They rent space at a private or public park for the open area they need. Then there's the red tape and forms required before permits can be secured. That can be tricky, especially when activities like archery and sword fights are involved."

Kit gasps. "Real sword fights?"

"No. They stage mock battles along with other entertainment, such as singers, troubadours, and jesters."

"Your parents have to hire all those performers?" Kit asks.

"There are a core number of regular employees, but many are volunteers. All of them need to be outfitted in costumes and scheduled on fair days. Since horses are used for jousting, there has to be a secure area to present the performance and for the spectators to watch. Both the crowds and cast need to be fed, so medieval-appropriate food is prepared and sold. The real money comes from liquor sales. Both the food and drink require special licenses and permits."

Stanford scratches his jaw, obviously confused by such an exotic existence. "Is your family able to make a living doing this?"

For the first time, Park hesitates. "To be honest, sir, my family has had to cover costs not recouped by ticket, food, or merchandise sales. They're very good at organizing and advertising the fairs to break even or make a profit. Most often it's bad weather that affects their financial success. But they're not in it for the money. They love what they do, and not many people can say that."

A warm, melting sensation fills me. Park doesn't favor his family's lifestyle, but he demonstrates his fierce loyalty to them. His attention to their financial welfare, as well as my mother and father's perception of them, is steadfast and endearing. Most of my childhood friends, at times myself included, denigrate our parents to anyone who will listen, while readily availing ourselves of the money, connections, and privileges, like expected birthrights. A niggling shame causes me to drop my head and stare into the depths of the wine I hold.

Mrs. Nichol exits one of the French doors to the patio. "Dinna is ready, Missus."

Park stands, his wineglass in hand. Betsy waves at him. "You can leave your drink here. The help will take care of it."

"Uh, oh . . . okay." His cheeks flush, and he sets the goblet down with unfamiliar awkwardness.

My father leads the way. Garrett and the children join us. A pleasant meal follows without any disagreement, drama, or overt hints about marriage. Park interacts effortlessly with everyone, especially my niece. He has an unexpected familiarity with Disney princesses.

The good feeling lasts until we say our goodbyes in the foyer. While Stanford shakes hands with Park, Betsy hugs me and whispers in a hushed tone, more contemplative than thoughtless. "Isn't it wonderful you and Park both love dogs? Otherwise, I wonder if he would have been interested in you."

More than the crisp, precise voice in my ear uttering the cruel words, her cheerful disrespect cuts deeper. Resentment fills the wound. "Yes, Mumsy, isn't it wonderful?" I head to the front door. "Park, we should be going now." I walk outside to the car like my trajectory is pre-programmed.

When Park opens the passenger door, I wait to hear the latch close then put the SUV in gear. Park clicks his seatbelt as I peel off, tires squealing on the driveway. I keep my gaze on the twin beams of the headlights.

"What's wrong?" His voice pierces the dark interior.

Grateful for the darkness, a lone tear trickles down my cheek. "Nothing's wrong. It's getting late. Didn't you say you have to work on Sunday since corporate day tax is at the end of the month?"

"You're sure you're okay?"

"I'm a little tired and have a long drive home after I drop you off." Although I don't look in his direction, I bet he's watching me.

I add several miles between us and Del Lago Al Mar before Park breaks the silence. "Your family's home is spectacular."

"It's too big. The taxes and maintenance are outrageously expensive."

"Will Kit inherit the property as well as you?"

"No. The estate is slated to be passed down only to Winslow heirs. Besides, Kit and Garrett could never afford to live there on his salary."

"So you'll sell it?"

"Unless I rent the place out for events and allow guided tours, but that really isn't my thing. The problem with selling is the land is more valuable than the buildings. It would break my Grammy's heart if her perfectly sound house is torn down to make way for a condominium or a modern monstrosity. Hopefully, Mumsy is around for years before I have to make that decision."

The clock on the dashboard reads five after nine when I pull up to Park's condo. I turn and look at him for the first time since entering the vehicle. "Thank you for coming with me today. My mother wouldn't have given me any peace until she and my father checked you out."

"I enjoyed myself. I worried how they would react to me, but your family is very nice."

"You held your own with them. I'm impressed."

"Well, I almost peed in my pants when you pulled up to the main gate." Park reaches across the center console and wraps his hand around my nape, drawing me close. "I better get inside and let Lamar out." His mouth closes over mine in a long, undemanding kiss. "Drive home safely, and send me a text when you get there."

"I will," I promise, a little breathless.

He climbs out and shuts the car door. A gust of ocean breeze teases his coattail and blows it away from his lean frame. I watch the curve of his butt as he walks toward the front entrance with his head high, shoulders straight.

You are turning out to be a man full of surprises, Mr. Robinson.

CHAPTER 30

FOR THE NEXT several weeks, Park and I meet for quick weekend dinners, close to either his home or business. One night I stop at his condo with homemade lasagna, Caesar salad, and a loaf of garlic bread.

He ushers me inside after a brief hug. "Thank you. I needed a break. I'm brain-dead."

Over dinner, Park bemoans not taking Lamar for their usual blocks-long outings. He scarfs down the food I brought like he hasn't eaten all day.

After dinner, I package the leftovers for him and put them away. "I'll head home now."

His eyes are bloodshot behind his spectacles. "You don't want to stay for a little while?"

I give him a rueful smile. "I'd love to, but you're tired. I'd rather you finish your work and get some sleep. If you want, before I go I'll walk Lamar."

He wraps an arm around my waist and pulls me close. "Are you trying to make me fall in love with you?" Before I can respond, Park releases me and lifts the dog leash off a hook next to the front door. "C'mon, buddy. You get to go out with a beautiful lady tonight."

The dachshund leaps from his bed, ready for a walk, which is why I make the offer. Due to my foresight in wearing sneakers today, I can go the distance with Lamar. My footwear also enables me to jog at the midway point of the walk when I notice several unsavory characters loitering up ahead. I run with Lamar two blocks east, to where more people congregate, and return to the condo from that direction.

An hour later when we enter, Park still sits at his computer. He rubs knuckles into his bleary eyes. "Did you tire him out?"

"Are you kidding?" I lift damp hair off my sweaty nape. "Lamar wouldn't get tired if we walked to Miami and back."

When I slip the leash off, the dog heads to his water bowl and slurps. I bite my lip. Should I tell Park how uneasy I was on Lamar's usual walking route?

He ambles over to me. "I'm sorry I haven't had much time to spend with you. It's going to be more of the same until the middle of April."

"Actually, my plans for Forever Homes Village have started coming together all of a sudden. I'm in meetings with site planners and architects, as well as my financial managers." I put my arms around his neck. "When things settle down, you and your Tantra chair better be ready."

Park kisses me then looks into my eyes with an unfathomable gaze. "We may not be physically together, but you have no idea how much you're on my mind."

Something warm and liquid flows over me, weakening and strengthening me at the same time. "Oh, Park."

Before I can say more, Lamar's wet muzzle and tongue lap my bare calf in a long swipe. The dachshund jumps up and places his paws on my leg. I bend over and received his grateful chin lick.

Park laughs. "He wants you to know he appreciates the walk."

"I was glad to do it." I straighten and sling my purse strap onto my shoulder. "Get a good night's sleep, and call me when you can."

When his front door clicks shut behind me, I can't stop smiling as I walk down the hall. Are you trying to make me fall in love with you? The words in his rich, velvety baritone echo inside my head. I push the elevator's down button and speak to my reflection in the shiny steel doors. "Maybe I am trying since I might be falling in love with you."

CHAPTER 31

THE NEXT AFTERNOON, I swing open the door into the foundation's lobby. I had been in meetings all morning as the construction plans for the village have gained momentum.

Kit sits behind the front counter. "How did it go?"

"Great. Site preparation should begin sometime next month. With any luck, the first of the houses will be ready by late next year. There's enough acreage to construct a multi-story apartment building in the northwest section. I can offer more homes for one-person occupancies, like a single person or a retired couple. Maybe I'll designate those for cats."

"Really? What a wonderful idea." Then Kit frowns, and her head jerks toward my office door. "You have a visitor."

"Who?"

"Trey Montgomery. Why would he show up here?"

"I'll have to ask him." I walk down the hall and open the door. Trey stands at the large window that faces a shady outdoor exercise area similar to my backyard. I shut the door, so Kit can't hear our conversation. From phone calls with my mother, I have an inkling of the reason for his unannounced visit. "Hello, Trey."

When he turns around, his disheveled reddish hair brushes the tops of his ears. He meets my eyes with a tired, empty stare and a weak smile.

I drop my purse and rush to him. "What's wrong?"

"It's Carmen."

I hug my friend. Betsy told me the Montgomerys were devastated to learn their golden boy had knocked up the landscaper's daughter. When informed of Trey's marriage to Carmen, his father banned him from the family home and said to not come back until he divorced her.

I run scenarios through my mind for Trey's anguish. Has Carmen left him? Is the baby not his? Does his wife want a divorce now that her WASP husband's family is no longer paying the bills? Then my thoughts shift from the usual Palm Beach expectations. Has Carmen lost the baby? Is she sick? Has her Venezualan family come between them?

After a minute, Trey straightens. "Sorry about that."

"Don't be." I lead him to two chairs but don't say another word.

"You probably know my parents have sort of disowned me," he says in a resigned voice. "I've got a part-time job and a position lined up with a state jurist after graduation." Trey's eyes narrow and his tone becomes bitter. "My father called him and demanded he rescind my clerkship. I had already warned Judge Linares that my parents wouldn't be happy about the marriage."

"Linares?"

Trey laughs. "His parents are from Colombia. I hope my father never has to try a case in his courtroom, especially after he said he didn't want a *Can* daughter-in-law."

"What do you mean—*Can*?"

"You know, a Mexi-*Can*, Puerto Ri-*Can.*"

I shake my head in disbelief at Mr. Montgomery's racism. "Why did you come here today?"

The animation drains from my friend. "When you offered to help me, I swore I would never ask you." Trey looks at me with a fierce expression. "And I wouldn't, except it isn't for me. Carmen and the babies need it."

"Babies?"

"A boy and girl. Last month, she went into premature labor and started bleeding. The doctor managed to stop both and saved the twins from being born early, but Carmen's on complete bed rest. Her family is taking care of her while I'm at work or school. The problem is—"

"Now she can't work at all, and your part-time job isn't enough."

"I can't ask her family. They're already doing so much, and they don't have the money."

I stand and walk to where my purse lays. I withdraw my checkbook, sit down, and open the leather folder. The skin around Trey's eyes bunches with a pained expression. I write out a check and hand it to him.

With obvious reluctance, he takes the paper and reads it. "Marin! This is too much for me."

"But it's not just for *you*. It's for your wife and babies."

He stares at me in open-mouthed awe. "Thank you so much."

"You're welcome. I'm glad you came to me."

"Do you want me to sign a promissory note? I can draft one if you give me access to a computer and printer. I promise to pay back every penny with interest, no matter how long it takes."

I smile at Trey. My Grammy Winslow once told me the best investments she ever made were in people. Those kinds of dividends proved to be more precious and worth more in the long-term. This principle guides me in the development of Forever Homes Village. The money I'm giving Trey is only a portion of my trust fund's monthly interest but a solid investment in his family's future.

"I don't want you to pay me back. I want the money reimbursed into an account for your children. I expect to be shown an annual statement in three years and for the next twelve after that. The bottom line should show an increase from the previous year. By the time your twins graduate from high school, I want there to be enough for them to pursue *their* dreams."

Trey glances up from the check in his hand. "I would prefer your parents don't know about this. Can it be our secret? I'll tell Carmen, of course."

"No problem. This is just between us friends."

"But I insist we put those terms you mentioned in writing. We'll have Kit witness our signatures."

After the copies are printed, signed, and witnessed, my sister and I stare out the main door as Trey walks across the parking lot to his car.

Kit asks, "What was the paperwork for?"

I tell her but omit the amount of the check.

Kit's eyes glisten with unshed tears. "How could the Montgomerys not want their grandchildren, their own flesh and blood? So what if they're half Hispanic? I wonder if Father knows about this."

"You can't say anything. Besides, Mrs. Montgomery and Mumsy are friends and—"

"Father has to work with Mr. Montgomery. Garrett has made comments about Trey's father alienating some foreign-born clients. Now I know why." Kit heads to her desk. "Don't worry. I won't say a word. I know how to keep secrets too."

CHAPTER 32

THE WEEK FOLLOWING Trey's surprise visit, I arrive at the foundation and this time it's Rita sitting in the chair across from my desk. When she twists toward the open door, her eyes are red and puffy.

I rush forward. "What's wrong?"

"It's Angelina."

Angie? I haven't seen her since the Renaissance fair, but we text or talk every week. That seems to be the way girl friendships evolve. Whatever free time we once spent together is now filled by the shiny, new men in our lives.

I sit in the chair next to Rita. "What happened? I spoke with her last Thursday."

"She and that *bastardo* she's dating came to dinner last night. He has her on a special diet and is starving her. She doesn't eat any carbs, fats, or dairy. He makes her go to the gym with him almost every day. She's gotten so skinny her clothes hang on her."

Angie first gained weight with the infamous Freshman Fifteen in college, but in her case, it was the Freshman Forty. Over the years of graduate and medical school, Angie whittled the extra pounds in half but always bemoaned the stubborn ones that resisted various diets and exercise. I know my friend works out with Brent but she said nothing about a restricted diet.

Rita dabs at her eyes with a wadded tissue. "She warned me she wouldn't eat my pasta. But then she refused Nonni's meatballs because they had bread crumbs and were browned in olive oil."

"How does she feel?"

Rita flicks her hand in a dismissive gesture. "When I ask, she says she's fine and happy, but a mother knows. She looks terrible and is too quiet. Like she's afraid to talk when the *stronzo* is around."

I reassure Rita about her daughter's diet and exercise program. As far as Angie's reticence around Brent, I cite my own experience. "When I went to dinner with Park's family he said very little. They wanted to know about me, and I wanted to know about them. The same thing happened when he came to dinner at my parents' house. I listened most of the time. It's kind of normal for those situations."

Rita sniffs. "I guess. But I still have the feeling there's more going on."

"What do Rudy and Mrs. R think?"

"He says I'm crazy. There's nothing wrong. Nonni doesn't like *Brent.*" She drawls his name and curls her lips like a bitter nastiness flooded her mouth. "Do me a favor. Go see Angie for yourself. Also, maybe you and Park could double date with them. A man might sense something off about the guy that a woman won't."

I agree to check out the situation. After Rita leaves, I replay the last few conversations I had with my friend. She relayed very little new information about her love life. I talked more about Park than she did about Brent.

Is Angie keeping a secret from me?

CHAPTER 33

ON FRIDAY, I arrive at Atlantic Veterinary Hospital with two rescues, Bobby and Maggie. Both seven-year-old dachshunds had been owned by an older gentleman who moved to an assistive living center due to health issues. When Angie enters the exam room, her weight loss is obvious. Yet, she appears healthy.

"Wow," I say. "You look great. How much weight have you lost?"

"Fifteen pounds, but I've lost more in inches." A broad smile stretches across Angie's face, as she slips her white lab coat off her shoulders, opens it wide, and twirls. My friend's muffin top has disappeared. With a sleek waistline, her bosom is more prominent.

Angie hefts the male dachshund, sets him on the exam table, and checks him out. "This big boy is about four to five pounds overweight. So, is his girlfriend. Looks like they weren't exercised much but never missed a meal. Of course, my mom would think they look just fine. She's upset with my weight loss and says I'm too skinny. She blames Brent. He suggested the diet, but I'm the one who chose to follow it."

"How long are you going to continue it?"

"I'm slowly adding back some foods to maintain the weight loss, but Mom acts like Brent forced me into hard labor with limited rations. Last Sunday when he told about our exercise routine, I heard her call him *herr commandant* under her breath." Angie places Bobby on the floor.

I hand Maggie to her. "How are things going with you and Brent?"

"Good. How about you? Is Park still busy doing taxes?"

"Things are easing up now. How often do you guys get to see each other?"

"Every day at the gym, Saturday evenings, and Sunday mornings."

By the time I leave with the two dogs, who are given updated vaccinations, and orders to cut down on food and increase physical activity, I have no new insight into Angie's relationship. We do promise to schedule a double date soon.

CHAPTER 34

AT THE END of April, the foundation's financial records are digitally transferred to Robinson Account Management. Several days later, Park calls. "I've looked over the Forever Homes financials. Did you know your CPA never prepared a Statement of Functional Expenses in the two years he'd been doing the books?"

"Is it required?"

"The statement is recommended if thirty percent or more of your revenue comes from contributions. You and the board would have benefitted from the details about how the foundation used its resources."

"We always know what the assets and liabilities are from the balance sheets provided for all our monthly board meetings."

Park draws in a deep breath, audible over the phone. "But he never broke down the expenses."

"Kit attaches checks to all the invoices for my review before I sign them. I know where and how much money is being spent." I pause. Why is Park so concerned about me not getting this report? "Do you suspect someone's stealing from the foundation?"

"No, but it would be difficult to tell. The money may not be important to you, but it's in a nonprofit's best interest to be vigilant."

A red haze blurs my vision for a second. "What do you mean *the money may not be important to me*? I care if my money and other donations are wasted or stolen."

Park's voice calms as my agitation increases. "I know, but without a Statement of Functional Expenses, it's easier to defraud an organization. You have a strong vested interest because, if money is needed to meet expenses, you make sure it's there. Forever Homes doesn't have to raise revenue from other contributors to cover a shortfall, but it doesn't mean you shouldn't take all possible precautions to prevent someone misusing the funds."

His rational, reasonable words settle me. "What would you recommend we do?"

"If it meets with your approval, let me conduct a forensic audit going back to the start of the foundation. I'd feel better if I knew every expense is properly accounted for."

"Maybe I should pay you for the extra hours of work?"

He chuckles with his deep-timbered voice. "I'll figure out an appropriate compensation and invoice you if I need to have the Tantra reupholstered."

CHAPTER 35

AFTER TAX SEASON ends, my relationship with Park transitions from weekend dates to overnighters, lunches, and dinners during the week. One evening in May when we return to his condo, he hands me his key fob for the door leading inside to the elevator lobby. "Open it."

After the latch releases, I push the lever and stepped inside. At the elevator, I flash the fob again to call the car then hold out the device to him.

He reaches into his pocket. "It's yours. I signed one out for you. And here's the key to my condo. If I'm late, I don't want you waiting on the sidewalk again."

The previous week he had been detained at the office. As I stood outside, a scruffy, young man on a bicycle approached me and asked for money, eyeing my Louis Vuitton bag. Lucky for me another couple exited the lobby, and I slipped inside. Unlike the time I felt unsafe on the walk with Lamar, I told Park about this latest incident.

We step into the empty elevator, and I push the button for his floor. Park pulls me against him. "Use the key if you ever want to stop by to walk Lamar or fix a meal . . . " He nuzzles my neck. "Take a shower . . . " His hand covers my breast. "Wait for me in bed or on the chair . . ." He kisses me long and deep.

When the elevator doors open, we rush down the hall. Park kicks the door shut behind him. I raise his shirt. As soon as it clears his head, Park unzips the back of my vintage sundress and pulls it to my waist. The cool air from the overhead AC vent feathers my bare breasts. I grasp the waistband of his pants and pull him down the hall toward the bedrooms.

Lamar steps into our path. Park stumbles, and I push him against the wall. My out-of-control need for him reaches the breaking point. I squint in the dim light and fumble with his zipper.

Lamar whines.

"Tantra," Park pants against my neck and steers me toward the guest room.

His zipper separates. I place one hand on his shoulder to keep him still. The other one reaches through the opening of his shorts. "Here."

"Oh, God."

The dog bumps against me when I drop to my knees. I ignore him. Lamar nudges my elbow with his wet nose. Park grows harder and longer. I look up. His lips part and his eyes close. With each new stroke of my tongue, he trembles.

His knees buckle and bump against my chest. "Please, love, stop."

I do—but not because he begs. He calls me *love*.

"The chair." Park slips his hands under my arms, and I stagger to my feet on shaky legs. My naked breasts brush against his hard-muscled chest. He stares into my eyes and in a hoarse voice says, "Forget the chair."

I drag his pants and shorts down his hips as I sink to the floor again. He kicks off his shoes. One hits the wall with a hollow thud. Park kneels. He flips up my skirt and slips off my panties. I wrap my legs around his waist. Our eyes lock, and he buries himself inside. The intensity of his gaze makes my chest hurt.

"I love you, Marin."

CHAPTER 36

LATER, AS WE lie side by side in the hallway, I ask, "Do you really love me?"

Park slips an arm under my neck and draws me close. "I do. Does it bother you that I said it?"

"Not if you mean it."

He raises himself on an elbow and looks into my face. "Why would I say I love you if I didn't mean it?"

I wet my lips. "Others have."

"I don't know about the others, but I meant every word. When we were apart because of my work, I never missed anyone as much as you. My office manager asked why I was driving myself so hard this year. I wanted to be with you and not have any looming deadlines. It's when I knew I loved you."

Do I love him? I want him more than any other man I've known. I ache to spend time with him, cook for him, eat with him, sleep with him. I've never felt so much like my true self with anyone else. With my other boyfriends, I had to make allowances to please them. Park never asks or demands I change anything.

His arm under my neck jiggles my head. "What's wrong?"

"I'm falling in love . . . with you too."

"You don't sound sure about it." In the dim hallway, his face is a dark, expressionless mask.

"Well, we met only four months ago."

"Are you saying that's not enough time to fall in love? Some people meet and are married in less."

"I know. It's just—"

Park sits up and stares straight ahead. "I get it. In the past, you've wondered if people cared more about you or your money. Right?"

"Yes." I say the word with conviction.

"The time we've been together is hardly long enough for a friendship, let alone love, but I do love you. I didn't intend for this to happen, but you're everything I wasn't looking for." Park stands and holds out his hands. "I'll wait until you're ready to say you love me. But first, let's find a place more comfortable than this hallway." He pulls me to my feet and steps back. All of a sudden, he teeters, dancing on one foot. "Dammit!"

"What's wrong?"

His gaze swivels around the floor. "You want confirmation I love you? I ignored Lamar's schedule, and now I'm standing in dog shit."

I smile. He really does love me.

CHAPTER 37

TWO WEEKS AFTER Park's *I love you,* I schedule a double date with Angie and Brent. Hopefully, we'll have a pleasant, uneventful evening, and the two men will get along as well as me and Angie. I pray Rita's paranoia won't color my perception of Brent. In the past, Angie's dating history has been less than stellar. She tends to fall for every man who pays attention to her, often settling for cheaters, liars, and fakes. Angie is a smart, loving woman and deserves a good man, one who knows how damn lucky he is to have her.

Park and I arrive first at Two Georges, a waterfront restaurant in Boynton Beach. A few minutes later when Angie and Brent join us, I inhale sharply. Since meeting Brent for the first and only time at Ren-Faire, I've only pictured him as Jack Sparrow. In reality, he looks nothing like the pirate or Johnny Depp.

Angie says, "Marin, you remember Brent, right?

I narrow my eyes at the stranger. "Have we met before?"

Brent studies me with his head cocked. "You look vaguely familiar too, but your ears are different."

Angie rolls her eyes at him. "Don't encourage her."

Brent stands a head taller than five-foot-two Angie. He has brown, curly hair and a clean-shaven face. His button-down, black linen shirt is tucked into shiny gray slacks that make him look like a muscular Miami gangster.

When the hostess asks if we want to be seated inside or out on the patio, Angie answers first. "I'd prefer inside."

The May temperature hovers in the low eighties but a stiff breeze blows off the water. Angie wears a long-sleeved, oatmeal-colored cotton tunic with wide-legged, long pants resting on the tops of her sandals. In contrast, my Stella McCartney sheer-yoked mini dress bares me down to mid-chest and up to mid-thigh.

During dinner, Angie seems more subdued than usual. On the other hand, I can't find any fault with Brent unless he is flawlessly impersonating a pleasant man with good manners. Angie and I listen to the men discussing the pros and cons of high-priced vehicles. After the wait staff removes our dinner plates, Angie stands and excuses herself to use the ladies' room.

I place my napkin on the table. "I'll go with you."

Brent grabs Angie's hand and pulls her close. It appears he kisses her cheek, but from my vantage point, his lips don't pucker but move in speech. Angie straightens with an almost imperceptible nod to him.

In the toilet stall next her, I talk to the metal dividing wall. "You're going to find this funny, but I've been picturing Brent with dreadlocks, eyeliner, and a mustache. When you guys walked in, I was like, who's this guy with my friend?"

A disembodied chuckle came from the other enclosure. "So you weren't joking? You didn't recognize him."

I finish using the facilities first, lean my backside against the wide vanity, and wait. Angie approaches one of the double sinks, turns on the water, and soaps up like the medical doctor she is.

I cross my arms over my chest. "You told me Brent worked for a company that sells pre-owned cars. But I didn't know the cars were luxury models. Somehow I thought he was just a salesman, not the head of finance."

I had the mistaken impression of Brent working at a converted gas station with a dozen cars scattered around a cinder block building, plastic flag garlands lining the perimeter, and hand-painted lettering on windshields. Instead, he handles both acquisitions and sales at a dealership located in an upscale commercial section of Boca Raton.

Angie rinses the suds off her hands. "The owner of the company is some rich guy who knows nothing about the business, but he's friends with people who want to sell their cars every year when the new models come out. Brent's been basically running the company for the last seven years."

As Angie places her wet palms under the hand blower, my eye catches sight of unusual multi-color bracelets when the long sleeves of her tunic ride up her arms. A second look confirms the marks are not jewelry.

I grab her. "What are these?"

Angie snatches her wrists away and shakes the sleeves down. "Nothing."

Before she can head to the door, I block her path, grab both her forearms and raise them in the air. The loose cotton sleeves drop away, exposing bruised, raw bands of skin above her hands. "What happened?"

Angie stares at me with hard, flat eyes I've never seen before. "Leave it alone."

Her anger doesn't deter me. "No! Tell me right now, or I'm going into the restaurant and punch Brent." I have a vision of his curly-haired head snapping back as my fist slams into his nose.

Angie deflates. "It was an accident."

"Bullshit! What did he do? Tell me now or—"

"He sometimes likes bondage, and it got a little rough last night." Angie raises moist eyes to meet mine.

So Brent knows more about BDSM than Angie originally told me. My only knowledge of the erotic behavior comes from the *Fifty Shades* books and movies. "You consented to being tied up?"

"Handcuffed."

"How did you get these marks?"

Angie shrugs. "Like I said, it got out of hand."

"Did he stop when you said the safe word?"

"We don't have one."

My mouth drops open. "Are you crazy? Not having a safe word, or not honoring it, changes everything. Sex is no longer consensual, it's a crime. He assaulted you."

"I'm fine, and he promised it wouldn't happen again." She casts a worried look at the restroom door. "Can we leave now?"

"Sure. Gimme a hug." Before Angie can protest, I put my arms around my friend and squeeze tightly.

Angie stiffens with a sharp inhale then steps away from the embrace. "Don't say anything to Brent. He's upset about it. And don't tell Park either. Please, just let it be our secret."

There it is. Our secret. The words uttered to secure my silence by people who know me well. "All right. I won't say anything as long as you tell me if he hurts you again. Promise?"

Angie nods and hurries out.

The wrist bruises aren't the only painful spots on my friend's body as evidenced by her reaction to my hug. For Angie's sake, I have to return to the table and perform the appropriate social amenities for the rest of the evening and act like I'm not carrying a devastating secret.

How am I going to do that?

CHAPTER 38

ON THE DRIVE to Park's condo after the double date, I say to him, "You and Brent really got into the whole car thing during dinner."

"Did we bore you?"

"Not really. What do you think of him?"

"He seems like an okay guy. A little obsessive about working out and expensive wheels, but that isn't what bothered me."

"What *did* bother you?" Aha! Rita was right. Men can pick up on issues with other men.

"You."

I arch in surprise. "Me? What did I do?"

"You were different tonight, especially after you came back from the ladies' room. It was like you were putting on an act and weren't yourself. What gives?"

Park already knows me so well after just a few months of being together. "Angie told me something in private and it really upset me. I guess I did a poor job of hiding my feelings."

Park doesn't ask any more questions of me. We drive on several more miles before he says, "I did learn something interesting about Brent while you were gone."

I sit up straight. "What was that?"

"He works for a company that I'll be doing their accounting starting next month."

I slump against the seatback in disappointment.

"With tax season over, I'm conducting a forensic audit at Excelsior Luxury Motors for the owner, Bartholomew Gubelmann."

I perk up again. "I know Barty. He dated my sister for a little while."

In high school, Barty Gubelmann had been a twiggy young man who Kit finally broke up with because of his inability to make a decision. He would stand at a fast food counter for an embarrassingly long time deciding between combo meals; then the process would be repeated for his drink selection.

Park stops at a red light and turns to me. "I don't know if getting his business will be worth all the aggravation. He's been talking to me for over two years about taking over his accounting. The problem is the guy couldn't make a decision if a gun was put to his head, and he was given one choice."

I laugh. Some people never change.

CHAPTER 39

I'M STAYING IN closer contact with Angie since the double date several weeks ago. I quiz her and, if we're together and she's dressed in long pants or long sleeves, I insist on seeing her skin. There are no new marks on her arms, legs, or back. Angie says she and Brent still engage in some bondage, but now they have a safe word which she says she has not had to use. Despite her reassurances, as far as I'm concerned, the situation remains like a stubborn hot spot after a forest fire. At odd moments, I bring it into the light and re-examine all the angles, in case I miss a vital sign or something which can lead to a potential disaster.

One day in June when I check my calendar, I see a special notation I made and call Park. "I just realized your birthday is on Saturday. We should celebrate. You're turning thirty."

"Don't remind me. Besides, I'm not big on parties."

"Why not? Bad memories? Your birthdays couldn't have been any worse than mine."

"Wanna bet? My mom read this article that said parents shouldn't throw lavish kids' birthday parties."

With dry humor, I say, "I wish my mother had read the article. There were more adults at my parties than kids. Once I disappeared into the boathouse, and no one noticed I was gone for two hours. They only came looking for me so I could blow out the candles. What did your mother do?"

"She had everyone make my gifts. For my twelfth birthday, my dad carved a wooden whistle only dogs and Superman could hear. Mom baked me a flourless, sugarless birthday cake. You can imagine how delicious that tasted. Meadow picked a bouquet of weeds, and River glued gravel on cardboard spelling out *Happy Birthday, Bro.* Afterward, I said no presents if I had to lie about how much I liked them. I told my parents all I wanted was a whole pizza and a liter of Coke I didn't have to share. Mom finally agreed I could poison myself once a year."

"Well, what can I do for your thirtieth birthday?"

"If you cover your naked body with the tiramisu you make, I'd be very happy and grateful."

A delightful shiver cascades over me. "You have a deal."

CHAPTER 40

WHEN PARK AND Lamar arrive at my house for the birthday celebration, only Mia and I are waiting for them. Two weeks earlier, Lili and Brewster found a forever home with an older couple who lost their eighteen-year-old beloved doxie. After their adoption, I replaced them with four Dachshund/Chihuahua puppies. I erected a large plastic playpen in my small living room to contain the not-yet housebroken babies. But now the dismantled enclosure leans against the wall.

Mia wags her tail as Lamar sniffs her all over. When he finishes, she plods over to the sofa ramp and, unlike her usual race up the incline, she places one foot in front of the other until she reaches the cushion. Lamar waits on the floor then climbs up, and settles himself with care beside her.

"What's wrong with Mia?" Park asks.

"She's been like that all week. I thought maybe she was depressed after Lili and Brewster left. I hoped the puppies I brought home would perk her up, but she snapped and growled at them which is not like her. So I gave the babies to Mrs. R to foster."

"How old is Mia?"

"Fifteen." I lean over the sofa and stroke both dogs' backs. "Looks like Lamar has a good chance of winning the Dachshund Derby next year. Angie warned me Mia might not get better."

Park places a comforting hand on my back. "C'mere." He enfolds me in a tight embrace. "I'm sorry you're worried about her."

The clamp around my chest loosens its grip with his warm, strong arms around me. Several times a day, my breath hitches with the warning of future heartbreak when my beloved Dachshund is no longer around. I step back and plaster on a smile. "I'm sure Mia will be fine. Come into the kitchen, and see what I have for your birthday."

"Did you make or buy me something?"

"Both." A large, beribboned box sits on the quartz countertop, but I point to a glass dish filled with ladyfingers dipped in coffee liqueur and layered with whipped mascarpone. "This is what I made as you requested. We can negotiate how it'll be eaten later." I place my hands on either side of the gift-wrapped box and lift. "This is what I bought you."

The bottom of the box is cut away. On the counter lay two sausage and mushroom pizzas from Four Brothers next to two liters of Coke, a fifth of Bacardi, and a bag of limes.

Park's face brightens. "My favorite birthday presents."

"I added the rum to make this into an adult party, especially considering your plans for the dessert."

CHAPTER 41

SIX DAYS LATER on Friday evening, my phone rings. I blow my nose before answering, but my voice still sounds feeble and clogged with tears. "Hello."

Park says, "Marin? What's wrong?"

"Oh, Park." At first, I can't speak through my emotional hiccups. "It's . . . Mia . . . She's blind."

"What? How did it happen?"

I sniff. "She has SARDS, Sudden Acquired Retinal Degeneration Syndrome. Dachshunds and miniature schnauzers are particularly susceptible to it, especially females."

"What causes it? Is it contagious?"

I dab at my eyes with a fresh tissue. "They don't know the cause, but it's not contagious."

"Is there no surgery or medication that'll help?"

"No."

"How's she doing?"

I stroke Mia. "She's fine. I'm the one falling apart. In fact, she spent most of today comforting *me*. I know I shouldn't be so emotional. It's not like she's dying or in pain. Angie and the eye doctor explained that she'll still have a good life and learn to compensate for her blindness. But she loved to play ball and race, and she won't be able to anymore."

"Is someone there with you? Angie? Rita? Your sister or mother?"

"No."

"Then Lamar and I are coming over."

"You don't have to. We'll be fine. I just need to come to terms with this. I think Mia already has."

Park's voice oozes compassion but also carries a thread of resolve. "If you want, you can kick us out after we get there, but we still want to check on you two."

His concern soothes my jangled nerves like the firm touch of massage. "I look horrible."

"You'll always be beautiful to me. How about I pick up something for dinner?"

"Thank you. I don't feel like fixing anything to eat."

"We'll see you in an hour." He disconnects the call.

I lean down and speak in a fake, high-octave tone used when asking dogs or babies questions they aren't expected to answer. "Guess who's coming over? Lamar will be here. Do you want to see Lamar?"

Mia's ears twitch. I drop my head against the sofa back. Traffic will be horrendous at this time on Friday. Why is Park so adamant about coming here? A sudden, overwhelming sensation of warmth and happiness fills me where moments before grief and sorrow had been.

He loves me.

And I love him.

I love an accountant who often dresses in tailored suits but isn't concerned if they are covered in dog hair. I've fallen in love with a stickler for tradition and rules who owns a Tantra chair. I'm crazy about a man who spent much of his childhood traveling like a gypsy on the Renaissance fair circuit but can hold his own in a mansion with the Palm Beach elite.

When my mind drifts to the birthday celebration last weekend with Park and Lamar, I sit up with a start. Mia's unseeing eyes swivel around the room, her tan eyebrow spots dancing.

Lamar knows she can't see!

He had been beside her or within a few feet the whole time. They hadn't played but walked side-by-side all around the house. He nudged her through the doggie door then raced to meet her outside. From there, they headed to the large rectangle of synthetic turf where they did their business.

I said to Park, "Look. Lamar is exercising Mia."

But he wasn't. Lamar had been teaching her how to navigate the environment. He recognized her recent disability and assumed the role of Mia's seeing-eye dog. Tears flood my eyes with gratitude and joy for the intuitive dachshund loved by the man I love.

CHAPTER 42

THE NEXT DAY Park modifies the doggie ramp for the sofa with wood side rails, so Mia won't walk off the edge. While he works, I order a new collar online which reads: *I'M BLIND*. If Mia ever becomes separated from me in an unfamiliar place, a rescuer will better understand her panic. Two days later, a plug-in bowl that circulates water arrives from Amazon. The bubbling sounds allow Mia to locate her drinking water and food bowl next to it. Carpet runners delineate the most-traveled parts of the house to assist her with navigation. I use my voice more, although I sometimes forget and point or give a hand gesture.

A week after the SARDS diagnosis, I dip a dog biscuit into some leftover beef gravy, hold the treat out for Mia to smell then toss it into the backyard. With her nose held up in the air or low on the ground, my dachshund tracks the biscuit, eats it, and comes back with a wiggle in her step for more. I clap with delight.

With Mia less tolerant of puppies or excitable dogs, I bring home two senior dachshunds to foster. For them, the most exciting part of their day focuses on mealtime. In a short period, Mia and the two older dogs bond like a group of Bingo players at a retirement center. Considering the two fosters' ages and health, I'm prepared for Harley and Davidson to live with me for the rest of their lives.

Park and Lamar spend the next three weekends at my place. Our time together cooking, taking care of the dogs, and working around the house seems more like a living, rather than a dating, relationship. As a result, it's been a month since we last used his Tantra chair. I almost ordered one, but my little bungalow is filled to capacity with existing furniture and dog paraphernalia. Besides, the chair makes going to his place a special treat.

Mrs. R volunteers to spend the weekend after the Fourth of July in my house. I call Park with the news. "Guess what? I can come to your house this Saturday and Sunday."

"Are the Rossetti's watching your dogs?"

"Mrs. R is. The AC went out in her house. Her nephew can't come until Sunday to fix it, so she's staying at my place, and I'm staying with you."

"Great. Let's plan on going out Saturday night."

CHAPTER 43

I ARRIVE EARLY at his condo on Friday. Only Lamar is there to greet me. I plan to prepare chicken Alfredo and a Caprese salad for dinner. I'll feed Park then, at the appropriate time, I'll tell him I love him. The words often hover in my thoughts, like a song lyric I can't get out of my head. My declaration of love for Park will be perfect, unlike when I said those words to my two previous boyfriends.

The first time it happened with Austin, the guy I lost my virginity to and dated in high school. Immediately after I uttered the words, his eyes rolled about like a terrified horse escaping from a barn fire. Then he dutifully and insincerely said he loved me too. With Blaine, my ex-fiancé, I again said those three little words first. A week passed before he said them back, followed by a sham proposal of marriage. Now that Park has told me first and demonstrated the sincerity of his words, I'm confident in expressing the emotion in my heart.

After I place a plate stacked with slices of tomato, mozzarella, and fresh basil leaves in the refrigerator, the lock clicks on the front door and Park enters. He greets Lamar then stands and kisses me. "Something smells good."

"It's another of Mrs. R's recipes." I scan his drawn face. "You look tired. Did you have a rough day?"

He sighs, and his eyes shift away from mine. "Yeah. Is there time for me to shower and change clothes?"

"We'll eat whenever you're ready."

Fifteen minutes later, I'm at the sink running cool water over the hot pasta. Warm lips caress the back of my bare neck. Delightful shivers run down my spine.

Park nibbles on my ear. "Is there anything I can do?"

I spin around and loop my arms over his shoulders, careful to keep my wet hands off his shirt and rub against him. "Well . . ."

"I meant with dinner."

"How about opening the wine?"

Park seems quieter than normal while they eat. His workday must have been unusually difficult. He pushes his empty plate to the side and turns to me with a sober expression. "I need to talk to you about the foundation."

I blink. "Okay."

"Let me get what I brought home to show you." He returns with a sheaf of papers from his briefcase, withdraws one from the stack, and slides it across the counter. "Do you recognize this?"

I glance at an invoice from Atlantic Animal Hospital. For the last four years, the agreement between the clinic and Forever Homes is for the foundation to pay for medications, surgeries, lab work, and radiology. Angie provides her veterinary services for free to reimburse me for paying off her medical school loans. The invoice in front of me billed for a dental cleaning ten months ago.

I push the paper back to him. "This is from Angie."

"Look at it again."

Everything looks fine, but I check once more and spot a typo. Or is it? The name at the top is not Atlantic Animal Hospital. It reads as *Altanic Animal Hospital.*

On the counter, Park places a one-inch thick stack of papers clipped together. "It's also on all these. Someone has been defrauding the foundation for the last eighteen months. They've been submitting false invoices, and you've been paying them. The Altanic bills are never received or paid in the same weeks as the legitimate ones. Here's a valid invoice from Angie."

I compare the false invoice to the actual one and note that payments are sent to the same address, but the post office boxes are different numbers. The knot in my stomach tightens. Someone has orchestrated the scam with attention to detail.

"I stopped at the place where the PO boxes are, but they wouldn't tell me who picks up the mail." He pulls another paper from the pile and shows me a photocopy of six endorsed checks. Altanic Animal Hospital is stamped on the back along with a series of numbers. "I contacted the bank where this account is located, and they confirmed there is a business checking account in the Altanic name."

"So it's a real company?"

"It's a real dummy company."

A headache throbs behind my right eyebrow. "How much money was stolen?"

"Over eighty-seven thousand dollars."

I gasp. This evening started with soft music, happy laughter, and good food. Then, without much warning, my world is rocked with the knowledge that someone I know swindled me.

Please don't let it be Angie.

As if Park reads my mind, he says, "I called Angie and made up an excuse about a missing invoice. I'm confident neither she nor anyone at her office is behind this. So I checked Sunbiz online to see who the registered agent is for Altanic Animal Hospital. Do you recognize the name, Mary Louise Reston?"

Why does that sound familiar? "I don't think so. What's a registered agent?"

"Usually it's someone who's an officer with the business, but any name can be given. The state doesn't require you to prove who you are."

I lick my dry lips. "What do you recommend we do now?"

Park gathers the papers into one pile and clips them together. "The first thing is to not sign any checks to Altanic Animal Hospital. Meanwhile, I'll look into things a little more to see what I can uncover. There hasn't been a fake invoice since I took over the books. So I suspect the embezzler is someone who knows you have a new CPA and is lying low."

Only my previous accountant, the Rossetti's, and my family know Park volunteered to do the foundation's books. It's unthinkable for any of them to be responsible. If they became mired in financial straits, I would be more than willing to help out. Even my friend, Trey, asked me for a loan despite his reluctance. But maybe someone on the periphery perpetrated the deception. Many volunteers cycle through as fundraisers, animal care helpers, dog walkers, foster parents, and event assistants.

With a cloud of suspicions fogging my thoughts, I struggle to enjoy the rest of the weekend with Park. I don't fake my orgasms, but everything else requires me to put on a false mask of pleasure. Ignoring the ache of betrayal in my chest, I soothe myself with the rationalization that the culprit has to be someone I don't know well or at all. My self-imposed anesthesia helps me not feel bad, except nothing feels good either.

As a result, I never tell Park I love him.

CHAPTER 44

PARK CONTACTS ME every day with questions about my efforts to weed out the embezzler. His level of intensity and frustration with my inability to identify the thief mimics a call to his cable provider who charged him for a premium channel he never ordered. In our last conversation, his voice acquires a harsh edge of annoyance. "It sounds like you don't want to find out who did this?"

"Of course, I do. But I don't want to accuse someone unjustly."

"Has anyone quit or stopped volunteering. It's usually a sign of guilt."

"Nothing's changed." I finally agree to call my employees and volunteers into my office one-by-one and lay out the evidence for them to see.

Park cautions me to remain alert to everyone's reactions. "Be ready if someone becomes confrontational with you and goes on the offensive. You need to be prepared."

On Monday morning, I spread the fake invoices across the conference table in my office along with several of the valid ones from Angie's veterinary hospital. When my sister comes into work an hour later and taps on the open door, I say, "Oh good, you're here. There's something I want to show you."

Kit steps inside. "What's all this?"

"We have a problem. Take a look."

My sister comes closer then stops. Kit's smile disappears, and all the color drains from her face. She takes a step back with eyes wide as if I transformed into an intruder who confronts her with a weapon. "I'm so sorry."

For several seconds, we stare at each other, one shivering with primal terror, the other stunned into immobility. While my heartbeat hammers in my throat, red splotches crawl up Kit's neck to her jaw, contrasting with her dead-white complexion.

At last, I jolt out of my speechless stupor. "You? You're the thief?" Each word sounds like a block of concrete hitting pavement.

"I didn't mean for you to find out."

I thrust my finger at the piles of paper. "This wasn't a one-time thing. You stole from the foundation for more than a year."

Kit tugs her hair, a gesture of contrition left over from childhood. Even though I'm the younger sibling, I often found myself soothing Kit when life's trials and tribulations laid her low. But this time, I will not placate my sister with the usual glass-half-full-you'll-feel-better-tomorrow routine. I turn my back on the sight of her tears.

Behind me, Kit says, "I'm so s-s-sorry. W-what are you g-going to do?"

Although her voice sounds full of over-the-top remorse, I say, "Maybe I should call the police. After all, this is grand theft." I wait for Kit to plead for understanding, appeal for time to make restitution, remind me we are family.

Instead, she speaks barely above a whisper. "Maybe you should."

I spin around. "You want to be arrested?"

Kit raises her beautiful, denim eyes, now red and watery. "No. What I want is to make it right. For months, I tried—"

"For months? You only stopped when Park took over the books." I walk on shaky legs to my office chair to get my bearings.

Kit follows and drops into a seat on the opposite side of the desk. She brushes at the wetness on her cheeks with the backs of her hands.

A sudden thought interrupts my state of shock. "Did Garrett make you steal the money? Is he the one who helped you set up the dummy company?"

Kit's chin wobbles and she stares back with brave humility. "No. It was all my doing."

My sister's acceptance of responsibility tugs at my heart. Garrett may not have ordered his wife to embezzle from the foundation but perhaps he applied pressure, so Kit had no other choice. I express a thought I have never spoken aloud before. "You've been dealing with Garrett's addiction for years, and now it's reduced you to becoming a thief. You should divorce him before he jeopardizes Trevor and Ainsley's future too."

"I can't."

"Why not? You don't owe him anything. He owes you. And now he owes *me*."

"I love him."

I throw my hands into the air. "Your *love* has enabled Garrett to manipulate you into committing fraud. How much money has Pops and Mumsy given you over the years? You've begged, probably borrowed, and definitely stolen to rescue him from his addiction."

Kit locks eyes with me. "He loves me, is a wonderful father, and works hard at the law firm. There hasn't been any gambling in months. I wanted to pay off the last debts, so we could start clean. I know I did wrong, but when you love someone you want to make them happy."

"When you love someone you want to make them healthy. *Then* they'll be happy."

"Don't blame Garrett for this. I thought I could pay it back, and no one would ever know."

"There's no way you could return eighty-seven thousand, six hundred, and forty-three dollars before someone discovered the missing funds."

Kit opens her mouth, but no sound comes out. The only noises come from the barking dogs outside the window and on the other side of the office wall. Both of us sit in silence. If I file charges, a greater chasm will be created between me and the rest of the family, one which could pit me against the people I love and cause an irreparable breach. To my way of thinking, having Kit arrested is an avenue of recourse I have to reject.

At once, a plan crystallizes in my mind. "Okay, here's what we're going to do."

"Can't we discuss this first?" Kit's voice sounds more like her old self, firm with a hint of whininess.

"No. Either you agree to my terms, or I tell Park who embezzled the money. He'll contact the authorities and present the evidence against you." All of a sudden, my brain makes a connection to the name Mary Louise Reston. "Oh, my God! You used your dead mother's maiden name as the registered agent for the dummy corporation."

When I finish outlining what Kit has to do to make restitution to the foundation, my sister grimaces then nods as if her neck is stiff with pain. "I'll do everything you say if you promise not to tell Father, Mother . . . and Garrett."

I frown. "Your husband doesn't know what you did?"

"No."

"Where does he think the money came from?"

"I told him Father gives me some every month as long as . . . he stops betting and gets help at Gamblers Anonymous."

I repeat the question I asked at Kit's birthday dinner. "How do you know he's attending?"

"We go to open meetings together."

"Good. I want to add Gambler's Anonymous to our agreement. You and Garrett will need to continue going to meetings."

"We would do it anyway."

"If there's evidence you aren't following these terms, I'll tell everyone what you did."

Kit sits up straighter in the chair. "Don't worry. I don't want anyone, especially my children, finding out."

"I'll just need to let Park know who stole the money."

Her head shoots up like I delivered an uppercut to her chin. "You can't tell him!"

"Of course, I have to tell him. He's the one who discovered the fraud. He has a right to know."

Tears spring from Kit's eyes. "Please, please, don't say it was me."

"Why not? He won't tell anyone."

"Park might be family someday, and he'd know the terrible thing I did."

I open my eyes wide. Does Kit really think Park might one day be her brother-in-law? "There's no guarantee our relationship will lead to marriage."

"But it might. Please," she pleads in a whispery voice. "I'm begging you to keep this our secret."

I tip my head back and stare at the ceiling with a clenched jaw. There it is again. *Our secret*. "Fine. I'll keep your identity from everybody."

I call in one of the volunteer dog walkers to witness our signatures after I draft a document, which may not hold up in a court of law. Although not written by an almost-attorney like Trey, the agreement will be proof of Kit's thievery. Then I send my sister to dissolve Altanic Animal Hospital on the Florida Division of Corporations' website followed by closing the checking account.

I sit with my head cradled in my hands. What am I going to tell Park?

CHAPTER 45

PARK REGISTERED TO attend a CPA conference the following weekend in Fort Lauderdale. The event provides Continuing Professional Education credits, so he can renew his accounting license.

In a phone conversation with me earlier in the week, he said, "Let's get together Friday evening. On Saturday, I'll be too wiped out from sitting on my ass all day. When I get home, I'll walk Lamar then go to bed. I have more workshops until noon on Sunday."

In our phone conversations during the week, I hadn't told Park about uncovering the thief and making arrangements for restitution without involving the police. I'll tell him when we're face-to-face. My only concern involves not revealing Kit's identity by accident. This fear causes my stomach to clench several times a day. After feeding the dogs an early supper, I drive to Park's condo for Chinese takeout and a rented movie. As I approach his front door, an Asian man hands him a cardboard box filled with small cartons of food. Park waits for me in the open doorway.

"You're just in time." He leans sideways and kisses me.

After greeting Lamar, I help open the various containers of chicken almond ding, pepper steak, shrimp egg foo young, and pork with vegetables. We sit at the kitchen bar with loaded plates. A strangling tension constricts my throat. Should I tell him I love him first? I push my food around for several minutes, unable to eat.

"Did you uncover the embezzler yet?"

I jerk upright, like when my phone rings in a moment of deep concentration. "Uh, yeah, I . . . I did."

His eyes brighten behind his lenses. "That's great. Who is—"

"It's one of the foundation volunteers."

"How did—"

"She saw the invoices on the table in my office and confessed."

"Why would—"

"She has a family member with a problem who created a lot of debt for her."

"What are—"

"We worked out an agreement of restitution rather than me taking any legal action."

Park throws his chopsticks onto the granite countertop. "What the hell!"

"Please understand. I decided having her arrested won't solve the problem."

"The *problem* is she committed a felony, Marin."

I researched the crime online after Kit's confession. Her embezzlement qualifies as second-degree grand theft, punishable by prison time and fines up to ten thousand dollars. "The most important thing for me is to get the money reimbursed. That won't necessarily happen if a woman with a family is sent to jail."

Park sits rigid in his chair with his arms crossed on his chest. "Then what good is having laws? Once every criminal is caught he or she could say: 'I'm sorry. I'll give you back what I stole'. Without punishment, the thief just becomes smarter about not getting caught the next time."

"I know this person will reimburse the foundation, and she'll never steal again."

Park's nostrils twitched. "And how do you know that?"

"She doesn't want anyone to find out what she's done. I've agreed to not have her arrested or inform her family. If she fails to abide by our agreement, I can take either action or both."

"If she didn't have the money to pay her debt before, how is she going to pay you now?"

I swallow hard. "I've upped her time at the foundation to thirty hours a week. She'll be an unpaid employee at ten dollars an hour until all the money is reimbursed."

He gives an exaggerated snort of disbelief. "My parents got rid of their thief, but you're giving yours a *job*?"

"She's not collecting a paycheck and has to report to work on the days and times she's assigned, unlike the other volunteers. The dogs don't care if she gives back the money in cash. They want someone to rescue them, care for them, and find them loving homes. If she provides eighty-seven thousand dollars' worth of time and labor, the animals will benefit more."

Park raises his eyes toward the ceiling. "Let's see . . . if she works thirty hours a week . . . at ten dollars an hour . . . it'll take her . . . more than five years to pay back what she owes."

I stare at him goggle-eyed. "You did that calculation in your head?"

"Don't look at me like I'm the Rain Man." The spinning ceiling fan in the living room casts shadows across Park's face like a whirling vortex. "I know I'm just your *volunteer* accountant, but aren't I entitled to see my efforts rewarded with justice served?"

"There's no justice in throwing the woman into the modern-day equivalent of debtor's prison. I want restitution, so I've made the punishment fit the crime. Instead of having her sit in a jail cell, she'll be reminded of the mistake she made for thirty hours every week."

"A mistake no one else knows about."

"Yes. As long as she abides by the terms of the agreement."

Park pushes his plate away. "Tell me her name."

"Why?"

"I can't force you to file charges, but I'll report her to the authorities, so there'll be a record. If she ever tries to do this again, the previous complaint is on file."

I hold my elbows in opposing palms, my body stiff as if I've turned into a fragile glass in danger of breaking. "I promised her I wouldn't."

He lowers his voice. "Come on, Marin. Tell me."

"No." I often take pride in refusing people's demands, especially my parents', but saying no to Park hurts like a stinging dart to my chest.

He looks me in the eye. "I see."

I reach my hand across the counter, although it falls short of touching him. "I gave my word. Can we just agree to disagree on this?"

He looks away from me. "I don't know if I can."

My thoughts swirl in uncertain circles. Will Park still report the fraud to the authorities? Will he be unable to accept my unwillingness to identify the fraudster? Will he quit as the foundation's CPA? Will he no longer love me?

Echoing my thoughts, Park says, "I'm not sure about the future of our relationship in light of your decision."

His words slice through me like an executioner's ax. "You won't . . . love me anymore?"

He sighs. "I'm pissed off. I thought we agreed on how this would be handled. I spent countless hours doing the audit, and for what? So a criminal can give you a sob story and get off scot-free."

"If you want to be paid for the extra hours, send me an invoice."

Park erupts like an overheated kettle. "This isn't about the money! It's about the law and letting the court system decide what the appropriate punishment is."

"I understand why you're upset, but I truly believe the agreement I made with my . . . volunteer is the best option for now." My heart stops with the near slip of Kit's identity.

Park shrugs. He picks up an egg roll and bites into it with a fierce chomp. "Then I guess we have . . ." More chewing. "Nothing else . . ." More chewing. "To talk about." Swallow.

We eat the rest of the meal in silence. I pick at my food while Park focuses on consuming what lays on his plate. We put the leftovers away and watch a Red Box movie with Lamar between us on the sofa, like a doggie demilitarized zone. When the credits roll, neither of us suggests a quickie on the Tantra.

I stand. "Do you want me to go with you and Lamar on your walk?"

"I'm going to let him out to do his business then come back inside. I have to be in Fort Lauderdale by eight AM tomorrow."

"Okay." I pick up my purse and head to the door.

"Marin."

I stop and turn around. He rises from the sofa and comes to stand in front of me. "I have a lot of thinking to do."

With his statement, something soft inside me splits open, and all my insecurities of being worthy of love begin to wriggle through the crack. I study his set face as a weighted heaviness settles on my chest and compresses my heart.

The corners of his mouth are tugged down. His mahogany-colored hair is rumpled from his fingers tunneling through it during the movie. The shadows under his eyes show from behind his glasses. "Give me a few days then I'll call you. I don't know whether to kiss you or shake some sense into you."

I raise my hand like a shy little girl. "Can I pick?"

Despite our weak chuckles, we end up kissing like warring spouses who have been counseled never to go to bed angry but find they are unable to reconcile yet. We don't hug but hold onto each other the way strangers do with stiff bodies and awkward shoulder pats.

On the way to the elevator, I come to a halt. I forgot to say I love you to him.

CHAPTER 46

BY WEDNESDAY, I'M a wreck. Every ring or text alert I receive sends me racing to my phone, but none of the calls or messages is from Park. In desperation, I send him a text.

How u doing?

He doesn't respond.

On Friday, a week after our argument, I call him. After a number of rings, I'm directed to voice mail and stumble through an unprepared response. "I . . . I haven't . . . heard from you all week. Are you okay? Please call me as soon as you can."

Over the weekend, I leave more voice and text messages. On Monday, I call his office, although he asked me to always contact him on his cell phone.

"Robinson Account Management. Ingrid speaking. How can I help you?"

"Uh, hello, this is Marin McAllister. I'm trying to get in contact with Park."

A pregnant pause occurs before the woman speaks again. "I'm sorry. He's not available. Is there anything I can help you with?"

Possibly his employees know he oversees the rescue group's account, but are they aware he's dating the director? Perhaps I should act more like a concerned client than a spurned lover to reach him. "He's doing the books for my non-profit, The Forever Homes Dachshund Foundation. I have some important questions I need to ask him."

Ingrid doesn't say anything for an awkward length of time then a man's voice comes on the line. "May I help you?"

It's not Park.

"I'm calling to speak to Park Robinson."

"He's not available."

Is he not available to everyone or just me? "When can I talk with him?"

"I'm sorry, but the best I can do is let him know you called."

"Do you have my name?"

"Ingrid wrote it down. Good-bye."

I stare at the screen then punch in the number for Park's cell phone. This time I'm not leaving him a message from his pleasant, or concerned, or anxious girlfriend. This time I'm going to be his angry, upset, hurt girlfriend. By now, he should have the finesse to say it's over between us. How dare he leave me dangling for more than a week, uncertain if we're still a couple or a couple of exes.

A recording says his mailbox is full.

CHAPTER 47

I FINALLY FINISH a three-hour-long afternoon meeting about construction delays at my Forever Homes Village project. At odd moments during the contentious conference, a knotty worry about Park pops into my consciousness. I focus on him instead of concentrating on what the construction managers are saying. Possibly this is why the meeting drags on so long. When I arrive home, I'm beyond tired and frustrated. I pour myself a large glass of merlot as soon as I get inside the house. When I finish feeding the dogs, my cell phone rings.

"Is this a bad time to call?" Angie's voice wobbles, thick with emotion.

I stiffen with instant alertness. "What's wrong?"

"Brent's gone."

A thought buzzes through my head. Has Rita discovered what he's done to Angie and contracted a hit with one of her Italian relatives? "What do you mean?"

"Last Friday, he told me he would be busy all weekend, so we couldn't get together, but he never said anything about leaving. I haven't seen him at the gym all week. I got a text from him yesterday saying he's taken a new job in another state and moved."

"What does his text say?"

"Here. I'll read it to you: *Babe, sorry. Got a new job. Leaving FL. Nice knowing u.*" Angie exhales a sharp breath. "Can you believe it? That's all he can say after six months together?"

Great. That makes two disappearing boyfriends. "Are you sure he's really gone?"

"I went by his apartment early this morning. One of his neighbors said he left during the week with a couple of suitcases."

"I'm so sorry, Angie. I know you cared for him."

"A couple of weeks ago we passed a jewelry store in the mall, and he asked me what kind of rings I liked. I thought he was going to propose. Instead, he sends a nice-knowing-you text?" Angie's voice breaks with a tiny fracture of grief.

Although my friend insists Brent never physically hurt her again, in my opinion, Angie's boyfriend is still a walking time bomb. For me, the breakup is a relief. Angie needs to find someone who makes love to her the way she likes and treats her the way she deserves. "I know it's weird, Angie, but—"

"You want weird? I called his office. The guy I talked to said Brent was taking a vacation and would be back on Monday."

"Did you tell them about the text?"

"No. I was so surprised I just thanked him and hung up."

Because of Angie's emotional low, I don't share the loss of my boyfriend too. The parallels between our dating relationships are uncanny in comparison. Both of us began dating these men in February and both of them appear to have dumped us in July. Perhaps Brent sensed me and Rita stomping through his relationship with Angie, giving our opinions, asking questions, and uncovering flaws. Maybe he worried Angie would begin to see him through the eyes of the people who matter to her, so he left rather than change his lifestyle. Or . . .

Rita did hire a hitman.

CHAPTER 48

THE FOLLOWING WEEK, I arrive at Atlantic Veterinary Hospital with a new dachshund rescue for Angie to examine. My friend takes one look at me and the dog and stops halfway into the exam room. "What happened?"

I rub the ear of a miniature short-haired. "Doxie Roxie was surrendered because the couple has six-month-old twins. The wife says she can't handle both *his* dog and *their* kids."

Angie moves closer and lays the file she carries on a nearby counter. "I'm not talking about Roxie. What's wrong with you?"

"Oh, Ang." My friend knows me so well it's pointless to lie. "Park broke up with me too. At least, I think he did."

Angie sits on the wooden bench next to me. "Talk."

With the little dog's warm, furry body against my abdomen like a soothing pillow, I tell her about Park uncovering the embezzlement and that I identified the person responsible as one of the foundation's volunteers. Again, I don't name my sister.

"I wondered why he called here asking about our invoicing procedures."

"He wanted to find out if the fraud occurred at your end or mine. Whatever you said confirmed it was someone from the foundation."

Angie picks up Roxie and places her on the exam table. "Why did this cause you guys to split up?"

I describe Park's adverse reaction to my handling of the fraud. "I haven't been able to talk to him at all. He won't answer my calls or messages. I even tried his office and got the runaround from his staff."

"Have you gone to his condo? Do you still have the key he gave you?"

"What if he isn't home?"

Angie writes a notation in the dog's chart. "Go inside. If there's no sign of another woman then keep trying to get in touch with him. But if you spot makeup in the bathroom or clothes in the closet, wash your hands of him." Angie picks up Roxie and strokes her head. "This girl seems to be fine. Her former owners saw to her physical well-being. I'm sorry you're going through the same thing I did. At least, Brent had the balls to tell me it was over and not leave me hanging."

When I return to the foundation with Roxie, Kit is at the front desk. "How did it go?"

I hand over the dog's leash. "Roxie is cleared for adoption. Photograph her then upload everything onto the website. I'll be in my office."

A stack of mail is piled on my desk. At the bottom is a large green and white envelope from Robinson Account Management, which had been sent by certified mail. Because of the foundation's scheduled board meeting next week, I'm expecting a monthly balance sheet and a Statement of Functional Expenses from Park. In the previous months, he emailed the documents rather than sending them by mail.

When I tear open the flap, I pull out a stack of clipped papers along with a form letter which says: *As of August 5th, Robinson Account Management CPA LLC has terminated our professional relationship with you and will no longer render services to The Forever Homes Dachshund Foundation.*

My breath comes in rapid heaves. The letter contains legalese concerning the final preparation of financial statements, unpaid fees that may be due, additional work in progress, and advice for selecting a replacement CPA firm as soon as possible. By the time I finish reading, the paper is dimpled with wet spots from my dripping tears. No longer do I need to wonder if Park is ending our personal relationship. The evidence is right in front of me. He's cutting all ties.

A tap at the office door sounds and Kit's blonde head appears. "I've finished uploading Roxie online. Is there . . . What's wrong?"

I sob into my hands as tears slide through my fingers. Kit slips a wad of tissues into my wet palms. I wipe my eyes, nose, and cheeks. When I glance up, my sister's beautiful face is crumpled into the mask of a sad clown.

Kit points to the letter on the desk. "Is that because of me?"

I nod.

"Does it also mean Park is ending his relationship with you?"

I bite my lip and nod again.

"Why?"

I take a deep breath, my voice cracking on the words. "He insisted on knowing your name. Don't worry. I didn't tell him. He doesn't agree with not having criminal charges filed. We argued, and he said he needed time to think."

"But that doesn't mean he wants to break up, does it?" A flash of something both hopeful and fearful crosses Kit's face as she reads the letter again.

"It's been three weeks, and he hasn't returned any of my calls or messages. I think he's given me a pretty clear answer."

"Sometimes I haven't spoken to Garrett for a long time when we've had a really bad fight. It doesn't mean I want to end the marriage. You need to talk with him and have him tell you the relationship is over."

I push the heels of my hands deep into my face and massage my swollen eyes with tiny circular motions. I lick my dry lips and taste salt like I've been swimming in the ocean. "And how am I supposed to do that?"

"Have you tried going to his house?'

"Angie suggested I confront him there too."

"She's right. Until he says the words to you, it may not be over."

After Kit leaves, I sit with my eyes closed. Park's love loosened the tight rein I had on my emotions. With his rejection, my heart clunks shut, like the heavy door of a safe. Once again, I'm unlovable and unloved. I check my Apple watch. He should be home from the office in another hour. Angie and Kit are right. I need a definitive resolution to this romantic limbo.

After helping feed the foundation's dogs their supper and settling them in for the night, I drive to Park's condo. His Prius is parked in its regular spot. I take an available guest space nearby. Several feet short of the building's front doors, I halt. What if Park had my key fob deactivated?

With trembling fingers, I hold the gray, plastic disk up to the electronic eye. A green light flashes, and a click sounds. I pull open the door. As the elevator ascends to the sixth floor, I inhale and exhale with deep, cleansing breaths. Despite the relaxation technique, my knees almost buckle as I wobble down the carpeted hall to his condo.

I stare at the white metal rectangle of his front door. Music filters through it. Sometimes Park has Alexa play tunes, but he keeps the volume on low. Now heavy, thumping rhythm pulses through the walls and is audible in the hallway.

I knock. No answer. I knock harder. No one opens the door. Inserting the key, I grasp the lever handle and press down. The music pours out like a tsunami of sound. I hurry inside and shut the door behind me.

The place looks like there had been a party last night. Dishes and glasses litter the kitchen countertop and living room tables.

"Hello? Park?" I'm not sure anyone can hear me over the loud music.

A man's voice shouts from another room, "Yes."

I take a couple of steps closer to the hallway. I halt at a shout with a higher pitch. For several seconds, the music goes silent then switches to another song, softer in volume. During the quiet lull, I recognize a familiar sound—the squeaking of bare flesh on the leather upholstery of the Tantra chair.

A sickening queasiness rises within me. I bend forward, my hands pushing on my abdomen. On the floor lays a trail of clothes leading to the guest bedroom door; a white tank top with its straps twisted, a mostly buttoned man's dress shirt, a filmy chiffon skirt, and a pair of jeans collapsed onto their bottom hems like chimneys felled in an implosion.

A woman's voice cries out, "Oh, God. Oh, God."

I back up to the front door and throw the fob and key onto the living room floor. Holding my tears in check until reaching my car, I sob with my forehead on the steering wheel. After a long bout of heaving shoulders, snotty sniffs, and flurries of tears, I exhale, exhausted and shaky. My body feels like I vomited up fetid food. On the drive home amid my heartbreak and fury, a thought comes to me.

Where was Lamar?

CHAPTER 49

I AM FORCED to cope with one heart-sinking realization. I fell for the wrong guy again. Park isn't the amazing man I thought, hoped, and prayed he was. Like my ex-fiancé, he has a major flaw I overlooked. Blaine claimed he respected me and would wait for sex until we married. Instead, he couldn't face intercourse until he was legally entitled to some of my millions. With Park, his control issues and adherence to rules have no gray area. Once I opposed him, he dropped me like I never mattered, and a new, possibly more compliant, girlfriend is my replacement.

Over the next couple of weeks, I work long hours at the foundation overseeing the ongoing construction of Forever Homes Village, organizing adoption events, doing social media blasts about available dogs, and driving in all points of the compass to rescue animals in dire situations. Often my heartbreak seems more physical than emotional. I reach for an over-the-counter painkiller then stop myself. Tylenol won't alleviate heartache. Instead, I fill every waking hour and arrive home each day like a wrung-out dishrag.

During this time, I receive notification that Sandy Hanna, my friend who manipulated Park into our first date, passed away. The woman, who suffered from congestive heart failure, died in her sleep. Her death devastates her husband, Ray.

Their daughter calls me with the sad news. "Mom's funeral is Friday."

"I'll be there. Is there anything I can do?"

The woman hesitates. "Uh, she left a file folder with all kinds of instructions and a note saying if Dad and I decide to sell the property, I should contact you first."

Sandy's ten acres run adjacent to a tract I purchased for future development. "Ray doesn't plan to live on the ranch?"

"Not without Mom. Besides, taking care of the place and the animals was getting too much for them. Thank goodness, Mom hadn't taken in any additional horses or cats for the last two years."

"Where will your dad go?"

"I'm moving him, the last two horses, and any of the barn cats we can trap to my place in Ocala. If we can come to an agreement, it would save us having to put the property on the market."

The note Sandy left includes a price. After having a real estate analysis done, I offer to buy Ray and Sandy's place with a thirty-day closing. Later, I'll decide what to do with the house, ten-stable barn, and acreage. Maybe I'll start a rescue for abused or neglected horses.

My mother calls near the end of August. We haven't spoken since my breakup with Park. Betsy says, "How are you? We haven't talked in weeks."

"I'm fine. I've been very busy." I wince at the falseness in my voice.

"You must be. Kit has been putting in longer volunteer hours too. We hardly ever see her during the day. Anyway, I'm calling because we're celebrating your father and Garrett's birthday next Sunday. I'm inviting you and Park, but no gift is necessary from him."

Obviously Kit hasn't told anyone Park and I are no longer a couple. The only punishment worse than having to attend a party at my parents' house is telling my mother about the breakup.

I sigh. "Park won't be there. We broke up."

"Oh, no. What happened?"

"We had a difference of opinion, and he ended things."

"I see. It's unfortunate you couldn't hang on to him. He seemed like a very nice man."

Yeah, a nice control freak who wasted no time in finding another Tantra playmate. "Well, that's what happened."

"Are you sure there's nothing you can do to resurrect the relationship? Your father and I are so pleased with him."

"It was his decision, not mine."

"Perhaps if you apologize and offer to change your opinion of whatever caused the disagreement, he'll reconsider."

In a harsh voice, I spit out, "Are you saying I should grovel to get a man back?"

"No, I'm just —"

"It's over, Mumsy. Deal with it."

When the call ends, I rub the knot of tension stretching across my forehead. Will I ever stop feeling like my radar has been knocked off-center by Park's magnetic force? Maybe I'll get back to normal when I finally stop loving him.

Or maybe I'll feel like this forever.

CHAPTER 50

ON THE FIRST Sunday morning in September, I help Everglades Angels pick up a mixed breed rat terrier and miniature pinscher dumped near a campground. Both little dogs sit by the edge of a dirt lane waiting for their family to return for them. They quiver with fear and skittishness, and it takes some creative and coordinated efforts from me and the other volunteers to get both of them safely caught and crated. At home, I hurry to clean up and dress for the birthday party. After showering, I skin my hair back into a damp ponytail, slap on eyeliner, mascara, and lipstick, dress in a pair of Dolce and Gabbana black skinny jeans and a black Michael Kors tank top. I insert silver hooped earrings ringed with tiny diamonds into my earlobes.

Arriving late to Del Lago Al Mar, I find Garrett's parents in attendance, as well as his brother, sister-in-law, and their two sons. The group also includes Trey's parents, but without their son, daughter-in-law, and two infant grandchildren. Once again, I'm the outsider; the only unmarried woman in the group who works rescuing animals that will never be designer pets.

All the guests congregate in the formal living room, except for Ainsley, Trevor, and Garrett's nephews. The four young cousins clatter up the main staircase to the media room when I open the front door. Ainsley, wearing a pink Princess Rapunzel dress, waves with enthusiasm before following the three boys.

The women, in pastels outfits like a summer paint chart, sit near the marble fireplace. The men cluster by the mahogany wet bar, no doubt jockeying for male dominance. My mother and sister greet me and motion to join them. I always strive to be different, and today I look like a crow among brightly-colored parakeets.

Mrs. Montgomery, Trey's mother, gives me a frosty stare as if I'm the reason her son is married to an unsuitable woman. But Garrett's mother smiles and scoots over to make room on the sofa. I nod to Jessica, the woman married to Garrett's brother. She's a near copy of Kit.

Conversations, which had been in progress, are resumed. Mrs. Nichol brings me a glass of white wine. I let the talk float around me without paying much attention.

During a lull, Jessica catches my eye. "I hear you're building homes out west where you live. I didn't know you were interested in construction."

"I'm not. I'm interested in helping animals."

"What do you mean?"

"I'm building a small community of homes for people who can't afford their own. They can live there as long as they foster and care for rescued dogs."

Mrs. Montgomery snorts. "I can't believe you're providing new houses for unemployed losers. Who would want to live next to these people and kennels full of barking dogs?"

"You have the wrong idea about Forever Homes Village. It's for families who can't afford a nice house but are willing to take care of rescued animals. I don't want the dogs and cats to spend their life in kennels or cages. They become more adoptable if they're used to being part of a family. I'm also planning an apartment building for retirees."

Kit pipes in. "The older residents are better suited to fostering cats."

Garrett's mother asks, "Do people bring the animals to your rescue group, or do you go out and find them yourself?"

"Both. This morning I helped pick up two family pets dumped in the Everglades."

Mrs. Montgomery in her usual brassy voice says, "Really?" She eyes my knees through the ripped designer jeans. "Too bad you didn't have time to change clothes before coming here."

I scowl at Trey's mother. Before I can say something inappropriate, Betsy says, "Let's gather our men and head to the dining room. I'm sure the birthday luncheon is ready."

The children eat in the media room while the adults are seated in the formal dining room with meal service from the staff. I toy with my food. While the men discuss the impact of possible import tariffs, the women launch into a discussion of the next Junior League charity gala to benefit the art museum. Should it be a full dinner with dancing or a champagne brunch? Should there be a silent auction for donations or a raffle ticket sale for a luxury item?

After the luncheon, Mr. and Mrs. Montgomery depart first. Garrett's parents and brother present him with two golf-related gifts then leave for home. The McAllister family gathers outside on the veranda for Stanford and Garrett to open their presents from us. I bought my father his preferred monogrammed dress shirts, one in white and one in bluish-gray, the only colors he wears with a suit. I also ordered two for Garrett in pale lemony yellow and charcoal gray. At the time, I chuckled when selecting the colors; yellow for the coward, near-black for the villain. After the gifts are opened and gratitude expressed, I place my hands on the arms of my chair to rise and say good-bye.

"Sit, dear." Mumsy's voice is more commanding than usual. "Trevor and Ainsley, why don't you ask Mrs. Nichol for some of those macarons you love. She also has fresh lemonade."

The children jump to their feet and run inside. Garrett rises as if sensing a family pow-wow involving only the McAllisters and their daughters. Stanford waves him back into his chair.

Betsy eyes us. "What we want to discuss involves all of you. Now, Kit, we know you offered to help out Marin's foundation, but four days a week you do not get home before six in the evening. This means your children have to be attended by Mrs. Nichol. At the end of the day, it is her job to supervise dinner, not Trevor and Ainsley."

I heave a near-silent snort. It had been Mrs. R's job to care for me when I arrived home from school or summer programs because neither of my parents was available.

Kit sits upright, her feet flat on the flagstones, like a kid outside the principal's office. "I talked with Mrs. Nichol, and she doesn't mind watching them until Garrett or I come home."

In an authoritative and patient tone, Stanford says, "Supervising your children is a duty she is not being compensated to perform."

Kit's eyes cut to her husband. "I guess . . . we can pay her ourselves."

"Dear, it's not so much the money," Betsy adds. "Trevor and Ainsley need you to be with them. It's not like you're working a regular job or volunteering your time for . . ."

When my mother trails off, I jump in. "Volunteering her time for what, Mumsy? A worthwhile cause like the art museum?"

Betsy turns toward my father. Stanford shifts his gaze to his son-in-law. "Don't you think your wife should be home seeing to your children?"

Garrett shoots a sideways look at Kit. "But helping out at the foundation means a lot to her."

Kit stares straight ahead. Her knee bounces with a frenetic rhythm.

I put a hand on her twitching leg. "Volunteering at Forever Homes is important work. Kit may not be earning a paycheck but is gaining valuable experience."

Stanford frowns. "Explain to me how sitting at a computer or cleaning out dog cages are valuable experiences."

"It's more meaningful than planning a gala which donates less than thirty percent of the money to charity." I tamp down my anger and moderate my tone. "The work Kit does is hands-on and beneficial to the animals. She gives them attention and affection which they need as much as shelter, food, and water. She's also been more successful than anyone else in finding them new homes."

Betsy lifts her chin and in a calm voice addresses Kit. "We applaud your efforts, but your father and I feel you should cut back until your children are more self-sufficient. You are a kind, sensitive woman with a caring heart. I'm sure when Marin told you how much the animals needed your help, you were compelled to assist. However, Trevor and Ainsley need you more. If you still want to be an active volunteer, there are many worthy causes closer to home."

I clutch the arms of my chair. "What the hell? Are you saying rescuing living creatures is not a worthwhile cause? Or are you saying Kit shouldn't be around a bad influence like me, because I might corrupt her into doing work that really matters?"

"Marin!" Betsy slaps a palm to her bony chest with a thump. "You are misconstruing my words and using inappropriate language. If you expressed your opinion with Park in this manner, it's understandable why he terminated your relationship."

Before I can respond, another surprisingly firm voice says, "This has to *fucking* stop right now!"

Everyone turns to stare at Kit.

CHAPTER 51

IN FRONT OF our family, Kit just said the most shocking swear word ever to cross her lips. She vibrates in her seat as if she can't contain her righteous anger. She resembles a peace advocate who suddenly transforms into an armed vigilante. Everyone wears open-mouthed, stunned expressions.

Betsy recovers first. "See, this is what I'm talking about. You would never have spoken so coarsely before doing manual labor with animals."

Kit hisses. "If you think what I *said* is coarse, wait until I tell you what I've *done*."

I twist in my chair and put both hands on my sister's forearm. "No, Kit. We've got this handled."

My sister's cornflower-blue eyes burn bright with a determination I have never seen before. "It's time for me to take responsibility. Step Five says we need to admit to ourselves and others the exact nature of our wrongs."

What's Step Five? "You have, and I'm proud of you."

Stanford growls, "What are you girls talking about?"

Kit faces our father. "I embezzled more than eighty-seven thousand dollars from The Forever Homes Dachshund Foundation."

Stanford blanches. "Oh, my God!"

"That can't be," Betsy murmurs.

Garrett appears baffled, like a sleepwalker waking up in an unfamiliar place. "You did? How?"

"I formed a dummy company and billed fake invoices to the foundation. Park discovered the missing money when he did a forensic audit."

I stroke my sister's arm to offer comfort and strength but remain silent, unable to stop this runaway train.

Kit stares into the incredulous eyes of her father. "I confessed to Marin when presented with the evidence. She refused to report me to the authorities. Instead, she's allowing me to use my increased volunteer hours to repay the money. In fact, it's why she and Park broke up. He didn't agree with her decision to not have me arrested."

"Really?" Betsy's one word contains equal parts astonishment and skepticism.

"The one request I made was for only the two of us to know who embezzled the money. Had she told Park it was me, he probably would have understood since I'm family. Instead, she had to claim the thief was just a random volunteer. So, not only am I responsible for the theft, but I'm responsible for breaking my sister's heart." Her voice squeaks in distress for the first time since beginning her confession.

Stanford eyes his elder daughter like she's an alien creature. "Why did you do it?"

Kit slides a glance at her husband. "To pay off the last of the gambling debts."

Garrett jerks upright. "What?"

Stanford jabs an accusatory finger at his son-in-law. "This is your fault! Because of your filthy habit, you've turned my daughter into a criminal."

Kit grabs her father's hand, pulling his index finger toward her. "Garrett isn't the one with a gambling problem. I am."

CHAPTER 52

WITH MY MIND in turmoil, I stare at my sister then out at the idyllic view, blinking against the setting rays of the sun. Gulping sounds draw my attention back. My father's mouth smacks open and closed like a dying fish. Betsy is slumped sideways in the chair like a gunshot victim, unaware of her wound.

Kit clasps her husband's hand. "Garrett agreed to take the blame. He let all of you think the worst of him to protect me. But it's time to come clean. According to my sponsor at Gamblers Anonymous, I can't proceed through the twelve-step process until I admit it's *my* problem."

Mrs. Nichol exits one of the French doors. "Excuse me. May I get you anything?"

Her words snap Stanford to attention. "No, thank you." He stands and offers a hand to his wife who sits in stunned silence. "We are going to my study for a while. Please send the children upstairs."

We relocate to the secluded room behind its thick walnut doors. The discussion continues for another half hour. In the beginning, Stanford and Garrett insist on reimbursing the stolen money.

Kit refuses with adamancy similar to a zealot's religious objection. "No! I did this, and I'm responsible for making direct amends. Don't deny me the step I need for my recovery. I deserve to do the work to repay the debt."

To my surprise and to show her support, Betsy offers to supervise Trevor and Ainsley after school when Kit is working at the foundation. "I can help them with their schoolwork and make sure they aren't playing video games."

Garrett insists on paying Mrs. Nichol when his mother-in-law can't watch the children. He turns to his wife. "What do we tell the kids?"

"Right now, nothing. They're too young. But one day, we will. I want them to know how an addiction can consume your life and cause you to do things you would never think you were capable of. They need to understand this can happen to anyone."

When the meeting ends, the family walks me to the front door. Kit hugs me. "I can't tell you how much I love you and appreciate all you've done for me. You have given me the strength to do this."

I approach Garrett and, for the first time in years, hug him. "I'm sorry I thought so poorly of you for so long. You've redeemed yourself . . . somewhat."

He smirks. "Only somewhat?"

"Despite your love for my sister, you're still a bit of an asshole."

"Marin!" Betsy gasps. "Your language."

"Accept it, Mumsy. Both your daughters have flaws."

"Maybe so, but you are wonderful women I wouldn't trade for the world." She pulls me into her arms. "I'm sorry for what I said about you and Park. One day he'll realize what a tremendous loss you are and regret it for the rest of his life."

CHAPTER 53

A FEW DAYS later, I receive a phone call from a female animal control officer in Broward County. "There's a dachshund here scheduled to be euthanized tomorrow. I think it might be a purebred but it's hard to tell. The dog's pretty aggressive and won't let anyone near. It looks like he's been living a rough life on the streets for a while. I don't know if they'll let you take him, but it seems a shame to put him down."

"I'll be there in an hour. Thanks for the call."

When I arrive at the Pompano Beach facility, a worker escorts me to the inside kennels. Quite a few of the cages house pit bulls and pit mixes. Some of these dogs will be reunited with their owners or adopted to new families, but most are dead dogs barking. The lives of many shelter dogs tend to be short and heartbreaking. More than half are euthanized. The statistics for cats fare even worse.

Officer Conway, a middle-aged woman with unnaturally black hair, joins me and the kennel worker. "You got here pretty quick. I assume you know how to approach an aggressive dog."

"Just point out the aisle and which kennel it is."

As soon as the dogs see us, many come forward barking. Others remain quiet or cower in back corners. As I creep closer, I squat-walk the last couple feet and stay in profile to the cage door. I keep my eyes on the floor and speak in a happy tone of voice. "Hi, buddy. I came to see you.

How're you doing? I want to be your friend. You're a good boy. Yes, you are."

Toenails click on the cement as short legs come into view. The dog sniffs then moves closer. Without warning, a loud howl splits the air, and a furry body launches itself at the door. The howling morphs into sharp barks and high-pitched cries.

I look at the dog and nearly fall from my position onto the concrete floor. "Open this door!"

Conway runs forward amid the cacophony of barking. "What's wrong?"

I poke my fingers through the holes in the chain-links. The dog frantically licks them. "I know this dog. Get him out of there."

The kennel worker fumbles with the keys. As soon as the door widens a few inches, the filthy, matted dachshund muscles his way out and takes a flying leap at me.

I hug his wiggling body. His tongue laps at every inch of my skin he can reach. "Oh, my God, Lamar. What happened to you?"

CHAPTER 54

I COMPLETE THE paperwork to take possession of Park's dog. "Was he wearing a collar when he came in?"

The shelter manager shakes her head. "No collar. No dog tags. We scanned him, found a microchip, and tried contacting his owner. The phone number was out of service. We sent an email but didn't get a reply. Unfortunately, too many dogs end up on the euthanasia list because we don't or can't get someone to contact us."

"I don't understand. The man who owns Lamar is devoted to him. He would have turned the state upside down looking for him." I glance at the dachshund. He faces the exit door, ready to bolt as soon as I give the word. "Where was he found?"

"He'd been hanging around a restaurant in Deerfield Beach. We think the workers fed him scraps, but someone eventually reported him as a stray."

Officer Conway kneels and pets the dachshund's head. "This little guy led me on a merry chase. When I finally cornered him, I had to use a catchpole. He turned vicious and fought me. I can't believe it's the same dog standing here. I'm really glad I called you."

"Me too. My little doxie will be thrilled. She and Lamar are great friends."

On the drive back to Palm Beach County, I call Angie and head to the veterinary hospital. "He's going to need a complete medical evaluation and a grooming."

"Let's hope he doesn't test positive for heartworms."

After dropping Lamar at Atlantic Veterinary Hospital, I drive to Park's office. I'll listen to his explanation for how he lost Lamar, but he better exhibit genuine concern for his pet, or I'll explode on him like a nuclear warhead. I find the office building for Robinson Account Management and ride the elevator to the third floor. When I reach the door, it's locked. A white paper is taped to a glass panel and reads: *At this time, we are temporarily closed due to an emergency.*

Is Park so devastated with losing Lamar that he can't work? A picture enters my mind of the trail of clothes on the floor leading to the bedroom. I shake my head in disgust. His lost dog didn't affect his ability to use the Tantra chair. I chide myself for getting rid of his key and fob. On the drive to his condo, I call Angie. "How's he doing?"

"Judging by his weight loss and the condition of his coat, he's been on the streets for about two months. Luckily, we dodged a bullet with heartworms. He's negative. But after shaving off the worst clumps of fur, we found an almost-healed injury on his hind leg. Something tore through the skin and a bit of muscle. He must have brushed up against something sharp. We cleaned the wound and put him on antibiotics."

"When can I pick him up?"

"He should be done with the groomer around five o'clock."

At Park's condo, I find his Prius parked in its assigned space. Does it mean he's home? And if he is there, is he alone?

At the lobby door, I press the call button for Park's unit. I ring it a second time. I wait, unsure if I should leave and come back later. Perhaps Park's car in the lot means he's out of town on a business trip—or a vacation with his new girlfriend.

A woman's voice crackles from the speaker. "Yes?"

Damn. "Is Park Robinson there?"

"No. Who is this?"

"I need to speak to him about his dog."

A long pause ensues then the woman says, "Have you found Lamar?"

"Yes, I have."

The woman's voice becomes shrill with excitement. "Is he with you?"

"No." I heave a frustrated sigh bent over the squawking box. "I need to speak with Park first."

"Where's Lamar?"

"He's at a veterinary hospital."

"Is he going to be all right?"

"He'll be fine. But then he'll be in the custody of The Forever Homes Dachshund Foundation."

"Marin? Is that you?"

"Yes." How does his new girlfriend know it's me? "Who are *you*?"

"It's Meadow, Park's sister. Come on up."

What is she doing here?

The door buzzer sounds and I pull on the handle. When the elevator door opens on the sixth floor, Meadow stands there. Before I can exit, Park's sister hugs me, grabs my hand, and pulls me toward the condo's open door.

She talks like she's ingested speed, at times slinging the words over her shoulder. "We wanted to get in touch with you, but Park insisted we don't. He didn't want to see you. Since we didn't have his phone, we couldn't look up your number. None of us could remember your last name and he wouldn't tell us. When he found out I was trying to find you anyway, he got really mad. After we told him Lamar was gone, he went into such a funk he wouldn't talk with anyone."

We enter the condo which is even messier than the last time I saw the place. Meadow picks up a pair of shoes and tosses them against the wall to clear a path. "Sorry about how the place looks. If Park saw this, he'd kill me. By the way, I love *your* shoes. Those are from Kate Spade, aren't they? Can I get you something? Beer, water, Coke?"

"No, I'm fine." I rub my forehead. "What's going on? Where's Park?"

Meadow squints as if something gives her pain. "Let's sit first, and I'll get us a drink."

I grab his sister's arm and draw her to a halt. "No. Tell me where he is and why you're in his condo."

In a low voice, Meadow says, "Back in July, Park was out walking Lamar when he was shot and left for dead."

CHAPTER 55

MY PURSE THUDS to the floor. Black dots dance in my vision. I squeeze the bridge of my nose between my thumb and forefinger as a bone-deep chill runs down my body. I fight a gray fog of faintness.

Meadow grabs my arm and leads me to the sofa. After sweeping a pile of randomly folded laundry aside, she lowers me to the cushion. "This is why I wanted you seated with a drink. I'll be right back."

She returns with a bottle of Dasani. I down a healthy swig of the lukewarm water and turn toward Park's sister who sits at the other end of the sofa. "T-t-tell me everything that h-h-happened."

"One night in July—"

"W-w-which night?"

"Saturday, the twenty-first."

Oh, my God! It was the day after their disagreement over the embezzler and the first day of his weekend conference.

Meadow's voice emerges hoarse, without modulation, almost monotonous. "He took Lamar out for a walk. Some guy approached him. He pulled a gun. Park turned to run. He got a few feet away, but two shots hit him."

The sickening vision makes me gasp.

Meadow sniffs back tears, her voice thick. "One bullet hit his hip bone and shattered his pelvis; one fractured his femur, the big leg bone. As he fell, his head clipped the corner of a concrete planter. Luckily, he only had a severe concussion and not a skull fracture. Still, with his head injury and the loss of blood, he nearly died. The doctor told my parents they had to revive him in the ER because his heart stopped."

A painful wrench forces my forehead to my knees. As I shiver, my heart races.

"Park didn't have any ID on him. His cell phone and his watch also disappeared. Because of the head injury, he was in a medically-induced coma the first week. His office manager finally identified him and got in touch with us." Meadow's hand stroked my hair. "It's okay now. The bullets missed all his organs, although some big blood vessels and his bones were damaged. He's had two operations so far, and physically he's doing better. But . . ."

I sit up despite the spinning in my head. "What?"

Meadow looks away as if reading something written on the wall across the room. "At first, the surgeon didn't know if he could save Park's leg. He said there was a chance it wouldn't heal properly and may need to be amputated. I had never seen my big brother cry before. He said if they took his leg, he would kill himself."

Tears on the edges of Meadow's lashes spilled over. We clasp hands and sit in mourning silence. I have a choking sensation in my throat as if a small ball is lodged there creating a paralyzing dry socket.

Meadow squeezes my hand. "But don't worry. Park won't lose his leg now. It finally started healing. But he kept asking about his dog until we had to tell him. It was awful when he found out Lamar was gone. He's been so depressed he hasn't wanted to do much in physical therapy and won't even try weight-bearing exercises." Meadow slaps her hands on her chest, like an excited preteen with badly applied eye makeup. "Oh, my God! I forgot. You have Lamar! How did you find him?"

I relate the call I received earlier in the day about Lamar's imminent death and his physical condition. "The vet found a wound on him. Maybe it came from being grazed by one of the bullets."

"That's probably why he ran away."

"The animal shelter retrieved Park's contact information from Lamar's microchip. But with his phone was out of service and his business shut down, no one responded to them." My gaze shifts to a large pile of mail, tilted at a precarious angle on the kitchen counter. "How are his bills getting paid?"

"His mortgage and utilities are debited from his account. I don't know about the rest."

"Is he still in the hospital?"

"He was moved to a rehab place last week."

"Will he be able to walk again?"

Meadow nods. "The doctors are optimistic. Once the metal rods bolted onto the screws had been removed, he got feeling all down his leg and into his foot."

"Metal rods?"

A faint revulsion flits across Meadow's face. "They were on the outside and attached to metal pins inside his leg. It was *really* gross. Mom couldn't stop crying. Finally, Park told her to go home, and I was elected to stay. Then he got super mad because I was trying to find you. He said he didn't want to see you and, for like two weeks, he refused to see me too."

Rather than being upset with Park's insistence not to have me at his bedside, I squash a feeble stirring of shame as though I am responsible for what happened to him. This area of town has had an uptick in the number of robberies and assaults with an undesirable element prowling for tourist and resident victims. I should have done more to warn him about walking after dark. "How often have your parents been back since he was injured?"

"Mom was here until we learned Park wouldn't lose his leg. Dad and River came for a few days, but they've had to run the fairs scheduled through the rest of the summer. I've been keeping all of them up to date on his progress."

Considering the Robinsons' financial situation, they likely can't afford frequent trips. Maybe I can cover the airfare and hotel costs for their next visit. "When will they be coming back?"

"The end of October. Okay, now I have a question for you. Did you break up with my brother? Is that why he didn't want me to contact you?" Meadow gave me the look of a parent who suspects a guilty child.

"We argued the night before he was . . ." Guilt and pain lodges at the back of my throat. "He said he needed time to think. He was scheduled to be at a conference all weekend. When I hadn't heard from him after several days, I called and left voice mails and texts, but he never answered any of them."

"Why didn't you call his office?"

"I did. He'd been doing the accounting work for my rescue group, so I called as a client rather than a pissed-off girlfriend. They didn't tell me anything, and later I received a letter saying his firm was terminating our professional relationship."

"They sent those letters to everyone. Without Park, money wasn't coming in. He had to let his office people go."

"I figured the termination letter was his way of ending our personal relationship too."

"You should know Park wouldn't do that." A touch of arrogance colors Meadow's voice with a slight I-know-my-brother-better-than-you superiority to it.

"I didn't think he would either, so I drove over here with the fob and key he gave me."

Meadow blinks several times. "You did?"

"I found his car parked in his designated space, so I figured he was home. When I walked in music was blaring, the place looked like a party had just ended, and there was a trail of clothes leading to the guest bedroom."

Park's sister looks away, pinkness tinging her cheeks.

My words roll off my tongue with delightful ease. "I heard a man shouting, and a woman saying, 'Oh God' over and over. I assumed it was Park and his new girlfriend, so I threw the fob and key on the floor and left."

His sister sags with relief. She licks her lips and lifts her flushed face to me. "Well, it wasn't Park. I had a . . . friend stay over."

"A very good friend from the sound of things."

"Are you going to say anything to Park? To my parents? They left me here to help him, but I got bored. Anyway, my friend's gone back to college."

"Don't worry. It's none of my business." My gaze shifts to the mail on the island counter. Filled with a sense of capability and purpose, I stand. In the kitchen, I separate the correspondence into smaller stacks. Mostly junk comprises the pile, but some invoices and notices of payments due have not been opened.

While I sort, Meadow gathers up the scattered clothes and shoes. She comes back from the bedroom and leans her hip against the counter. "Want me to help?"

I grab a garbage bag from under the sink. "Go pick up all the empties and trash."

When Meadow returns with the bag half-full, I dump in advertisements, catalogs, circulars, and magazines. I find a rubber band in Park's desk drawer, bundle a packet of bills together, and put them in my purse.

Meadow knots the ends of the trash bag. "What are you going to do with that mail?"

"I'm going to pay the bills that are still owed. Do you have the fob and key I left here?"

Meadow retrieves them from a kitchen drawer. "I was weirded out when I found them on the living floor. I didn't think I was that messy."

I pocket the set. "I'm keeping Lamar with me until Park is home. Right now I need to go pick him up at the vet's office. You can tell your brother I found his dog. The poor little guy was so matted and dirty, the groomer probably had to shave him down to his skin. With his wound and how skinny he is, I don't think Park should see him yet."

"Can I tell him what happened?"

"It's up to you, but make sure he understands that for now, Lamar is mine."

Meadow squeezes me in a tight hug. "Thank you."

After we exchange cell numbers, I say, "Let me know how everything goes."

"I will. I can't wait to give Park the news."

CHAPTER 56

WHEN I ARRIVE home, I can't tell who's happier, Mia or Lamar. Both whine in delight, bump and sniff each other. At one point, they stand silent and still with Lamar's head resting on top of Mia's, the dachshund equivalent of a hug.

My phone rings an hour later and Park's sister's name appears on the screen. "Hi, Meadow."

"It's not Meadow."

Park's husky baritone with its underlying sexy sweetness makes my heart stop. "Hello, Park."

"My sister told me everything."

"Don't worry. Lamar is with me and Mia."

"How is he?"

"Right now he looks more like a short-haired dachshund, except for his ears and tail. The groomer gave him a boot camp buzz cut." I smile at the two dogs curled together in one bed.

"When can I see him?"

I came to a decision on the drive home. Will Park hate me for doing this? "When will you be standing upright?"

"What?"

"Meadow said you've been refusing to do therapy. They want you to get on your feet."

His voice carries a hint of defensive anger. "It hurts like hell. I've tried, but one minute is too long."

"Well, when you can do it, I'll bring Lamar to see you."

"You don't get to decide that. He's *my* dog."

"Not anymore. He's now registered to the foundation. I'll be waiting for your call. Bye." After hitting the disconnect button, I sit with my phone still pressed to my ear. Is keeping Lamar away from Park for his own good? Or is it payback for keeping me in the dark for months? "No!" I say aloud. "This is the right thing to do."

For several days, Park uses his sister's phone to demand Lamar be brought to the rehab center. Each time, I ask, "Are you standing for a minute yet?" Today my phone rings while I'm working in my office.

When I answer, Park says, "I'm in PT right now and calling to tell you I stood for one minute today." He follows this with a sound like a snarling dog. "Now bring—"

"Let me talk to your therapist."

"You don't believe me?"

I don't answer.

"Fine!" Muted music plays in the background then Park growls, "She wants to talk to you."

An unfamiliar voice comes on the phone. "Hi, this is Doug. How can I help you?" His enthusiastic tone probably feels like salt on sore skin to his hostile client.

"Did Park really stand for a minute today?"

"Yeah, he did. Of course, I was holding him with a gait belt, in case he fell."

"What's a gait belt?"

"It's made of canvas with a buckle. We wrap it around the client's waist to safely help with sitting, standing, or walking."

"So you weren't holding him up?"

"Nooo."

Doug's hesitance tells me he may not have held Park up, but he is holding something back. "Are you saying he was upright but mostly on his good leg?"

"Yeah, but he's come a long way in just a week."

Meadow fills me in daily on Park's progress along with the epithets he mutters, which often include my name. The problem is now Lamar. The dachshund has gained weight but still looks like a concentration camp survivor. He needs more good food and time for his hair to grow out. Will the dog's changed appearance have a detrimental effect on Park's recovery? "Tell him I want you to call me when he's able to stand for one minute, unassisted, and on both legs."

Even over the phone, I sense Doug's grin. "You sure you don't want to tell him yourself? Sounds like you get off on living dangerously."

CHAPTER 57

THAT EVENING, MEADOW calls and, in a wheedling voice, says, "Park is really trying hard. Why aren't you letting him see Lamar?"

"It's for the dog's sake. Before the shooting, Park was the leader of the pack, and Lamar was the follower. Now with his human in a weakened state, the dog will take over as the alpha male and become protective. Lamar could become aggressive toward others, like me and my dog. After all, his fierceness kept him alive on the streets but nearly got him killed at the shelter. I've seen it happen before."

"Wow, I didn't know about that."

"People dump or give away their family pets all the time because they attack other animals or people. The dogs are just doing what comes naturally as leaders of the pack. None of the owners stepped up to assume the role, so they had to do it. I can't allow that to happen with Lamar. Psychologically, he's still recovering from his ordeal too. When Park is strong enough to be the leader again, we'll come to visit. But right now, I'm the alpha Lamar needs to get over his trauma."

After Meadow relays this information, she reports her brother no longer follows the therapist's instructions with angry protestations but grits his teeth and does the work, often more than is asked. Also his insistent phone calls to bring Lamar to the rehab center stop.

A week later, Doug calls. "I'm letting you know Park is not only standing for more than a minute on his injured leg but taking a couple of steps too. I wish all my clients had a dog they wanted to see as much as he does."

"That's great news," I say, all hale and hearty, but sad because Park doesn't want to see *me* as much as Lamar, if at all. "When can I bring his dog to the center?"

"Anytime, just let the front desk know." He pauses. "Meadow wants to talk with you."

His sister's voice rushes through the phone in an excited torrent. "Isn't it great? Park is doing so much better now. I couldn't believe it when I saw him *walking* today. Of course, he held onto the parallel bars but he crossed from one end to the other. Listen, can you wait until tomorrow afternoon or the next day to bring Lamar?"

"Why?"

"Park wants me to arrange for a barber to come here. He hasn't had a haircut or shaved since he was hospitalized. He looks scruffier than River."

I laugh. "Lamar won't care how he looks."

"No, but my brother cares how he'll look to you."

A feeling bordering on euphoria fills my heart. "Just let me know the day and time."

Two days later, I prep for my visit to the rehab center. I part my hair in the middle and secure it in a long ponytail. I dress in tight, white jeans, despite my mother's admonition that, even in Florida, it is fashion suicide to wear white after Labor Day. I pair the jeans with a gold-chained, crystal-embellished Gucci belt, and a loose, white silk blouse. I want to appear casual-chic and sexy. Park once said he was more turned on when I wore white rather than black. Of course, at the time, he was referring to my bra and panties.

The October weather remains unseasonably warm with no hint of cooler autumn temperatures during the day. I park my SUV in a space under the shade of a magnificent Florida maple soaring into the sky. I eye the cream-colored Mediterranean-style rehab center where Park waits for me and Lamar.

After unlatching my seatbelt, I turn to face Kit in the passenger seat. "As soon as I've talked with someone in charge and with Park, I'll come out to get the dogs."

I leave the car running and the AC on. A low hedge, trimmed with startling symmetry, and unoccupied teak benches line the path to the double sliding front doors. Despite the facility's cleanliness, the faint smell of powerful antiseptics and boiled potatoes wafts through the air. Lights glare too bright and sounds bounce off hard surfaces, magnified to an uncomfortable loudness. I locate the nursing supervisor and discuss Lamar's introduction to the center. With the arrangements settled, I head to Park's room.

Taking a deep breath, I enter. Meadow sits on the end of his hospital bed, her legs crossed, leaning forward with her elbows on her knees, like a kindergartener listening to an enthralling storyteller. Park is in a wheelchair, silhouetted against bright sunlight streaming through a window.

On the outside, I smile at the brother and sister. Inside, I shatter into tiny brittle pieces.

CHAPTER 58

I HAD PREPARED myself for Park to look different. Meadow said he lost weight. But the contrast between the man who used to swing me up into his arms and dance around the room and the one before me is unbelievable. Without Meadow there, I might think I'm in the wrong room.

Park appears to have lost twenty to thirty pounds from his already lean, muscular frame. The fresh haircut makes his head look smaller and vulnerable, like a little boy on the first day of school. His usual ruddy skin is dead white, his face all sharp bones and gaunt cheeks. The tiny dark hairs of his facial stubble contrast sharply with his paleness, like a miniature crop poking through a snowy expanse.

I stifle my rage at the injustice of this beautiful man damaged by such a senseless act of violence. The suffering he's endured is etched on his drawn face. His once-powerful body sits in the prison of a wheelchair wearing clothes that hang limply on him.

Park turns a disinterested gaze on me then surveys my feet. "Where's Lamar?"

His first words hit me like an invisible fist punching the air from my lungs. I step forward. "Hello, Park. It's nice to see you again after all this time."

His eyes blink behind a drab pair of brown glasses. Likely his Cole Haan designer frames are lost or broken. "Sorry. Did you bring Lamar?"

"He's out in the car with my sister and Mia. Before you can see him, there's some training I need to do first."

The dark pupils of his eyes flare. "What kind?"

"Has he ever been around wheelchairs, walkers, or canes before?"

"No."

"He has to be introduced to the different smells, noises, surfaces, and people here. After all, he's been through a lot too. I need him to be okay with the equipment and all the other new things in this place."

Park speaks in a hollow, shaky voice. "What if he's afraid?"

"We'll go home, come back tomorrow, and do it again. I take it you don't want to see him only today. You'd like him to visit as often as possible, right?"

He nods.

"Then we'll do this my way. If everything goes well on the way to this room, the next step is how *you* react." Park leans forward in the wheelchair, exhibiting the first sign of interest, so I continue. "You have to be Lamar's leader the second he enters this room. Don't try to touch him, talk to him, or make eye contact. If he starts to rush you, make noises, or jump around like he used to, redirect him." I turn my head toward Meadow. "That goes for you too. Lamar needs to remain calm."

Park shoots his sister a brooding glance. "We'll do whatever you say."

"Okay. I'll go get him. It might take a while, so be patient."

Meadow scoots toward the edge of the mattress. "Do you need any help?"

"No, I've got this."

She looks at me in a searching, almost disappointed way, as if she hopes for something to do other than entertain Park. "By the way, I *love* your belt."

When I walk outside the rehab center, Kit exits the vehicle. "How did it go?"

I look around, like I stumbled into a strange neighborhood, unsure how I ended up here. "He looks so . . . so broken. But right now, he's only interested in Lamar."

"Not you?"

Instead of answering, I head to the rear of my SUV and open the hatchback. Mia and Lamar press close to the front gate of the dog crate. I grab the dual dog leash that allows the two canine companions to walk next to each other in the same way a visually impaired person holds onto a sighted person's elbow. With both dogs coming to the center for the first time, my hope is for Lamar to be more focused on his duty to guide Mia and less on his fears. Kit follows me inside.

The residents and staff are ready. As we walk the hallways, various people roll past in wheelchairs, cross in front of us with walkers, or thump a cane on the floor. I instruct everyone to follow The Dog Whisperer's *no talk, no touch, and no eye contact* rule. The people and Lamar do remarkably well.

Outside Park's door, I say, "We're coming in."

I stop halfway across the room. At first, Lamar doesn't respond. Then his nose twitches and he sniffs the air. Seconds later, he fixates on the figure in the wheelchair.

Park's hands grip each other with white knuckles as if to prevent himself from reaching out for his beloved pet. "Lamar, come."

With tentative steps, the dog moves forward. His brown eyebrow spots bob up and down like a seesaw. Lamar stops next to the chair's footrest.

Park points to the floor, his gaze averted. "Sit."

Lamar sits. The dog pins back his ears, and small quivers of anxiety run down his back. The tip of his tongue pops out for tiny air licks. Everyone freezes into a suspended state then Mia emits a snort of impatience and stretches out on the laminate floor. Lamar looks at her, slides his feet in front of him, and rests his head on his paws.

I breathe a sigh of relief. "Do you want to hold him now?"

Park's thin hand rubs his forehead as he shifts his hips with a stifled grunt of pain.

Meadow clambers off the bed. "Do you need to lie down?"

He nods and stares at me, as though to telepathically reject any offers of assistance or sympathy.

I tug the leash, and the dogs stand up. "Let me see if Lamar has to go out. Get in bed, and I'll bring him back, so the two of you can rest together." I walk out rather than watch Park transfer from the wheelchair to his bed.

Kit leans against the hallway wall, bent over her cell phone. "Done already?"

"I'm bringing Lamar back in a few minutes."

When we return, I put his dog on the bed with Park. But as soon as Mia and I turn to leave the room, Lamar whines and sits on the edge of the mattress, readying himself to jump off. In the end, I set Mia on Park's other side. "You'll have to keep both of them with you. Meadow and I will grab some coffee and be back in thirty minutes."

Meadow leads the way to a visitors' lounge after being introduced to Kit. When we seat ourselves in plastic chairs, I take a sip of overheated coffee. "He's . . . so different."

An emotion that is akin to sharp pain flashes in Meadow's eyes. "I forgot how he must look to someone who hasn't seen him. When he was in the hospital with half his head shaved and ugly black stitches, his eyes swollen shut, and tubes going in and out of everywhere, I could barely stand to look at him myself." She stirs her coffee with a thin, wooden stick and stares into its creamy depths. "He's been really sick for the last week."

"Why?"

"In the hospital, he took a lot of pain meds. He needed them to cope with the surgeries. After being transferred here, the doctor started to wean him off, but a few days ago Park insisted on going cold turkey. Yesterday is the first day he didn't throw up or shake like a wet dog. The pain and withdrawal made his physical therapy hard. Finally, he agreed to take prescription-strength Tylenol but nothing stronger."

If my guilt right then was paint, I'd have enough to cover this entire building inside and out. "Why didn't you tell me? I made him stand for one minute before he could see Lamar."

"It's okay. Doug knew he wasn't taking any heavy-duty painkillers. He said he'd rather patients gut it out because the pills can mask results. Like the old saying goes: No pain, no gain. Doug expects him to make really fast progress now."

Upon our return to Park's room, Kit says she'll wait in the hall. For whatever reason, my sister doesn't want to see Park. When Meadow and I walk in, each dog presses against Park's body like furry bolsters, their heads at his feet. He lies with his hands resting on their backs like a poolside sun worshipper on a lounge chair.

All three of them snore.

CHAPTER 59

EVERY DAY FOR a week, I bring Lamar to the rehab center for a visit. The first time I don't bring Mia along, both dogs experience separation anxiety. When I put Lamar in the crate without his friend, he whines and whimpers. In turn, Mia stumbles to her doggie bed, the picture of dejection.

I frown at my unhappy pet. Too bad Park and I haven't bonded like our dogs. He only needs me as a temporary caretaker. During each visit, he gives no indication we have ever been in an intimate relationship. Our interactions border on unnatural animation and politeness, like in-laws meeting for the first time. On Friday, I bring Lamar to Park's room, hand him over, and turn to leave for their hour of alone time.

Park says, "Can you stay with us today? I need to talk with you about something important, and I can't do it with Meadow around."

My heart lurches. Every day I ache with a physical need to be close to Park, but his indifference riddles me with invisible wounds. I often weep in my car after he visits with Lamar. Taking a composing breath, I spin to face him and return to his bedside.

Park's amiable countenance flattens into a serious expression. "Is Angie okay?"

Why is he concerned about Angie? "Uh, yeah. She's fine. Why?"

Park closes his eyes and sinks back against his pillow. At last, he lifts his lids. "Two weeks after I was shot, I told the detectives that her boyfriend, Brent Hoover, was the person who tried to kill me."

CHAPTER 60

I LET OUT a helpless laugh. "Sorry. I . . . Are you sure?"

"When I regained consciousness, I didn't remember anything. But then the medication wore off and my memory came back."

"How did you know Brent was the gunman?"

"When I was walking Lamar, I didn't pay attention to the guy who approached us, but he called out my name. When I looked up, Brent said, 'This isn't personal' and pulled out a gun. I turned to run but not fast enough."

Oh my God! This explains why Angie's boyfriend left suddenly and without warning. He found out Park was still alive. "But why would he want to kill you?"

"I discovered he embezzled from Bartholomew Gubelmann's used car business."

My mouth falls open. Not because Brent defrauded the company he worked for, but my shock comes from the realization that, once again, Park uncovers illegal activity; first, with Ren-Faire, then with my foundation, and now with the car dealership. Is embezzlement now the crime du jour?

Park says, "I found purchase orders and sales invoices at Excelsior Motors that weren't adding up."

"Did you tell Barty?"

Park flashes a slightly rueful smile. "I should have, but considering how clueless he is about his business, I contacted Brent instead and asked him questions. I think I spooked him. He must have decided to kill me, so the complete forensic audit would be stopped or postponed, and he would have time to get away. A couple of weeks after the shooting and before I shut down my office, I instructed the staff to send everything to another CPA. He found the evidence showing Brent had stolen over two million dollars in the last five years." Park explained a convoluted bookkeeping program that allowed Angie's former boyfriend to collect deposits from buyers and not have the monies reflected in the final purchase price.

"Have the police located the money or Brent?"

"The funds were traced to an overseas account. They're not sure where he and the money are now, but he has an arrest warrant for attempted murder and fraud."

I tell him about Brent's abrupt departure and how much it shocked Angie. "Why didn't the police question her after you told them about Brent? I mean, she doesn't know anything, but wouldn't they want to talk to his girlfriend?"

"I didn't tell them about Angie."

"Why not? She didn't do anything wrong."

"That's why. I didn't want the police showing up at the veterinary hospital asking questions she couldn't answer or getting her family upset."

I tap a loose fist against my chest, grateful for his discretion. "I have to tell Angie about this."

"Of course, you do, especially if he tries to contact her. Has he?"

"I don't think so. She would let me know."

"Not if he convinced her to keep quiet."

Brent's nice-knowing-you text flashes across my thoughts and Angie's resulting anger. "After the way he left and now with what's he done to you, I'm sure there's nothing he could do or say to redeem himself with her."

When I leave the rehab center with Lamar, I call and invite Angie for wine and pizza at my house that night. After we polish off half a bottle of expensive Pinot Noir and a thin crust veggie supreme, I tell Angie what I learned from Park. My friend's reaction surprises me.

Instead of being ashamed of her poor choice in men or displaying her volatile Italian temper, Angie narrows her eyes, in a somewhat analytical manner. "Now it makes sense. He left to avoid being arrested. Still, what he did to Park is horrible. I'm so sorry, but none of us could have possibly seen *that* coming."

Except for Rita and me.

Angie shakes her head. "I can't believe *your* former boyfriend uncovers the fraud perpetrated by *my* former boyfriend."

I tilt my ear toward my shoulder. "And *your* former boyfriend tries to kill *my* former boyfriend."

"Then *my* former boyfriend sends me a *nice knowing you* text and flees the country. I guess I should trust my mother's instincts more. She said Brent had shifty eyes. Considering how many of my *uncles* are in the mob, she knows firsthand about thieves and murderers."

"I worried how you would take this. I didn't know if you had gotten over Brent yet."

Angie tips her wine glass and takes a long swallow. "You know, they say the recovery period from a failed relationship is half the time you were together. Brent and I dated for six months, and it's been three months since he sent his awful text. Trust me. I got over him way ahead of schedule."

Unlike Angie, I haven't gotten over Park according to the same formula. "You're not just saying that, are you?"

"No. I really mean it. I hoped Brent would be Mr. Right because he was buff, handsome, and had a full-time job. I even put up with him saying I had a fat ass."

I gasp. Never had Angie allowed a boyfriend to use the F word before.

My friend pours herself another glass. "It's hard to believe, huh? You know, growing up I assumed I would marry young, like my mom and grandmother. They told me nice girls could always find nice boys to marry. Like being nice was all it took. They can't understand why it's been so hard for me to meet Mr. Right." Angie twirls a long strand of her natural red locks around her finger. "Maybe it's my hair."

"What does your hair have to do with it?"

Angie sighs. "There are just so few men brave enough to play with fire."

I laugh and refill my glass. "You may be right."

"When I closed in on thirty, I decided to have a positive outlook and keep my heart and mind open to all possibilities. But it was hard when each relationship ended, whether by my choice or his. Despite all my breakups, I always thought if I tragically died, many of my former boyfriends would come to my funeral. Brent is the only one I wouldn't want there. But I'll be front and center at his and probably get kicked out for bad behavior. Can you be arrested for spitting on a corpse?"

"I don't know, but I'll be sure to bail you out of jail." I raise my goblet in the air.

Angie taps the rim of her glass to mine. "That's what friends are for."

CHAPTER 61

PARK'S PROGRESS IN regaining his strength and mobility increases daily, but I worry about him walking Lamar upon his release from the rehab center. What will happen if he's stopped by another criminal on the street?

I search the Internet and find a low platform treadmill for dogs with a wider belt and less motor vibration than ones for humans. I discuss the exercise equipment with Park. "I saw this online and thought it might be a good thing for Lamar until you're able to take him for long walks again."

Park studies the information sheet I printed out. "Doug reminded me again today that I would need to take it slow when I go home. With this, I wouldn't have to worry about Lamar getting the exercise he needs."

I offer to have one set up in his living room before his discharge from the rehab center. Park vows to reimburse me, but I brush him off. "We'll settle up later. Right now I can train Lamar on it. The treadmill might also be good for Mia."

At the last moment, I buy an extra one for my house. After only twenty minutes of introduction, Lamar trots away on the belt, tongue hanging out, and his tail high and wagging. I slow the speed and lift Mia onboard. The two dogs exercise side-by-side. Despite her blindness, Mia exudes walking confidence since nothing blocks her forward progress.

The following week, I can't drive Lamar to the center for several days. I have numerous meetings with the village's construction crew. I call Kit into my office. "Starting tomorrow, I need you to take Lamar to see Park. I'll bring him here."

"Can't Meadow do it? I could drop Lamar off at the condo."

I shake my head. "No, it's not a good idea to leave Lamar with Meadow. I'd feel better if he was in your charge."

As far as I can see, Park's sister isn't a very responsible twenty-one-year-old. Every time I visit his condo, it looks like a pigsty. Gentle reminders and admonitions have little or no effect. After several sets of Park's white sheets become tinged pink because Meadow doesn't separate the wash, I call a cleaning service to come twice a week.

One day at the rehab center, Meadow wore a tank top turned inside out. With a sheepish grin, she said, "I spilled something on it and haven't done the laundry."

I rolled my eyes because she looked like she had gotten dressed in the dark or in a hurry. A week later, I received a frantic phone call when Meadow ran out of gas on the expressway. I dropped everything and rushed to meet her with a one-gallon can. Cars and trucks zoomed past, some honking, as we filled the tank with enough fuel to start the engine.

I also have a second reason for finding a substitute dog transporter for the week. Park's parents and brother are due to fly in tomorrow. I don't know if they are aware I'm only Lamar's temporary dog sitter, but I can't face them or their pity. I pinch the bridge of my nose and will away the slight headache behind my eyes.

Kit's voice radiates concern. "What's wrong?"

"I hoped by now Park would show some interest in me." I tell Kit about not saying I love you to him before his near-death injury. "I've been trying to look and be the kind of woman he would be attracted to again, but he still treats me like a . . . friend."

"Park isn't interested in a Barbie doll in a business suit." She eyes my black pencil skirt and white silk blouse. "He fell for you and all your wackiness. He wants a woman with weird-colored hair, mismatched clothes, and more than the usual amount of body parts showing. I saw his family and, although he looks different than them, he seemed thrilled that you fit right in."

Is Kit right? Have I turned into the woman I think Park wants?

". . . and get Rita to dye your hair. Wear something that shows off your low back tattoo. Something skimpy and sexy will turn him on. Once he's good and interested, you can tell him how you feel."

In a neutral voice, as if negotiating the release of a hostage, I say, "If I say I love him now . . . maybe he'll think I'm doing it out of pity."

"Not if he still loves you. Does he?"

"Meadow asked him how he felt. He never gave her a straight answer, but she's sure his feelings haven't changed. The problem is his body. He has a long road ahead of him to even get physically close to where he was before the shooting. When I first met him, his looks attracted me. But what I feel for him now is way more than skin-deep. There's no one else I'd rather be with. I'm hoping as his body gets stronger, his heart will too."

Kit straightens her shoulders like a boxer ready for the next round. "Don't worry about Lamar. I'll take care of everything and make sure Park gets nice, long visits with him."

My sister's new confidence pleases me. Kit had always preferred to hide in the shadows behind me, her outrageous younger sibling. Betsy used to tell people in an audible whisper, dripping with cheerful disrespect, "Our girl, Kit, is a bit shy." As a teenager, my sister made herself physically ill worrying what people thought of her. As a result, her aloofness and reserve had often been misinterpreted as snobbery. Maybe her reticence accounts for the online gambling addiction. Kit can experience the highs of risky behavior without having to interact with real people.

The following week when my phone rings, I nearly drop it when I see Park's name on the screen. Fumbling with the device, my finger trembles when I hit the button to answer the call.

Is Brent calling me from Park's phone, or is it someone else?

CHAPTER 62

"HELLO?" MY VOICE sounds small and uncertain.

"Hi, it's me."

The deep baritone sounds like Park, but I can't be certain. "*Who* is this?"

No one answers for several seconds. "It's me."

"Me, who?"

A gusty sigh blows from the phone. "It's Park. Who did you think it was?"

Blissful relief runs through me like a shot of brandy. "Brent or a scavenger who found your phone."

"What are you talking about?"

"I know your phone went missing after you were shot. Brent might have taken it or some druggie who searched your pockets before the police showed up. When I saw your name on the screen, I thought one of them was calling me."

Park's voice rumbles in my ear. "Don't worry, it's just me. While Mom was here, she bought me a replacement."

"And she was able to get you the same number?"

"My office manager handled that after mine wasn't recovered. Mom also brought in my laptop, so I've been catching up on things. Listen, I want you to know I'll repay you for all the money you've laid out the last several weeks, including Lamar's treadmill."

"You don't have to. I—"

"No, I do. I have the money, but Meadow couldn't access it. I appreciate all you've done, but it's more than I can ask of a friend."

A friend?

In our six months of dating, we hadn't developed nicknames for each other, made joint purchases, or taken a trip together. In a sense, our relationship had still been shiny and new. But is calling me a friend Park's first step in an official breakup? Rejection is tough to go through once but twice borders on cruelty.

The sting of his words fills me with petulant resolve. "We're more than *friends,* and you know it."

"Yes, we once were. Still, I feel we should probably not—"

"Even if we are no longer a couple, the fact that I had to find out what happened to you all on my own is not something one friend would do to another."

"I'm sorry, but I just felt it was in your best interest to not have to deal with what I was going through."

"You left me dangling for weeks. If you didn't want me to visit you, I would have been upset but complied. Keeping me in the dark is not what one of my friends, let alone my lover, would do even if they're upset with me."

"You're right. It's just that I was in a bad way physically, and then emotionally when I found out Lamar was gone."

"If I had known he was missing, I could have used my resources to find him before he spent weeks on the street."

"I realize that now. You have every right to be angry with me. I appreciate all you've done, but I still feel that we can't . . ."

I don't want to hear his reasons for repaying me, for no longer loving me, for ending a relationship which had barely begun. His words wash over me like an unfamiliar language as my eyes burn, and my throat knots into a tight ball.

"Marin? Are you there?"

"I'm . . . I don't . . ." My face grows hot as I struggle to speak.

"I can't understand you. There's something wrong with this damn phone. We're breaking up."

A juvenile, vengeful anger fills me. "We're breaking up? How dare you do this to me over the phone?" My voice is thick with emotion, but my words come out loud and clear.

"That's not what I—"

I hit the disconnect button, needing time to organize my thoughts, bring my emotions under control, and plan. I ignore the ringing and allow Park's call to roll over to voice mail. My phone dings with a text.

We have to talk.

I wait for a moment before my fingers fly across the keypad. *Not today. Tomorrow.*

OK.

With the air of one determined to take charge, I smack my phone onto the desk blotter. I will be the one behind the wheel when it comes to the future of their relationship. Not Park. He may be the brake pedal, but I'll operate the accelerator, driving us forward or causing us to crash and burn.

CHAPTER 63

KIT DRIVES LAMAR to see Park on Saturday afternoon and tells him I'll visit that evening to talk. To pull off my plan for being dressed like a jet setter with money to burn, I enlist Meadow and Angie's help. In exchange, I'm taking them to dinner at Ta-boo on Worth Avenue then we're going to several Palm Beach nightclubs. The two women remain in my SUV when I park at the rehab center.

That morning, Rita added scarlet color to my ebony hair from my jawline down. I squeezed into what Angie calls my *Come Get Me Dress,* a nude and black lace body-hugging mini with a hem that ends well above my knees and just below my private parts. I'm wearing my Jimmy Choo ankle strap heels, smoky eye makeup, skin bronzer, and deep red lipstick.

Meadow laughs as I slide out of the SUV, careful not to flash anyone in the vicinity. "I almost pity my brother. Remember he's not at full strength yet."

"I'm counting on it. If I'm not back in twenty minutes, come inside."

Two of the afternoon shift nurses recognize me and stare with open mouths when I ass-shay past their work station. One heavyset, black woman gives me a wide smile and waves her hand. "You go, girl."

An elderly man in a wheelchair looks stunned as I shimmy around him in my tight dress and nose-bleed heels. At Park's door, I stop and take a deep breath before stepping into the room.

The TV is tuned to a football game. Park reclines with the head of his bed raised. He wears a V-necked T-shirt and a pair of plaid pajama bottoms. I pose with one hand on my hip and wait. His glance shifts to me with a quick sideways movement of his eyes then his whole head jerks in my direction. Without looking away, he points the remote at the screen and turns off the TV. Neither of us speaks for several seconds.

Park breaks the silence first. "You, uh, look . . . nice."

"Only nice? You must need new glasses."

"No, I mean . . . you look great. Is the dress new?"

I run my palm over my breast, down my abdomen, and onto my thigh. "I've had this for years. It's one of my favorite party dresses."

Park's eyes follow my self-caressing hand. His Adam's apple bobs like a red rubber ball. "Are you going to a party?"

"I'm taking Meadow and Angie to dinner then we're going clubbing for a girls' night out." Little does he know that I'd rather be clubbed over the head than go clubbing tonight.

"What's the occasion?"

"I need to take my mind off you only wanting me to be your *friend*." I put my hand on my jutted hip as though I'm posing on the red carpet, waiting to be photographed. A movement catches my eye. Park's pajama bottoms rise with a slight tenting. I glide toward his bed like a supermodel on a catwalk. Before he can stop me, I lay my hand on the bulge. "But it looks like you have more than friendly feelings toward me."

His eyes open wide behind his lenses as he stares at his lap then looks at me. Meanwhile, the physical contact with him sends shockwaves zinging through my body. In the silence, Park and I regard each other like survivors of a surprise attack after the all-clear.

His voice is low and full of wonder. "Damn. I'm not impotent."

"Obviously not."

He focuses on my hand. "Before I was shot, you always turned me on. I was instantly hard. Like someone flipped a switch. The first time you brought Lamar here, you looked gorgeous. But nothing happened. Each time I saw you, I was dead from the waist down."

Tenderness engulfs me. "Park—"

"Doug said it was because I was physically weak. So I worked more, but no matter how much I pushed myself, I couldn't . . ."

My heart softens. Park exerted himself in therapy, not only for Lamar but for me as well. His workouts added a hard layer of muscle to his still too-lean body. Even his injured leg is fleshed out more. His arms, shoulders, and chest show the benefits of weight lifting. But I never considered sex might be the reason he put me in a friend zone.

I wrap my fingers around him. "You needed time to heal. And it appears you have. Am I still only a *friend?*"

His face contorts, so I move my hand and place it over his heart. A lone tear runs under the bottom edge of his glasses and down his cheek. "I couldn't let you be with half a man. You deserve better."

My eyes dampen, and I lay my cheek against his. He pulls me down on the mattress beside him and holds me close. I have never seen a man express bittersweet joy with tears before.

Then he kisses me.

At first, his lips touched mine, slow and gentle, a delicate tasting. He draws back with a curious expression. His irises expand until they swallow all but a narrow ring of chocolate as his eyes linger on my crimson-colored mouth then rise in increments to meet my gaze. We are close, almost nose-to-nose.

He whispers, "I could get lost in your emerald eyes."

He kisses me again, this time parting my lips and opening my mouth. His tongue touches me, withdraws then returns. Park deepens the kiss as he explores the hard edges of my teeth and the softness within. As his passion grows, his mouth demands more of me.

Under the hem of my dress, he rests his warm hand on the inside of my bare thigh. His fingers inch between my legs. I press my thighs together. His hand slides higher until he touches me intimately, probing.

After a time, he breaks away from my lips and nuzzles his face into my throat. "God, you smell good."

I straighten, and his head falls back against the pillow. Something hard pokes me. I raise one hip and pull the TV remote from under my thigh. I smile at a possible joke, but I meet his fierce eyes and falter. His gaze dips downward, cruising over my breasts to where my dress bunches, his hand hidden beneath. I avert my face and my lashes drop to shield my eyes. With a jerky movement, I dislodge him, rise from the bed, and tug down the hem of my too-short dress.

I accomplished my goal to force him to respond to me, but rather than a smug sense of satisfaction, my pulse hammers, and my voice contains a raspy huskiness. "What did you want to talk about?"

He looks at his erection and chuckles. "We could talk about what just came up, or you could lift up that hot dress and do something about it."

My face burns with my plan gone awry. He is supposed to express regret for throwing me aside, not laugh and proposition me. Park relaxes against the pillow, gives me a devilish grin, and sniffs his fingers.

Flutters in the pit of my stomach make my breath catch. I cross my arms over my chest to still my trembling hands. "You called me here to talk. So, talk."

Before Park can respond, Angie and Meadow stagger into the room with high-pitched laughter. Like me, they wear mini-dresses and CFM heels which they teeter on like drunken gazelles. Meadow doubles over, her arms wrap around her abdomen.

I turn to face the two women. "What's going on?"

Angie is less hysterical than Park's sister. "Some old guy in a wheelchair pulled Meadow onto his knees and offered her money for a lap dance."

Using the knuckles of her index fingers, Meadow wipes her lower lashes. "He said the other stripper got away, but he was willing to pay for the two of us."

Angie smiles at me. "A nurse had to help get her loose. You ready to go? Our reservation is at eight, right? Hi, Park."

He waves one of his hands as the other strategically covers his lap.

Although I'm anxious to hear what Park has to say, maybe another day's delay is a good thing. After all, I've been waiting for months. Now it's his turn. I flash him a false smile. "Sorry. I've got to go. We'll talk the next time I visit."

He frowns. "Wait, I, I—"

I link arms with Meadow and Angie and head to the door. "See ya."

CHAPTER 64

AS SOON AS the car doors close, both Angie and Meadow say in unison, "What happened?"

I explain how Park has not been able to respond to me sexually. "That's the whole reason he treated me so coolly and called me a *friend*."

"Men!" Angie sneers with faint disgust. "What did he expect? He was shot twice and nearly died. Did he think the first time he saw you he'd start drooling and step on his penis?"

I start the engine. "I don't know, but this dress did the trick. He got a hard-on the minute I walked into the room."

Angie's coffee-colored eyes sparkle. "What did *you* do?"

"I wrapped my hand around him and pointed out that he must still have feelings for me. He pulled me onto the bed with him then—"

"Puh-leeze!" Meadow scrunches her face in comic revulsion. "Can we please stop talking about my brother's junk?"

All of us laugh as I steer the vehicle out of the parking lot and head to Ta-boo. After a delightful dinner of sea bass for me and Angie and a New York strip steak for Meadow, we head to Clematis Street where a string of clubs dot the area. Our first venue is a popular karaoke club with several rooms catering to different groups and musical styles. Meadow volunteers to perform and has a decent voice for pop tunes. She sings with her face twisted in rock star anguish.

From there, we move to a club where a DJ plays a variety of music. We dance together until all three of us moan about our aching feet. Our last stop is a three-storied Irish pub and nightclub. Music videos blast on projection screens. On the rooftop deck, we watch the lights of West Palm Beach. During the evening's bar-hopping, Meadow and Angie drink mixed drinks, some purchased for them by wannabee hookups while I chase three glasses of white wine with ice water. When the night ends at four AM, I call Uber to drive us from the club to my car rather than walk the dark and mostly deserted streets, even though it's only a few blocks. The driver turns out to be a woman paramedic named Liz.

"Sorry your fare isn't going to be more," I say after Meadow and Angie tumble into the backseat.

"That's okay. I'm beat after working two shifts and ready to go home." Liz taps the drop-off information into her cell phone app.

"Two Uber shifts?"

"No. I worked one at the fire station first."

Angie leans forward and drapes her arms over my shoulders. "I'm really hungry. Can we stop somewhere for breakfast?"

When we reach my car, I shift in my seat and face Liz. "There's an all-night diner near the condo where Meadow is staying. Why don't you follow me and have breakfast with us?"

Meadow's head appears between the front seats, and she slurs, "Marin's paying for everything, so my brother will fall back in love with her." She topples sideways in the seat, eyes closed.

When the Uber driver raises her eyebrows, I shrug. "It's a long story."

"And one I'd love to hear over pancakes."

A short time later, three party girls and a woman in a PBFD T-shirt enter the diner. We grab a free booth and soon have white ceramic mugs of coffee in front of us. Liz insists that Meadow and Angie drink water and orange juice to combat the effects of the alcohol in their systems. We order blueberry pancakes, sausage, and hash brown potatoes. While waiting for our food, we regale Liz with my love story and Park's injuries at the hands of an unknown assailant. Neither Angie nor I identify her ex-boyfriend as Park's attacker. It will remain a secret from everybody for now. After all, what does one more secret matter to me?

Liz pauses with a dripping forkful halfway to her mouth. "I heard about that shooting. At first, they didn't know who the victim was."

Meadow tells about the tense first days of Park's hospitalization when his survival was in doubt followed by the possible loss of his leg.

Liz turns to me. "It must have been really hard for you to see him in such bad shape."

Once again, a fierce pain like a sharp needle pierces my flesh. "I didn't know he had been injured. When I couldn't get in touch with him, I thought he'd decided to break up with me. I'm hoping our relationship will get back on track again."

After breakfast, Liz offers to drive Meadow home. I push a one hundred dollar bill into her hand.

Liz's mouth drops open. "Whoa. This is too much."

"No, it's not." Waving good-bye, Angie and I head to my car.

I drop off my friend around six, drive home, and slip off my shoes and dress. Grateful that the dogs are with Mrs. R, I crawl into bed. My phone chimes two hours later.

The screen name reads Park.

CHAPTER 65

"WHAT?" I MUMBLE beneath the sheet.

Park's voice sounds crisp and cheerful. "Are you sleeping?"

I make no effort to sound awake. "Yes."

"You must have had a late night. Meadow didn't even answer her phone this morning. All of you got home safe and sound?"

"Uh-huh." I yawn. "Good-bye."

Two hours later, my phone rings again. I pull the pillow over my head until the ringing stops. Typing keys and a bell sounds with an incoming text. A minute or an hour later, the ringing wakes me for a third time.

"What do you want?"

Park says, "I have a favor to ask."

"Yes. I can bring Lamar later today."

"What I need is for you to take Lamar and me home to the condo. The doctor has given the orders for my release. I'd have Meadow come, but I doubt she's in any shape to drive. Will you do it?"

I sit up and squint. The right side of my bedroom glows brightly with morning sun while the left remains dim with long shadows. I pull my hair into one long dark rope over my shoulder. The tresses caress my bare breasts and the tops of my thighs with a sensual thrill. "Can it be later this afternoon? I need more sleep."

"Yes. Thank you for doing this."

"Well, what are *friends* for." I disconnect the call and fall back on my pillow.

A few minutes after two, I retrieve Lamar, Mia, and my two senior adoptees, Harley and Davidson, from Mrs. R's house. I drop the three older dogs at home, settle Lamar into the car crate by himself, and send Park a text: *OMW*. I also manage to get Meadow to answer her phone and give her a heads-up about Park's release.

"Why today?" His sister groans.

"You can't blame him for wanting to get out of there. You've got at least two hours to clean the place up."

When I enter Park's room with Lamar, he is dressed in street clothes with an aluminum cane hooked over the arm of a chair. His jeans and polo shirt are still a little large on his frame. His skin has a ruddy glow from sitting in the sun on the rehab center's outdoor patio.

I drop the leash, and Lamar scurries toward him. After petting his dog's head, Park eyeballs me from head to toe and smiles. "You look . . . great."

I'm wearing low-rise skinny jeans with a black midriff halter top and my white majorette boots, the same ones I had on when I met Park at the Dachshund Derby. My hair is pulled into poufy anime pigtails.

A wheeled, carry-on suitcase and several reusable grocery bags sit on the bed. Park picks up Lamar's leash and the footed cane while I grab his belongings. Well-wishes and good-byes from the staff on duty delay our departure from the facility. Once outside, I instruct Park to wait on a teak bench at the front entrance with Lamar while I bring the car around. Although my SUV has running boards that extend out when the door opens, I brought a small plastic stool, in case Park can't hoist his leg up to the assist step.

I leave the vehicle idling at the front entrance and approach him. "Let me get Lamar inside then I can help you."

After closing the dog crate, another door clunks shut. The silhouette of Park's head shows from the passenger seat. I glance at him when I slide behind the wheel. His lips are pressed tight, and the long line of his jaw is bunched. He stares out the windshield as if the landscape appears new and foreign.

I crane my head forward. "Are you okay?"

He clears his throat. "Yeah. Seems like years since I've been more than a few feet from a hospital bed."

Having never been bedridden or deathly ill, I can only image the fears that haunt him about what his future will entail. My breath hitches with a new realization. Bringing his dog to the rehab center allowed me the opportunity to see Park whenever I wanted. He was a captive on display for me. Will he still want me around once he's home with Lamar?

CHAPTER 66

I DRIVE THROUGH a brief, but ferocious, tropical shower. With the passing of the rain, the air smells fresher and the afternoon sunlight is golden and rich. Park opens his window a few inches. The warm wind blows in his face and ruffles his hair. He closes his eyes and inhales, his chest rising with each deep breath.

Should we have our talk now? When we reach his condo, Meadow will be there. This time in the car may be our only opportunity to speak, but Park seems to revel in his release from the sad sights, alien sounds, and chemical smells of confinement. I decide not to interrupt his enjoyment of freedom from the rehab center and his reintroduction to the outside world.

Ten minutes later, I park the SUV on the street in front of his building. Park stares at the lobby doors like he's never seen them before.

I reached for my handbag. "Here are my key and fob for the condo doors. I'll meet you inside the lobby after I park."

He opens the passenger door, places his cane on the ground, and gingerly slides off the seat. Once on the ground, he closes the door and, leaning heavily on the cane, he approaches the main entrance and enters. He hobbles to the elevator and keys the button with one hand braced on the wall. The doors open, and he disappears inside.

I throw my hands into the air. Why didn't he wait for me? Now I'll have to call for access. After parking, I release Lamar from the crate and tie his leash to one of my belt loops. I grab the handle of the roller suitcase and loop the canvas bags over my arm.

I make the trek halfway across the parking lot when Meadow runs toward me. "Let me help."

I hand off bags and suitcase. "Did Park send you down?"

Meadow snorts. "He just walked in. I asked where you were, and he got this OMG look on his face. I left before he commented on how the place looked."

"There's a box of Lamar's things still in the back. Let me get it."

When we enter the condo, Park isn't in the main living area. I put the box on the counter and unclip the dog leash. Lamar sniffs the floor and trots down the hall toward the bedrooms.

"Park?" Meadow calls. "Where are you?"

"I needed to lie down."

I step toward the bedroom hallway. My boot heels echo on the tile floor.

Park calls out in a flat voice. "Thanks for the ride, Marin."

I shudder to a stop. "Uh, you're welcome. I—"

"Meadow, will you come in here and lift Lamar onto the bed with me."

"Sure." Her eyes meet mine with a thread of apology in them. "Be right there."

Park says, "Thanks again, Marin."

"Okay. Good . . . bye." I walk to the door and open it.

Meadow follows and speaks in a hushed tone. "He gets like this in the afternoon. His leg hurts, and he's really tired. After resting, he'll be fine. Why don't you stay here with us?"

Park had been awake since early morning as evidenced by his phone calls to me. After receiving his discharge from the doctor, he probably didn't rest while waiting to be picked up. Being the tough guy he thinks he still is, he may have overextended his stamina readying himself to come home.

I can stay and help his sister clean. The place looks better but not near to Park's exacting standards. His belongings and Lamar's need stowed away then I can prepare dinner. Or maybe I'll crawl into bed with him to talk.

Park's deep baritone echoes down the hall. "Is she gone yet?"

The welcome home scenario playing in my head vanishes in a puff of mental smoke. I waggle my fingers at Meadow in a weak farewell.

His sister calls over her shoulder. "She just left."

"Good. Can you . . ."

I head to the elevator with long strides, the tassels of my majorette boots flicking in the air like dismissive little fingers.

CHAPTER 67

AS I DRIVE away from Park's condo, a wave of pure misery and heady anger sweeps over me. At present, I'm the sturdier and healthier one, but the vulnerability Park and I share should be the basis for a stronger relationship, not one dependent on his ability to walk and get an erection.

I stop at a liquor store, purchase a fifth of tequila and two fresh limes. After letting the dogs out, I cut one of the tart fruits into four mouth-wide wedges, retrieve the salt shaker, a shot glass, and open the bottle of Patron. The first hit of tequila is pleasant on the surface with a welcome burn beneath. I feed the dogs then down a second shot. Hours later, I ready the dogs for bed, cry a bit, and do a third shot. I take a shower and drink a fourth shot, I think. At some point, I fall into a sodden and restless sleep.

The next morning Meadow calls. "Park is back in the hospital."

"Whaaat?" I blink, like a sleeping airline passenger waking up to an announcement about the plane landing.

"Soon after you left yesterday, I had to call an ambulance for him."

I sit up with small, painful movements, one hand holding my phone, the other clasping my aching head. I keep my eyes closed. "What happened?"

"He dislocated his hip. The doctor called it sub-something, like a partial dislocation."

"When? How?"

"Park thinks it happened when he got into your SUV."

"I told him I'd help him after I put Lamar inside. I even brought a small stool so he wouldn't have to step up too high, but he didn't wait."

"He felt the pain in his groin on the drive home, but it wasn't until he walked inside the building that he knew something was seriously wrong."

"Why didn't he say anything to me?"

"Oh, I don't know. Maybe because he's a pig-headed man, like most of them are. I had to call an ambulance because I couldn't get him to the car without a wheelchair. He was in so much pain he didn't care."

With my eyes open to slits, the whiteness of the duvet blinds me like a laser beam. "Will he have to have another operation?"

"No. His surgeon fixed it with a mild anesthetic and pain medication."

"It's done? He's going to be okay?"

"The doctor said he was lucky because the joint didn't come all the way out of the hip socket."

Meadow informs me that Park has to stay overnight in the hospital. Then he's ordered to remain on bed rest and restricted movement until the muscles heal. She asks about Lamar's feeding and walking schedule before the call ends.

I rub my aching temples. Sunlight casts a striped pattern across the tile floor causing my stomach to roil. I plod into the kitchen to make a cup of coffee. On the counter, I find an empty plate with droplets of lime juice, a salt shaker lying on its side, and a half-empty bottle of tequila. Somewhere in my woebegone evening of excess, I lost track of an entire lime and six to eight additional ounces of booze. In a panic, I check my phone, but I made no drunken calls or texts last night. The only reminders of the drowning-my-sorrows interlude are a dry mouth and a raging headache.

After drinking several cups of coffee, water, and orange juice, I don low-rise Urban Outfitters camo pants, tan suede, peep-toe ankle boots, and a black tube top. I send a text to Meadow: *Ok to see Park in H?*

Yes. Must rest. Home tomorrow.

I stop at the foundation then head to the hospital to tie up the loose ends of our relationship.

CHAPTER 68

WHEN I ENTER Park's hospital room, a sleeping young man in a leg cast occupies the bed closest to the door. A smattering of pimples dots his forehead. As if to compensate for the restriction of one leg, he's flung his other limbs at odd angles around his body.

The pulled curtain obscures the occupant on the far side of the room. I round the fabric barrier and find Park asleep, flat on his back. Standing at the foot of the bed, I stare at his recumbent form.

This is a bad idea.

Although Park has no IV hook-up, he might still be in pain or doped up, and unable to carry on a rational conversation with me. Also, his roommate lies a few feet away and can eavesdrop on our discussion. I turn to leave then stop. I might as well wait for him to wake up and visit for a few minutes to gauge his mood and physical condition. Sitting on a vinyl armchair in the corner, I take out my phone and check emails.

Sometime later, Park's husky voice says, "How long have you been here?" He presses the controller to raise his head.

I look up from my phone. "Maybe an hour. How do you feel?"

"Sore and worried about Lamar."

"Why?"

"I may have been in a lot of pain yesterday, but I could still see how bad my condo looks."

"Don't worry. He'll be fine." I drop my phone into my purse and stand. "Why didn't you tell me you hurt your hip getting into my car? I could have driven you straight here."

"Until I got out, I didn't know how bad it was."

I approach the side of the bed. "I told you to wait. I brought a stool for you to use, in case something like this might happen. On top of that, you go walking into the condo without waiting for me. Just because I finally gave you a hard-on, it doesn't mean you're at one hundred percent."

A disembodied voice from the other side of the curtain says, "Dude, I hope that's not your sister talking to you."

A swoosh of embarrassed heat filled my cheeks. I forgot about the teenage boy.

Park smiles at me. "She's not my sister."

The world grinds to a halt as I wait. Will he say I'm his friend or his girlfriend?

"She's the most beautiful girl a guy could ever love."

The teen's voice squeaks with adolescent disbelief. "She is?"

"I am?" My voice drawls in wonderment.

An impish light gleams in Park's eyes. "Come closer."

I bend down and whisper, "I love you too."

He stills. "You do?"

"Uh-huh. And I have for a long time."

Park wraps an arm around my back and pulls until my head rests on his chest. He strokes my hair and kisses the top of my head. "Why didn't you tell me?"

"I wanted the time to be right, but it never was."

"Any time is a good time to say I love you."

I straighten so we can see each other. "I'm sorry I didn't tell you before your injury. With the fraud at the foundation, the construction project, and our argument about the embezzler —"

"You mean your sister, Kit."

I work to keep my expression neutral. "What are you talking about? Why do you think my sister stole the money?"

"Because she told me."

I lean back further and raise myself with a palm on his chest. "When?"

"One day when she brought Lamar to the rehab center. She confessed she had a gambling problem and begged you not to reveal her identity." He shakes his head. "I shouldn't have given you such a hard time. You handled the situation the way you thought best. Almost dying made me realize how rigid I had become."

I can't bear his pained look. "You're not rigid. You just have strong convictions."

"If I only had strong convictions, I wouldn't have gotten so angry with you. I'm sorry I demanded you do things my way."

"We're past that now."

"But you thought I had broken up with you." Park covers my hand over his heart. "I wouldn't have stopped talking with you because I was mad."

"I know. It's why I tried so hard to contact you. I even called your office, but they gave me the runaround."

"Did you tell them who you were?"

"No, I just said I was a client." I let out a deep breath. "If I hadn't found Lamar—"

"Thank God, you did." Park's face twists with anguish. "I wanted to die if—"

I place my finger on his lips. "Shhh. His rescue brought us together again. And when you think about it, our dogs are responsible for us meeting in the first place."

"No, we met because you failed to follow the rules."

With mock outrage, I say, "Look who's talking, Mr. No-Balls."

A snorting chuckle sounds from the other side of the room. Park grasps the raised bedrail closest to the curtain and, with slow, cautious movements he scoots to the far side. He straightens the sheet then pats the open space next to him.

My gaze flicks from the empty spot on the mattress to the separating curtain. "I don't want to hurt your hip."

"You won't."

I look in the direction of the room's doorway. "What if someone comes in?"

"So what?"

If Park wants to bend the hospital rules, how can I refuse? After toeing off my shoes, I lie beside him, afraid to place any weight on his fragile pelvis. He pulls my upper body toward him. The warmth of his skin permeates my clothes, and a divine limpness creeps through me.

Park's mouth touches my ear. "Before you showed up in that *dress*, which I can't get out of my mind, I had decided you were better off without an impotent gimp for a boyfriend. Even though this latest injury has set me back, I know I can again be the man you deserve. I love you."

I lift my chin and cup his cheek. "I love you so much."

"Then kiss me."

I place my mouth on his. Park's jaw moves beneath my palm, shadowing the languid movements of his tongue. The taste of him and his familiar scent quicken my pulse. He rolls toward me, forcing me to lie flat. His free hand lowers my tube top and covers my breast.

Park presses his erection against me. "I want you so bad."

"I want you too."

Breathtaking sensations surge through me, thrilling and unnerving, as I lose myself in an intimacy I didn't anticipate. The curtain which separates the two beds twitches. A grunt sounds and the fabric divider skitters on its attached metal rings toward the wall. I lift my head and stare over Park's shoulder. The teenage roommate elbows himself into a semi-sitting position.

"You guys are killing me over here." The young man meets my gaze with unabashed curiosity. "Hi, I'm Evan."

CHAPTER 69

PARK IS RELEASED from the hospital the following day. Meadow picks him up since I have to meet with construction people. Upon my return to the office, I call Park. "How are you feeling?"

"Better now that I'm home. Could you show us how to use the treadmill with Lamar? He isn't staying on it."

"Sure, but I can't get there until later this afternoon. How about I make you guys some supper?"

"Great. I've missed your cooking but not as much as I've missed you."

A bubble of euphoria rises in my chest. "I wish Mia could come. She would love to spend time with Lamar."

"Bring her."

"But what about violating the building's one-dog rule?"

"Screw the rule. She's only going to be here for a few hours and, if there's a problem, I'll claim she's a therapy dog."

Although Park improves daily, he no longer pushes himself to the breaking point. The hip subluxation and painful trip to the hospital are brutal reminders of what his body cannot yet do. On Saturday, Meadow removes herself from the condo for the day giving her brother and me the privacy we haven't had in months. We talk and drive each other crazy with kisses and caresses.

At one point, he gulps in air and leans his head against the sofa back. "I have a doctor's appointment on Friday. I'm going to ask when I can make love to you. Also, I want to get permission to drive. Then I can send my sister home."

I sit up and refasten my bra. "Don't rush yourself and set back your recovery."

"I won't. But sex has to be as good an exercise as water aerobics." He flashes a smile full of sin. "Just with a little more sweat."

I research online sexual positions recommended after hip surgery and find the Tantra chair will come in handy.

With the upcoming Thanksgiving holiday, Meadow makes plans to attend dinner with the family of a friend. I suspect *the friend* might be her Tantra playmate. Betsy invites Park to dinner at the country club with our family. He declines, not yet ready for a social outing. Rather than leave him alone all day, I plan to cook and eat with him.

He says, "Why don't you bring Mia, Harley, and Davidson so you can stay all day?"

"Are you sure you won't get into trouble?"

"We'll take them outside one at a time. No one will notice they aren't the same dog."

I kiss him. "You're becoming such a rebel."

On Thanksgiving Day, I prepare a small turkey along with several side dishes. We enjoy a quiet dinner while sitting on the sofa and watching football with the four dachshunds.

Park calls me Friday evening following his doctor's visit. "We're good to go. I've been given the green light to drive and . . . for other things."

In the background, Meadow speaks but I can't decipher the words. "What did she say?"

Park laughs. "My sister said she knows what the other things are and can't wait to get out of here. I bought her a plane ticket for next Friday afternoon."

"Are you driving her to the airport?"

"No. I won't be back from physical therapy. She can take Uber or Lyft."

"Why don't I take her then stay at your place for the weekend?"

"I was going to ask if you wanted to come here, or if I should go to your place."

I pause. "I, uh . . . think if we're going to do *other things* we'd better use the Tantra chair."

"Good idea. Bring Mia with you. Lamar and I want to spend the weekend with our ladies."

CHAPTER 70

ON FRIDAY, I pick up Meadow two hours before her flight to Philadelphia and grab the handle of her carry-on. "This is all you're taking with you?"

"I'm leaving most of my summer clothes here. I won't need them up north at this time of year. I'll get them when we come back for Ren-Faire in February." Park's sister slings a backpack over one shoulder.

After stowing the suitcase in the back with Mia in the dog crate, I head toward Palm Beach International Airport. When the first overhead highway sign appears with a silhouette of an airplane, I say, "I bet you'll be glad to see your family again."

Meadow shrugs. "It was kinda nice living alone in Park's condo, especially after you hired the cleaning lady. My mom does all the laundry and housekeeping in the RV. She's always saying, 'A place for everything and everything in its place.' I guess that's why Park is such a neat freak."

"What will you do until the Renaissance fairs start again?"

"My dad has signed me up to help out at the foundation. Last year, they put me in the housekeeping department." She looks sheepish. "It was a disaster. You know how good I am at cleaning."

The Robinson family has a foundation? "What does the foundation do?"

"It runs Terre Bella."

"What's that?"

Meadow fiddles with her dangly earring. "Park never told you about the estate our great-great-grandfather built?"

Estate? "Not yet."

"Grandmother inherited the property but never lived there after she got married. She did keep the gatekeeper's cottage and gave it to Dad in her will. The foundation has run the place since before I was born."

"What do they do with it?"

"All kinds of things. There are tours, and car shows, and special holiday events. During the summer, they book outdoor weddings, bar mitzvahs, things like that. It can be a pain in the ass getting home or leaving the cottage when one of those is going on."

I blink, stunned. Why hasn't Park said anything, especially after seeing Del Lago Al Mar?

I've treaded so carefully around him when it comes to my family's wealth as if I suffer from an embarrassing condition. When strangers discover I'm one of the Palm Beach elite, they view me with the same sidelong looks given to a celebrity in public or someone with a disfigurement. Now I learn Park's family had once been socialites too.

Outside the Delta terminal, Meadow hugs me and thanks me for the ride. "I'm so glad you and Park are back together again. He's a different person when you're around, almost human."

I head back to the condo with my foot heavy on the accelerator and a multitude of questions for Park.

CHAPTER 71

PARK'S PRIUS IS in its parking spot. He's returned from therapy. After walking Mia around the fringe of grass bordering the parking lot to do her business, I load a fold-out cart with groceries, my clothes, toiletries, and her dog bed.

When I enter the condo, the shower is running in the master bathroom. Lamar greets Mia with enthusiastic tail wags. I stow the food then pour myself a glass of wine. The shower shuts off. I rinse off brined chicken thighs and preheat the oven for a prepared cauliflower casserole to bake. Then I sip my wine and stare out the kitchen window.

A few minutes later, the sound of bare feet slaps on the tile floor in a slow, careful gait. Park approaches in a pair of jeans riding low on his lean hips. Water droplets glisten in his damp hair.

I set my empty wine glass down. "You're not using your cane."

"Doug wants me to walk short distances without it." He wraps his arm around my waist, kisses me then studies my face. "What's wrong?"

"We need to talk." I step away and head to the living room sofa.

"About what?" Park doesn't follow but leans against the kitchen counter.

"Meadow told me about Terre Bella on the way to the airport."

His brows draw together. "What about it?"

"Why didn't you tell me your family owns an estate in Pennsylvania?"

"Because they don't."

"Meadow said a foundation runs it, but your parents still live on the property."

Park shambles to the sofa and sits next to me. "Why are you upset? Terre Bella no longer belongs to the Robinsons."

"You should have told me anyway." Park stares at me over the tops of his glasses like a grandmother looking at a silly child, and I fume. "I'm not overreacting. Your grandmother grew up in a mansion. Obviously, her family was wealthy. Why didn't you say anything?"

"Because they lost most of their money before I was born." Park relates the story of Terre Bella, his family's thirteen-bedroom, red-brick Georgian house built in the late 1800s. "The property once covered over a hundred acres, but the 1929 stock market crash hit my great-great-grandfather hard. His son was forced to sell off parcels of land to pay the taxes until there was nothing left but a few acres. When he died, the house was almost uninhabitable. My grandmother set up a foundation and donated the property to the state."

"Your father never lived there?"

"Dad grew up in downtown Philly." Park pats my leg. "Trust me. I wasn't hiding anything from you."

I relax, mollified by his explanation. "Good."

"I don't even think about Terre Bella because having wealth and a mansion is more than two generations in my past. Besides, unlike you, I'm terrible at keeping secrets."

I stiffen. "What do you mean, *unlike me*?"

"You know. You didn't tell me you're the director of The Forever Homes Foundation. You make me think you were just a fundraiser. You kept Kit's identity as the embezzler a secret. Who knows how many other secrets you're holding?"

I risk an uncertain sideways glance at Park. He looks neither angry nor upset. "It doesn't bother you that I can keep secrets?"

He wraps his arm around my shoulders and pulls me close. "No. It means you're trustworthy."

For me, the power of secrets is in keeping them. Once revealed, they became like a hot air balloon with a hole, nothing but useless material. "You know I would never keep a secret that could hurt you or somebody else, right?"

"Of course. It's one of your qualities I admire most."

"I have qualities you admire?"

He drags my hand to the top of his thigh and covers it with his. "Many."

"Like what?" I raise my eyebrows and wait.

"Such as how loyal you are to your family."

I lean back and stare at him. "Are you kidding? I don't even *like* some of them."

"But you still love them and are loyal to them."

"Okay, I can keep secrets, and I'm loyal. So far, I sound like a good dog. Anything else you admire?"

"You're a great cook; you love animals in general and dachshunds in particular; you're sexy as hell and your best quality is . . . you fell in love with me."

I soften like warm caramel and ooze over onto his lean, but hard chest. "You're right. Loving you is my most admirable quality."

He lowers his head and the light touch of his lips on mine stills the air in my lungs. Park's hand slides across my cheek toward the back of my head. He plows his fingers through my hair as he places soft kisses everywhere, teasing and coaxing. The tip of his tongue touches the seam of my lips.

I murmur, "Park?"

"Hmmm." He tugs on the ruffled elastic neckline of my palm tree-printed mini dress.

"I need to . . . turn off . . . the oven."

One nipple pops out. He palms the puckered tip. "Do you know what I need?"

"I have a pretty good idea." I close my eyes as an ache spreads from my breasts to my belly. The tingling tugs at me, turning into a full-blown desire to have him buried inside. "Park?"

He slides his hand between my legs. "Mmm."

"The oven."

He raises his head. "Any food in it?"

I stare into the depths of his dark eyes. "Not yet."

"Good." He stands. "We're having dessert first—on the Tantra."

CHAPTER 72

IN THE GUEST bedroom, the setting sun casts long, striped shadows as its beams pass through the partially-closed blinds. A golden light splashes onto the cream-colored leather of the Tantra chair, giving it an exotic glow like the altar of a heathen god.

Park unfastens his jeans and lets them slip down his legs before he sits on the edge of the Tantra. He kicks his feet out of the puddle of his pants. In the shadowed room, the still-red scars on his hip and leg appear less prominent.

I shimmy out of my dress and thong panties. Leaning down, I purr, "Top or bottom?"

In answer, Park scoots backward, turns, and lifts his legs onto the lower hump of the chair. He grasps my hand and pulls me up to straddle his lap. He covers my breasts as I bend forward. My hair surrounds us like a silky black curtain. He draws my nipple into his mouth, bathing the taut peak, and sucking with gentle pulls. I gasp and arch my back, craving his touch, his taste, the way he once filled me.

By slow agonizing inches, I lower myself, gauging my weight on his pelvis. Despite how hot, wet, and ready I am, I hesitate to move. "Does this hurt?"

"It's okay," he murmurs.

I slip off his glasses and drop them onto a nearby table. Park's eyes become heavy-lidded with pleasure. His delicious mouth curls into a heart-stopping smile. Flipping my hair over one shoulder, I meet his lips in a wild kiss. Without conscious thought, I move slowly, sliding back and forth against his hard length.

His fingertips dig into my hips. "Stop."

I freeze. "Am I too heavy?"

"No. Feels . . . too good. I want in you. Raise yourself up."

Planting my feet, I lift a few inches, and Park thrusts up at the same instant I sink. We join in a white-hot synchronization. Park closes his eyes, his mouth slightly open, and his head thrown back with a rapturous expression. A shaft of sun shines on his face and creates shadows in the contours. When he opens his eyes, a beam of light sparks a chocolate diamond in the split second before he blinks.

My heart expands. It's too large for my chest and overflows with love for this man. I move on him with care. Watching his face, I evaluate my movements. "Park?"

He moistens his lips. "Yeah?"

"Is this good?"

"Oh, yeah." A laugh bubbles from him and causes vibrations to ripple through me.

I tighten my muscles and move faster. His flesh grows hotter as he thrusts upward, thick and long, stroking, massaging, and filling the empty place inside me. Park wraps a hand behind my neck and pulls me close, kissing me. I curl my fingers into his chest as if clinging to a cliff but slip by inches into a fiery abyss. Arching and crying out, the first wave of a turbulent release crashes into me, stealing my breath away. Instead of falling, I sail higher than ever before, filled with lighter-than-air happiness and pure joy.

Park lets out a throaty groan. His grasp on my hips tightens. He pulsates beneath me. I collapse onto him and breathe in the scent of his skin. Our racing hearts beat wildly against each other.

At last, I lift my head. "Are you okay?"

"I'm great!" He roars.

I giggle. A snorting noise comes from the doorway. Lamar sits next to Mia as she seconds his response with a short, impatient yip.

Park says, "It's past somebody's suppertime."

"I guess I better feed them and us too. I have a feeling we're going to need to keep up our strength."

CHAPTER 73

OVER THE NEXT couple of weeks, Park's stamina and stability continue to improve. He reopens his office in the middle of December, and two of his staff members return. He acquires several new clients who tell him Stanford or Betsy McAllister recommended his firm. Bartholomew Gubelmann switches his car business to Robinson Account Management in appreciation for uncovering the theft.

During one of our evening dinners, the detective assigned to the attempted murder case calls. After Park hangs up the phone, he says to me, "They've traced Brent to somewhere in the Middle East, possibly Saudi Arabia."

I lay down my fork. "Why there?"

"No extradition treaty with the United States and it's a good place to work in the luxury vehicle business. But he better think twice before stealing again. The punishment for grand theft over there is having your right hand cut off at the wrist."

With Christmas a week away, the Robinsons express disappointment when Park tells them he can't visit because of his work and therapy schedule.

I give him a rueful smile. "Too bad Christmas isn't on a Friday or Monday this year. You could have flown up for a three-day weekend."

"Yeah, if I sold a kidney to buy a ticket."

"If you want to go . . ." I hesitate then rush my words. "I can charter a private jet." Park opens his mouth, but before he can speak I rush on. "Kit has been doing such a great job with adoptions that we're low on dogs right now. I could contact some foster groups in Pennsylvania and bring back some hard-to-place dachshunds. Of course, we'd have to fly back with crates of dogs, but I've done it before."

Park asks more questions and finally says, "If the charter is for the dogs, I accept."

I arrange to bring back to Florida a total of eight dachshunds; a blind black and white piebald, a paralyzed adult male, and six seniors. Mrs. R volunteers to dog-sit my dogs and Lamar at my house for the weekend.

Late on Friday afternoon, I finish overseeing the loading of empty crates and supplies onto the jet when Park arrives. He hands off his bag to a crew member standing by the sleek white Citation CJ3 and eyes me like an airport scanner, lingering on my over-the-knee boots and short skirt.

I grab his hand and lead him to the drop-down stairs. "They're ready for us to board."

Soon the jet taxies to a runway and climbs airborne. Park keeps his face to the window until we ascend to cloud level. He looks around the cabin at the six toffee-colored leather seats and LED lighting. "This is a great way to fly. Do you do it often?"

Across the aisle from him, I shake my head. "My mother hired charters for our family ski vacations. It was almost the same cost as first-class tickets on a commercial flight. I did use a private jet two years ago when the foundation took in twenty dogs from a puppy mill in Oregon."

He glances over his shoulder to the back of the cabin. "I take it here's no flight attendant."

"No. The lavatory is in the back." I point to a small cabinet in the front. "That's the refreshment bar. It has drinks and snacks."

"Do the pilots ever leave the cockpit?"

"Not for a short flight like this. Why?"

"I don't want them to see what we're going to do."

I pretend to be shocked. "Park, we can't make love in here."

A beep sounds and the pilot announces, "We have reached cruising altitude. You may now move about the cabin."

Park unclips himself, stands, and smiles down at me. "Your nipples are hard." He cups one breast and brushes the stiff tip with his thumb through my black cashmere sweater. "Are your panties wet?"

"No."

"Liar." He leans in to kiss me. "I know you want me as much as I want you."

"You're right. I do. That's why I went commando." I lift the short hemline of my plaid skirt. "Is there anything else you want me to take off?"

A pulse beats at the base of Park's throat. "Everything but the boots."

CHAPTER 74

WHEN WE RETURN to Florida, Mrs. R takes the paralyzed foster to live with her. The foundation has a donated wheelchair that fits Buster fairly well. Angie's grandmother will help him learn to use the prosthetic. If needed, I'll have him measured and fitted for a custom piece.

On Christmas Eve, Park and Lamar arrive to spend the night. After dinner, he and I sit on the floor and open presents. From me, he receives new Ray-Ban sunglasses, a blue dress shirt with his initials monogrammed on the cuff, a navy blue tie imprinted with red dachshunds, a carved wood eyeglasses stand, and an iRoomba. The robotic vacuum makes his eyes come alive.

Then he glances at his dog. "What if Lamar attacks it?"

"We'll train him not to."

When it's my turn, Park hands me the first wrapped box. "You're a tough lady to shop for since you can buy anything you want." He gives me an umbrella imprinted with dachshunds and a grow-your-own-shitake log. "Every six weeks you can harvest your own mushrooms for the next three years."

One particularly heavy box contains three bottles of infused olive oil from Lovin Olive. I ask him, "Did you go to the Coconut Creek store to get these?"

"Meadow and I went." He warns me that the last two are typical boyfriend presents.

The first one I open contains two bra and panty sets, one in pale pink, and the other in citrusy lime. "I can't wait to wear these for you."

The final gift from him is a palm-sized box.

"I had to get you jewelry."

Instead of metal, the cuff bracelet is constructed of interlocking bands of maple, cherry, and rosewood.

"It's so different and so me." I slip it onto my wrist. "I love it, and I love you."

I kiss him, settling into his embrace. As the kiss became hotter and wetter, my hand skims over his hair, neck, and shoulders. A soft moan escapes me. Park slips his fingers beneath the hem of my Miu Miu cotton sweater. I palm his erection, ready to make love on the floor under the Christmas tree. The razor's edge of desire twists inside my belly. An aching need adds to the heat of my pleasure.

I tip backward, bringing Park with me. In an embarrassingly short time, the first wave of an orgasm crashes into me and rolls me over and over. I gasp, my breath snatched away by the power of my response. Just as the white heat eases, I drop into another storm of sensation, twisting and writhing. When the tempest subsides, I stare into his dark eyes, alight with passion and male pride. "You gave me my first multiple orgasms."

"Merry Christmas, my love."

CHAPTER 75

ON CHRISTMAS MORNING, Park and I drive to my parents' house for a holiday luncheon and gift exchange. Betsy insisted Park not buy them presents, but he places a bulging gift bag inside the SUV.

I twist in the driver's seat. "What's that?"

"A basketball autographed by the Miami Heat players for Trevor. I do the taxes for someone in the front office. He gets one for me every year. I usually donate it or give it to one of my employees."

"It's so nice of you to think of him." I hope my sullen nephew will show some appreciation for the present.

His second gift is for my niece. He bought Ainsley a pink Disney Aurora dress, complete with tiara and wand. "The last time we had dinner at your parents' house she told me which outfits she still doesn't have."

I laugh. "Kit blames me and my funky style for inspiring her. The clothes only go up to size six, so she can't wait until Ainsley outgrows the costumes."

"She would fit right in with my family. They never outgrow costumes."

When we enter the mansion, the sentimental music of someone dreaming of a white Christmas is playing throughout the foyer. When I hear this song in Palm Beach, I'm reminded more of rich Caucasians than snow.

A professionally-decorated, twenty-foot artificial tree towers in the center of the marble foyer. This year Mumsy and her designer chose a classic theme. Red is the dominant color with glass candy canes, wooden nutcrackers, hand-painted gingerbread men, and feathered robins. Yards of the McAllister tartan surround the base. A monstrous bow with the clan's plaid tops the tree, its streamers snaking through the branches to the floor. A real pine garland studded with white lights, pinecones, and wired ribbon gives off a woodsy scent as it loops up the marble staircase. Holiday wreaths at every window add to the grandiose and festive air.

All my family emerges from the drawing room, except for my father. Ainsley runs to me, dressed in a green and yellow traditional Chinese dress with long sleeves, worn by the Disney character, Mulan.

"Merry Christmas, Auntie."

I hug her. "How perfect! You're dressed as a Buddhist on Christmas Day."

After releasing Ainsley, I wait, holding my breath. Will Pops do it this year with Park here?

When I was ten years old, I insisted on buying everyone a present with my own saved allowance. I asked Mumsy what to get my father.

Betsy said, "Since we'll be skiing in Vail, buy him a Christmas sweater."

I interpreted my mother's suggestion literally and purchased a sweater with reindeer and snowmen prancing around a Christmas tree. Mumsy and Kit laughed when my father opened the gift. I raised damp eyes to meet his neutral gaze. Without a word, he left the room and returned wearing the sweater I gave him. To his credit, he kept the hideous thing on all day, even when we ate dinner at a local restaurant. Every year since, including unseasonably warm Christmases in Florida, he dons my long-ago present, even if it only for the length of time to open gifts.

Stanford steps into the foyer. I run to him and wrap my arms around his neck. "Merry Christmas, Pops. I wasn't sure you would wear your sweater today."

He hugs me and whispers, "It's the gift that keeps on giving."

And it remains so to this day. The sweater shows how much he loves me, although he never says the words. Garrett and Trevor troop to my SUV to carry in the presents since Park still uses his cane for navigating long distances, which the size of Del Lago Al Mar dictates.

I drop my purse on the credenza and turn to my sister and mother. "I better get started on lunch." Since I'm comfortable in the kitchen and the staff has the day off, the food is prepared in advance with instructions for me to mix, heat, and serve the dishes.

"It's all taken care of," announces my sister with a note of pride in her voice. "I made sure the food is ready."

Garrett enters from outside with an armload of boxes. "She's becoming quite a good cook."

"I am not. At least, not yet." Kit's self-deprecation contains a fierce pride overlaid with her innate vulnerability.

"The chicken last night was really good." Garrett disappears into the drawing room.

In answer to my raised eyebrows, Kit says. "Mrs. Nichol and Chef Phillipe have been teaching me some basic dishes. I remember how Mrs. R taught you to cook, and I decided it was time I learned too."

I hug my sister and turn to our mother. "Isn't it wonderful, Mumsy?"

Betsy throws up her hands. "I don't understand why you modern women want to do everything. We have people for that."

In the dining room, the table is set with tasteful Christmas decorations on the snowy white linen. Through the floor-to-ceiling windows, the ocean outside glints in the sun and beams of light reflect rainbows in the Waterford crystal glassware. A printed menu on a silver easel lists shrimp cocktail as an appetizer; an entrée of pork Wellington with spinach-mushroom stuffing; sides dishes of arugula salad with Meyer lemon dressing, rutabaga and sweet potato mash; and three different desserts—eggnog crème brûlée, peppermint ice cream, and homemade Christmas cookies. All the dishes are artfully displayed on a carved mahogany sideboard.

Kit points to the beautifully constructed meat in puff pastry. "I transferred this from the refrigerator to the oven this morning. The chef left very clear instructions for the temperature and time."

At previous McAllister holiday dinners, the men and children sat and waited to be served. Instead of the hired staff, Betsy, Kit, and I prepared their plates from the buffet and brought them to the table.

Park places his hand at the back of my waist. "What do you want me to do?"

"I'd like you to break with tradition, except you need your cane for walking."

"What do you mean?"

In a soft voice, I say, "The women serve the men and children."

His gaze follows my mother setting a filled plate in front of Stanford. Park walks to the table and hangs his cane on the chair designated by his name card. He returns to the buffet and picks up a plate. Stanford opens his mouth, but I catch his eye and shake my head. He shrugs, folds his hands on the edge of the tabletop, and waits in silence.

When Kit spots Park behind her, spooning salad onto his plate, she says, "Marin can get that for you."

"I prefer to do it myself."

Garrett appears at his wife's side and lifts the plate from her hands. "Is this for Ainsley?"

Kit stammers, "Uh . . . yes. Or you can give it to Trevor."

"He's in line behind Marin. You get yours, and I'll get mine after I deliver this."

Betsy returns from the kitchen with a chilled bottle of sparkling cider. She stops upon seeing everyone, except her husband and granddaughter, at the sideboard.

I hold up a martini glass filled with crushed ice, shrimp, and cocktail sauce. "Welcome to our brave new world, Mumsy."

After the luncheon ends, everyone helps clear the dining room. The family congregates around the real pine tree in the corner of the drawing room where the children receive their gifts from me then Park. Trevor shows a genuine spark of pleasure upon seeing the signed basketball. Ainsley hugs her new Disney dress to her chest and accessorizes her Mulan costume with the glittery tiara. Betsy and Stanford give Park several beautiful silk ties like the ones my father prefers and a Rolex watch. He offers gracious thanks to my parents, having been warned they may gift him with something expensive.

As usual, I receive clothes from my parents and sister that match their style of dress more than mine. Then my mother, father, sister, and brother-in-law open the gifts I purchased for them.

Thank yous are expressed to all when Park stands, pulls an envelope from his pocket, and extends it to my father. "I'd appreciate it if you and your wife read the message inside to yourselves."

I frown and I tilt my head at him. Betsy rises and stands behind her husband's chair as he lifts the envelope's flap and pulls out a Christmas card. Both put on reading glasses. At first, their expressions display curiosity. The more they read, the more they smile. Stanford flips the card over and reads the words on the back. He looks at his wife who nods.

After placing the card back in the envelope, he says, "My wife and I are both in agreement with your offer."

I turn to Park who no longer sits beside me. He is kneeling on bended knee, holding a small jewelry box with a beautiful Art Deco ring. My field of vision narrows to the vibrant rectangular emerald adorned with accent diamonds on each side. A sharp pinch in my chest and a frightening flutter in my stomach steal my breath away. I shift my gaze to Park's warm brown eyes.

With a smile, he says, "Marin, this is my grandmother's engagement ring. The emerald reminds me of your beautiful eyes; the ones I want to look into for the rest of my life. You've already given me the best gifts in the world. You gave me back Lamar, my will to live, and your love. Will you marry me?"

My eyes dart around the room at the smiling faces of my family. Then my gaze returns to Park and the most perfect ring I've ever seen. I put my palms on his cheeks. "You know I will, my love."

CHAPTER 76

SINCE AGREEING TO Park's marriage proposal on Christmas Day, my life's become an endurance test. Mumsy insisted on contacting Nancy Robinson the next day to discuss wedding plans. I placed faith in Park's mother to not slip over to the dark side and allow Betsy to create the spectacle of a royal wedding. After all, my future mother-in-law is a sweet woman who named her children after their nature-location conceptions, espouses healthy eating habits, wears gypsy-like clothing, and simplified childhood birthday parties.

But in a matter of days, I stare into the maw of a formidable prenuptial monster. Getting pressure from both sides, I agree to the actual ceremony and a buffet lunch at Ren-Faire on the last Friday in March. The following evening, there will be a more upscale dinner and dancing at my parents' country club.

Then Betsy calls me at the end of January. "I've canceled the reception at the country club."

"Why? Did they refuse to repaint the room to match your color scheme?"

"No. I told a number of our friends about the ceremony at Ren-Faire. To my surprise, they want to attend dressed in costume. Your wedding has become the highlight of the season. My phone hasn't stopped ringing with people angling for an invitation."

"Mumsy, do your friends realize the wedding is outdoors at a public park with port-a-potties, live animals, and people who sleep most of the year in tents and RV's?"

"Don't worry," Betsy says. "Nancy and I are coordinating everything. Not only will your wedding be the season's most special event, but this year's Ren-Faire will be the Robinson's most spectacular ever."

"What are you talking about?"

"I can't go into all the details, but all you and Park have to do is show up and enjoy yourselves."

CHAPTER 77

A MONTH BEFORE the wedding, I suffer through an hour-long conversation with my future mother-in-law about bouquets with traditional blooms paired with succulents and fresh herbs. When I hang up, I sit with my eyes closed. Nancy has drunk the Kool-Aid.

My wedding started out as a simple ceremony and meal with the Ren-Faire folks followed by a sanitized reception at a country club. Now it has mutated into Renaissance glamping with the construction of a medieval chapel, a tent large enough for a three-ring circus, and portable air-conditioned trailers with flushing toilets and overhead music.

On the afternoon of the rehearsal, Park and I drive to the Broward County location of Ren-Faire. Rather than the usual placard signs directing traffic, black iron posts with filigreed signage painted in ancient script announce: *Carriages Proceed Ahead.* Heraldic banners sway in the gentle breeze on strands of thin wire lining the asphalt drive.

Park stops the car next to the front entrance which mimics the dropped drawbridge of a medieval castle. We enter to find a stone church with a steeply pitched roof and tall columns. *St. Peter's Chapel* is carved into the lintel above double doors hung with iron hardware.

I stare with amazement at the construction. "How did your father and brother build this in three months? This is unbelievable."

"Everything is made from carved and painted polystyrene panels."

"All this is not wood and stone? It's fake?"

Park nods. "I have to admit it looks pretty spectacular now. Let's pray it doesn't rain tomorrow, or our church may disintegrate."

Past the chapel, complete with real wooden pews and an elaborate medieval altar, is a tent the Ringling Brothers would have envied. Four thirty-foot-long pavilions have been seamed together to create the enormous structure which sports jewel-toned stripes, scalloped edges, and colorful braiding. Dozens of thick wood poles support the twelve-foot-tall walls and high-pitched top. Vibrant flags on finials march across the peaks. Benches and tables with royal blue cloths, matching plates, napkins, and jeweled goblets fill three of the tents. Every few feet are iron birdcages with battery-operated candles, ivy and grape clusters, and artificial birds. Garlands of fresh myrtle dotted with red roses stretch side to side in loopy swags over the tables. On an elevated platform is a large trestle table for the wedding party lined with sparkling candelabra and silver epergnes for holding fruits and nuts. Gold-rimmed lapis lazuli plates top shiny metallic chargers.

A number of the pieces look familiar to me. Did Mumsy empty Del Largo Al Mar's locked silver closet?

Betsy never trusts anyone with the key, but now the valuable pieces dress a table in an outdoor tent. Park and I cross a wood dance floor with a fenced-off area of chairs and musical instruments. An overhead banner proclaims *Ye Royal Minstrels.*

An armed guard in a uniform stitched with the words Platinum Security over his breast pocket blocks our exit. "What are you doing here?"

In a firm voice, Park says, "Checking out what our mothers have planned for our wedding tomorrow."

The guard looks at his clipboard. "Your names?"

I lift my chin. "Marin McAllister and Park Robinson."

He eyes us and his paperwork, comparing photos to our actual likenesses. He points farther down the path. "Your parents are over by the dressing rooms."

I follow Park with the stunned aimlessness of a child entering Disney World for the first time. More guards mill around in golf carts. We pass outlying tents with signs proclaiming *Wickedly Funny Singing Wenches, The Queen's Mime,* and *The King's Acrobatrix.* Black metal markers at a fork direct us to *The Privies* on the left or *The Knights' Room* and *The Ladies' Chamber* on the right.

We head toward the sound of voices and two large tents staked across from each other. Park's family and mine are gathered there. My nephew, Trevor, sits on a nearby chest, his eyes glued to a cell phone. His sister, Ainsley, plops a pearl-covered Juliet cap on her head from a pile of accessories on a table outside *The Ladies' Chamber* tent.

Nancy Robinson spots us. "We wondered when you would get here."

"What do you think of the place?" Bob asks his son as he enfolds him in a hug.

"It looks great, Dad. I can't believe all you've done in such a short time."

"We didn't have much choice with your mom and Betsy cracking the whip over our heads." In a soft voice, he says, "Helps if one of them has deep pockets."

I study the tents. "Are those the dressing rooms for the wedding party?"

Betsy says, "No, we have air-conditioned RV's for us to use. These are for any guest who wants to wear a costume but didn't come dressed in one. Bob and Nancy are allowing them to borrow clothing from past Renaissance fairs."

Park's mother says, "I found the Queen Elizabeth dress I wore when we got married. Believe it or not, it still fits."

"It ought to," her husband drawls. "You were six months pregnant at the time."

Nancy tightens her lips and shoots Bob a furious look.

Betsy checks her clipboard. "Stanford, make sure the electricians have everything ready. The truck generators are behind the jousting field."

He salutes his wife and ambles down the path. In the past several weeks, I have not heard my father utter a word in the flurry of wedding planning. Maybe Pops had to sell his tongue to pay for all this.

Betsy checks her dinging cell phone. "The caterer is ready to go over final preparations. I'll meet you at the chapel in thirty minutes."

Nancy pulls out her phone and addresses her husband. "Have the saddles and bridles for the horses in the wedding parade been moved to the tack tent yet?"

"River and I'll check." He and his younger son take off.

Park's mother scans her phone again. "I hope Meadow gets here soon with the bouquets. Kit, we should make sure everything for the wedding party is in the appropriate trailer. I don't want someone's boots or . . . their gown to be missing tomorrow." Nancy gives me a pointed stare.

The look reassures me that my chosen wedding dress will be ready for me. I shocked my mother by ordering one without her knowledge or approval. I love the ruby-colored lace appliqués and crystals covering the low-cut heart-shaped neckline on the red silk corset bodice. An open back bares my spine with functioning laces that crisscross, allowing most of my skin and tattoo to be visible.

When I modeled the dress for Betsy and Nancy, my mother gasped. "It's red!"

I held out the ecru satin skirt with hands and arms covered in tight lacy sleeves ending in points. "And off-white too."

"In Renaissance times," Nancy adds, patting Betsy's shoulder, "brides often wore red to invoke fertility."

I fist my hands on my hips. "It's still my wedding, Mumsy. I've let you have your way with everything else, but I get to choose my own gown."

"Don't forget the wedding invitations," Betsy reminds me.

Park and I insisted the announcement include a message that all leashed and friendly dogs could attend with their owners. After all, Mia and Lamar will be part of the ceremony.

After Nancy and my sister leave, Park and I are left with Garrett and the children, the only ones not given an assignment. I am stunned with all our parents accomplished in such a short time.

Ainsley approaches and grasps my hand. "Guess what, Auntie? I'm going to be a fairy flower girl with real wings that move. Later I can play dress-up with them and make wishes come true. What are you going to do after the wedding?"

I look at Park. "Cartwheels."

CHAPTER 78

TO MY RELIEF, The Wedding of the Season goes off without a glitch. No freak thunderstorm destroys the wedding chapel. None of the Ren-Fair entertainers slug a Palm Beach do-you-know-who-I-am snob. No one is caught having sex, regular or BDSM, in one of the tents.

I delight in my father's Henry the VIII costume. He wears a jacket trimmed in faux fur with a chain stretching from shoulder to shoulder and a black velvet hat. I stare at his well-shaped calves in white stockings as we wait for the wedding march to begin. "Pops, I forgot what good-looking legs you have."

Stanford shakes his head and rolls his eyes.

Everyone in the wedding party chose their own outfits. My mother wears an Arthurian Queen Guinevere dress. Her jewel-studded tiara appears genuine and might well be the real thing. Garrett and Trevor garb themselves as two of the Three Musketeers. Kit and Ainsley dress in mother and daughter faeries outfits with metallic mesh wings and filmy dresses. The Robinsons continue in their usual roles as the Ren-Faire king, queen, knight, and lady-in-waiting but with new and more elaborate costumes. Park's college roommate and the third groomsman chose a wizard outfit with a fake white beard. He's paired him with Angie, who covers her red hair with a white wig and wears a skimpy gown like Daenerys Targaryen in the *Game of Thrones*.

Tears come to my eyes when I walk down the aisle and see Park. Not only is he dressed as Prince Charming, but he holds Mia under one arm while Lamar stands by his side. The marriage officiant, dressed as a hooded friar, bears a striking resemblance to Obi-Wan Kenobi. Kerry Kowalski, the wedding photographer, wears a Little Red Riding Hood costume with pockets in her long skirt and hooded cape for her equipment.

At the reception, I spot Kerry's son, Dylan, his grandmother and their pit bull, Angel. When I kneel to pet my most harrowing rescue and touching adoption, the dog's tail wags, and she licks my cheek.

Kerry snaps a series of pictures. "She remembers you."

Dylan hugs the dog's neck. "My A-gel."

I smile to hear the little boy talking. "You're her angel too."

A surprise occurs when Trey's parents walk in with him, Carmen, and their eight-month-old twins. Even though Mrs. Montgomery is polite and reserved with her daughter-in-law, she gushes and shows off her grandchildren. I'm confident Carmen will eventually win over her frosty mother-in-law.

Three hours later, Park and I slip away from the still going strong reception. In one of the trailers, we change out of our wedding clothes in record time. I sigh. I'm going to miss seeing him in the fitted white and gold tunic, leg and crotch-hugging pants, leather boots, and long cape. Maybe I can talk him into wearing the costume on our first anniversary—at least the boots and cape.

At the beachside hotel where we plan to spend our wedding night before flying to Fiji in the morning, Park unlocks the door. "Wait here." He wheels our overnight bags inside the room and returns with outstretched arms.

"What are you doing?"

"I'm going to carry you over the threshold." He bends and scoops one arm behind my knees, the other around my waist, and straightens. A small noise escapes his lips.

"Put me down!"

He places me back on my feet. "What's wrong?"

"You grunted."

"That's my I-can't-wait-to-get-my-wife-into-bed sound."

"Right." Grinning, I brush past him into the room. The last thing I need is for him to hurt his hip before the honeymoon.

Park closes the door. "I was trying to be a good husband."

I wrap my arms around his neck. "I know, but I would —"

"Prefer me as Prince Charming?"

I stare into his dark eyes. "You already are since your love came to my rescue."

The End

Look for the next Love on a Leash book in the series at www.janetfrankslittle.com
Part of a Whole: A Pit Bull Love Story

Text #1: Our lives together can be like a fairy tale.

"LET'S HOPE THE Florida Highway patrol doesn't stop us. We'd have a tough time explaining why we're wearing these clothes." I loosen the tie holding the red hooded cape around my neck and lift the elastic neckline of the white peasant blouse onto my shoulders, adjusting the laces of the black stomacher that indents my waistline a bit.

India takes her eyes off the road and smiles at me. "You make a lovely Little Red Riding Hood. That was a clever idea to sew pockets into your skirt and cape to hide the equipment."

A glow of pride warms me as I survey my mother who, for once, looks like the grandmother she is in real life. Mom wears a gray wig, wire-rimmed spectacles, and a heavy cotton nightgown envelopes her small frame. I glance over my shoulder into the back seat where my son and his dog sleep. Dylan is dressed in brown pants and a vest. The fake ax in an arrow quiver lies on the seat beside him. He portrayed the woodcutter who saves Red Riding Hood in the fairytale.

He's my hero too.

But Dylan's pit bull, Angel, who snoozes close by is a far cry from The Big Bad Wolf. She had sported a frilly white nightcap all afternoon, staying close to his side, and calming him when the noise and people overwhelmed his fragile nervous system. The undersized tan dog has become a true heroine by breaking through Dylan's barriers.

Facing forward again, I ask Mom, "How did Dylan do at the reception? I got so busy taking videos I lost track of you guys."

"A few times he became anxious, but Angel was able to settle him down. I did take him outside when the drummers did their act. The noise was too much for him."

I had been hired to photograph and film the Renaissance wedding and reception of the woman who had rescued Angel as a young dog. Because the event was outdoors and dogs were invited to attend with their owners, I brought Dylan and Angel. I prayed the sights, sounds, and people would not be too much for my son to handle. But thanks to his four-legged friend he coped much better than I expected.

As we drive northward into Palm Beach County, the setting sun creates beautiful bands of pink and purple on the horizon. The turnpike was once a less-traveled highway on the weekends, but with the influx of people on the western edge of the county, it is now as busy as I-95 to the east. When we exit the toll road and head toward the farm, I flip down the sun visor to block the brightest rays of the Easter egg-colored sunset. I close my eyes and don't see the SUV and trailer until the car slams to an abrupt stop.

"Oh, my God!"

With India's exclamation and the sudden braking, my eyelids snap open. Blocking our narrow drive is a storage trailer. One of its rear wheels is in the ditch which runs between the fence line and the asphalt county road. Hitched to the U-Haul is a Chevy Tahoe with its doors open. A young man has a cell phone to his ear, talking and pointing as if the caller can see the dilemma. Another man kneels on his hands and knees and peers under the tilted trailer.

My heart stops at the sight of the man on the ground. I recognize the Type 1 NWU he wears. My husband, Vic, sometimes donned his old blue camo pants and T-shirt during weekends around the house. Next to the unknown man in the U.S. Navy Working Uniform stands a footed aluminum cane like a silver sailor at attention.

My faulty brain finally kicks in after a paralyzing moment. It's not Vic. He's dead.

ABOUT THE AUTHOR

Janet Franks Little is a former speech language pathologist, artist, and contemporary romance novelist living in Florida and Ohio. She began writing and submitting short stories to publications at the age of twelve. Drawing upon her own experiences, her romantic comedies touch on real life issues. She loves a good book, dachshunds, and rehabbing Tudor houses.

Janet loves connecting with readers! Find her:
Website: https://www.janetfrankslittle.com/
Facebook: https://www.facebook.com/janetfrankslittle
Instagram: https://www.instagram.com/janetfrankslittle/
Twitter: https://twitter.com/franks_little
Amazon: https://www.amazon.com/Janet-Franks-Little/e/B00MYERSO6
Goodreads: https://www.goodreads.com/author/show/8409180.Janet_Franks_Little
Bookbub: https://www.bookbub.com/profile/janet-franks-little

Made in the USA
Las Vegas, NV
23 September 2021